THE
LIGHT
WE
LOST

THE
LIGHT
WE
LOST

JILL SANTOPOLO

ONE PLACE. MANY STORIES

HQ
An imprint of HarperCollins*Publishers* Ltd
1 London Bridge Street
London SE1 9GF

HarperCollins*Publishers*
1st Floor, Watemarque Building, Ringsend Road
Dublin 4, Ireland

This paperback edition 2018

10
First published in Great Britain by
HQ, an imprint of HarperCollins*Publishers* Ltd 2017

Copyright © Jill Santopolo 2017

Jill Santopolo asserts the moral right to be
identified as the author of this work.
A catalogue record for this book is
available from the British Library.

ISBN: 978-0-00-822460-8

MIX
Paper from
responsible sources
FSC
www.fsc.org
FSC™ C007454

This book is produced from independently certified FSC paper
to ensure responsible forest management.

For more information visit: www.harpercollins.co.uk/green

Printed and bound in the UK using 100% renewable electricity
at CPI Group (UK) Ltd

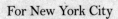
For New York City

prologue

WE'VE KNOWN EACH OTHER FOR ALMOST HALF OUR lives.

I've seen you smiling, confident, blissfully happy.

I've seen you broken, wounded, lost.

But I've never seen you like this.

You taught me to look for beauty. In darkness, in destruction, you always found light.

I don't know what beauty I'll find here, what light. But I'll try. I'll do it for you. Because I know you would do it for me.

There was so much beauty in our life together.

Maybe that's where I should start.

SOMETIMES OBJECTS SEEM LIKE THEY'VE WITNESSED history. I used to imagine that the wooden table we sat around during Kramer's Shakespeare seminar our senior year was as old as Columbia—that it had been in that room since 1754, edges worn smooth by centuries of students like us, which of course couldn't be true. But that's how I pictured it. Students sitting there through the Revolutionary War, the Civil War, both World Wars, Korea, Vietnam, the Persian Gulf.

It's funny, if you asked me who else was with us that day, I don't think I could tell you. I used to be able to see all their faces so clearly, but thirteen years later I remember only you and Professor Kramer. I can't even recall the name of the TA who came running, late, into the classroom. Later, even, than you.

Kramer had just finished calling roll when you pushed

open the door. You smiled at me, your dimple making a brief appearance as you slipped off your Diamondbacks cap and stuck it into your back pocket. Your eyes landed quickly on the empty seat next to mine, and then you did too.

"And you are?" Kramer asked, as you reached into your backpack for a notebook and a pen.

"Gabe," you said. "Gabriel Samson."

Kramer checked the paper in front of him. "Let's aim for 'on time' for the rest of the semester, Mr. Samson," he said. "Class starts at nine. In fact, let's aim for 'early.'"

You nodded, and Kramer started talking about themes in *Julius Caesar*.

"'We at the height are ready to decline,'" he read. "'There is a tide in the affairs of men / Which, taken at the flood, leads on to fortune; / Omitted, all the voyage of their life / Is bound in shallows and in miseries. / On such a full sea are we now afloat, / And we must take the current when it serves, / Or lose our ventures.' I trust you all did the reading. Who can tell me what Brutus is saying about fate and free will here?"

I'll always remember that passage because I've wondered so many times since that day whether you and I were fated to meet in Kramer's Shakespeare seminar. Whether it's destiny or decision that has kept us connected all these years. Or a combination of both, taking the current when it serves.

After Kramer spoke, a few people flipped through the

text in front of them. You ran your fingers through your curls, and they sprang back into place.

"Well," you said, and the rest of the class joined me in looking at you.

But you didn't get to finish.

The TA whose name I can't remember came racing into the room. "Sorry I'm late," she said. "A plane hit one of the twin towers. It came on TV just as I was leaving for class."

No one knew the significance of her words; not even she did.

"Was the pilot drunk?" Kramer asked.

"I don't know," the TA said, taking a seat at the table. "I waited, but the newscasters had no idea what was going on. They said it was some kind of prop plane."

If it had happened now, all of our phones would've been blowing up with news. Pings from Twitter and Facebook and push notifications from the *New York Times*. But communication then wasn't yet instant and Shakespeare wouldn't be interrupted. We all shrugged it off and Kramer kept talking about *Caesar*. As I took notes, I watched the fingers of your right hand unconsciously rub against the wood grain of the table. I doodled an image of your thumb with its ragged nail and torn cuticle. I still have the notebook somewhere—in a box filled with Lit Hum and Contemporary Civilizations. I'm sure it's there.

ii

I'll never forget what we said when we left Philosophy Hall; even though the words were nothing special, the conversation is burned into my memory as part of that day. We'd started down the steps together. Not exactly together, but next to each other. The air was clear, the sky was blue—and everything had changed. We just didn't know it yet.

People all around us were talking over one another:

"The twin towers collapsed!"

"School's canceled!"

"I want to donate blood. Do you know where I can donate blood?"

I turned to you. "What's going on?"

"I live in East Campus," you said, pointing toward the dorm. "Let's go find out. You're Lucy, right? Where do you live?"

"Hogan," I said. "And yeah, Lucy."

"Nice to meet you, Lucy, I'm Gabriel." You held out your hand. Amid everything, I shook it, and looked up at you as I did. Your dimple came back. Your eyes shone blue. I thought then, for the first time: *He's beautiful.*

We went to your suite and watched TV with your roommates, with Adam and Scott and Justin. On the screen bodies dove out of buildings, blackened mounds of rubble sent smoke signals into the sky, and the towers fell in a loop. The devastation numbed us. We stared at the images, unable to reconcile the stories with our reality. The fact that this was happening in our city, seven miles from where we sat, that those were people—actual human beings—hadn't set in yet. At least not for me. It felt so far away.

Our cell phones didn't work. You used your dorm phone to call your mom in Arizona to tell her you were fine. I called my parents in Connecticut, who wanted me to come home. They knew someone whose daughter worked at the World Trade Center and no one had heard from her yet. Someone else whose cousin had a breakfast meeting at Windows on the World.

"It's safer outside Manhattan," my father said. "What if there's anthrax? Or some other biological warfare. Nerve gas."

I told my dad the subways weren't running. Probably not the trains either.

"I'll come get you," he said. "I'll jump in the car now."

"I'll be okay," I told him. "I'm with some friends. We're fine. I'll call you again later." It still didn't feel real.

"You know," Scott said, after I hung up. "If I were a terrorist organization, I'd drop a bomb on us."

"What the fuck?" Adam said. He was waiting to hear from his uncle, who was part of the NYPD.

"I mean, if you think about it academically . . ." Scott said, but he didn't get any further.

"Shut up," Justin said. "Seriously, Scott. Not the time."

"Maybe I should leave," I said to you then. I didn't really know you. I had just met your friends. "My roommates are probably wondering where I am."

"Call them," you said, handing the phone back to me. "And tell them you're going to the roof of the Wien dorm. Tell them they can meet you there if you want."

"I'm going where?"

"With me," you said, and you ran your fingers absently along my braid. It was an intimate gesture, the kind of thing that happens after all barriers of personal space have been breached. Like eating off someone else's plate without asking. And all of a sudden, I felt connected to you, like your hand on my hair meant something more than idle, nervous fingers.

I thought of that moment, years later, when I decided to donate my hair and the stylist handed me my braid, wrapped in plastic, looking even darker brown than usual. Even though you were a world away then, I felt like I was betraying you, like I was cutting our tie.

But then, that day, right after you touched my hair you realized what you'd done and let your hand drop into your lap. You smiled at me again, but it didn't go to your eyes this time.

I shrugged. "Okay," I said.

The world felt like it was cracking in pieces, like we'd gone through a shattered mirror into the fractured place inside, where nothing made sense, where our shields were down, our walls broken. In that place, there wasn't any reason to say no.

iii

WE TOOK THE ELEVATOR UP TO WIEN 11, AND THEN you pulled open a window at the end of the hallway. "Someone showed me this sophomore year," you said. "It's the most incredible view of New York City you'll ever see."

We climbed out the window, onto the roof, and I gasped. Smoke billowed up from the southern tip of Manhattan. The whole sky was turning gray, the city shrouded in ash.

"Oh my God," I said. Tears filled my eyes. I pictured what used to be there. Saw the negative space where the towers had stood. It finally hit me. "There were people in those buildings."

Your hand found mine and held it.

We stood there, staring at the aftermath of destruction, tears dripping down both our cheeks, for how long I don't know. There must have been other people up there with us, but I can't recall them. Just you. And the image of that smoke. It's seared into my brain.

"What happens now?" I finally whispered. Seeing it made me understand the magnitude of the attack. "What's next?"

You looked at me, and our eyes, still wet with tears, locked with the kind of magnetism that ignores the world around it. Your hand slid to my waist, and I rose up onto my toes to meet your lips halfway. We pressed our bodies together, as if that would protect us from whatever came after. As if the only way to stay safe was to keep my lips on yours. The moment your body enveloped mine, that's how I felt—safe, enfolded in the strength and warmth of your arms. Your muscles fluttered against my hands and I buried my fingers in your hair. You wrapped my braid around your palm, tugging it and tipping my head back. And I forgot the world. In that moment, there was only you.

For years I felt guilty about it. Guilty that we kissed for the first time while the city burned, guilty that I was able to lose myself in you in that moment. But later I learned that we weren't alone. People told me in whispers that they'd had sex that day. That they'd conceived a child. They'd gotten engaged. Said *I love you* for the first time. There's something about death that makes people want to live. We wanted to live that day, and I don't blame us for it. Not anymore.

When we broke for breath, I leaned my head against your chest. I listened to your heart and was comforted by its steady beating.

Did my heartbeat comfort you? Does it still?

iv

WE WENT BACK TO YOUR DORM ROOM BECAUSE YOU promised me lunch. You wanted to go onto the roof with your camera after we ate, you told me, and take some pictures.

"For the *Spectator*?" I asked.

"The paper?" you said. "Nah. For me."

In the kitchen I got distracted by a stack of your photos—black-and-white prints taken all over campus. They were beautiful, bizarre, bathed in light. Images zoomed so far in that an everyday object looked like modern art.

"Where's this one?" I asked. After looking for a while, I realized it was a close-up of a bird's nest, lined with what looked like newspapers and magazines and someone's essay for a French literature class.

"Oh, that was incredible," you told me. "Jessica Cho—

Do you know her? She sings a cappella? David Blum's girl-friend?—she told me about this nest that she could see out her window that someone's homework got worked into. So I went to check it out. I had to hang out the window to get this shot. Jess made Dave hold my ankles because she was afraid I would fall. But I got it."

After that story I saw you differently. You were daring, brave, committed to capturing art. Looking back, I'm guessing that's what you wanted me to think. You were try-ing to impress me, but I didn't realize it at the time. I just thought: *Wow.* I thought: *He's wonderful.* But what was true then, and has been true as long as I've known you, is that you find beauty everywhere. You notice things other people don't. It's something I've always admired about you.

"Is this what you want to do?" I asked then, indicating the pictures.

You shook your head. "It's just for fun," you said. "My mom's an artist. You should see what she can do, these gor-geous enormous abstracts, but she makes a living by paint-ing small canvases of Arizona sunsets for tourists. I don't want that kind of life, creating what sells."

I leaned against the counter and looked at the rest of the photographs. Rust leaching into a stone bench, cracked veins of marble, corrosion on a metal railing. Beauty where I'd never imagined it could be. "Is your dad an artist, too?" I asked.

Your face closed. I could see it, like a door shutting behind your eyes. "No," you said. "He's not."

I had stumbled into a fault line I didn't know was there. I filed that away—I was discovering the landscape of you. Already I was hoping it was terrain I'd learn well, one that would become second nature to navigate.

You were quiet. I was quiet. The TV was still blaring in the background, and I heard the newscasters talking about the Pentagon and the plane that crashed in Pennsylvania. The horror of the situation rushed over me again. I put your photographs down. It seemed perverse to focus on beauty then. But looking back, maybe that was exactly the right thing to do.

"Didn't you say we were going to eat lunch?" I asked, even though I wasn't hungry, even though the images flashing across the television screen made my stomach churn.

The door opened behind your eyes. "That I did," you said, with a nod.

All you had the ingredients for were nachos. So, mechanically, I sliced tomatoes and opened a can of beans with a rusty can opener while you arranged tortilla chips in one of those throwaway foil trays and grated cheese into a chipped cereal bowl.

"What about you?" you asked, as if our conversation hadn't gotten derailed.

"Hm?" I pressed the top of the can into the beans so I could lever it off.

"Are you an artist?"

I put the metal disc down on the counter. "Nope," I said. "The most creative thing I do is write stories for my roommates."

"About what?" you asked, your head cocked to one side.

I looked down so you wouldn't see me blush. "This is embarrassing," I said, "but they're about a teacup pig named Hamilton who accidentally got accepted into a college meant for rabbits."

You let out a surprised laugh. "Hamilton. A pig," you said. "I get it. That's funny."

"Thanks," I said, looking up at you again.

"So is that what you want to do after graduation?" You had reached for the jar of salsa and were tapping its lid against the counter top to loosen it.

I shook my head. "I don't think there's a big market out there for Hamilton the Pig stories. I've been thinking about going into advertising, but saying it now, it sounds silly."

"Why silly?" you asked, twisting the lid off with a pop.

I looked over at the TV. "Does it mean anything? Advertising? If this were my last day on Earth and I'd spent my whole adult life coming up with campaigns to sell people . . . shredded cheese . . . or nacho chips . . . would I feel like my time here was well spent?"

You bit your lip. Your eyes said, *I'm thinking about this*. I learned more of your topography. Perhaps you learned a bit of mine. "What makes a life well spent?" you asked.

"That's what I'm trying to figure out," I told you, my mind turning as I was talking. "I think it might have something to do with making a mark—in a positive way. Leaving the world a little bit better than it was when you found it." I still believe that, Gabe. It's what I've been striving my whole life to do—I think you have too.

I saw something blossom in your face then. I wasn't sure what it meant. I hadn't learned you well enough yet. But now I know that look. It means perspectives are shifting in your mind.

You dipped a chip in the salsa and held it out to me.

"Bite?" you asked.

I crunched it in half, and you popped the rest into your mouth. Your eyes traced the planes of my face and traveled down the length of my body. I could feel you examining me from different angles and vantage points. Then you brushed my cheek with your fingertips and we kissed again; this time you tasted like salt and chili pepper.

When I was five or six, I drew on my bedroom wall with a red crayon. I don't think I ever told you this story. Anyway, as I was drawing hearts and trees and suns and moons and clouds, I knew I was doing something I shouldn't. I could feel it in the pit of my stomach. But I couldn't stop myself—I wanted to do it so badly. My room had been decorated in pink and yellow, but my favorite color was red. And I wanted my room to be red. I *needed* my room to be red. Drawing on the wall felt completely right and absolutely wrong at the same time.

That's how I felt the day I met you. Kissing you in the middle of tragedy and death felt completely right and absolutely wrong at the same time. But I concentrated on the part that felt right, the way I always do.

I SLID MY HAND into the back pocket of your jeans, and you slid your hand into mine. We pulled each other closer. The phone in your room rang, but you ignored it. Then the phone in Scott's room rang.

A few seconds later, Scott came into the kitchen and cleared his throat. We broke apart and faced him. "Stephanie's looking for you, Gabe," he said. "I put her on hold."

"Stephanie?" I asked.

"No one," you answered, just as Scott said, "His ex."

"She's crying, dude," Scott told you.

You looked torn, your eyes going from Scott to me and back again. "Would you tell her I'll call her back in a few minutes?" you said to him.

Scott nodded and left, and then you grabbed my hand, weaving your fingers through mine. Our eyes met, like they had on the roof, and I couldn't look away. My heart sped up. "Lucy," you said, somehow infusing my name with desire. "I know you're here, and I know that makes this strange, but I should see if she's okay. We were together all last school year and only broke up last month. This day—"

"I get it," I said. And weirdly, it made me like you better, that while you weren't dating Stephanie anymore, you still cared about her. "I should head back to my roommates anyway," I said, even though I didn't want to go. "Thank you for . . ." I started the sentence without knowing how to end it, and then found I couldn't.

You squeezed my fingers. "Thank you for making this day about something more," you said. "Lucy. Luce. *Luz* is light in Spanish, right?" You paused. I nodded. "Well, thank you for filling a dark day with light."

You'd put into words the feeling I couldn't express. "You did the same for me," I said. "Thank you."

We kissed again and it was hard to tear myself away from you. It was so hard to leave.

"I'll call you later," you said. "I'll find you in the directory. I'm sorry about the nachos."

"Stay safe," I said. "We can always eat nachos another time."

"That sounds good," you answered.

And I left, wondering if it was possible for one of the

most horrific days I'd ever experienced to somehow contain a small nugget of goodness.

You did call me a few hours later, but it wasn't the conversation I'd expected. You said you were sorry, so sorry, but you and Stephanie had gotten back together. Her eldest brother was missing—he worked at One World Trade—and she needed you. You said you hoped I understood and you thanked me again for bringing light to such a horrible afternoon. You said it meant a lot to have me there. And you apologized once more.

I shouldn't have been crushed, but I was.

I didn't speak to you for the rest of fall semester. Or spring semester either. I changed my seat in Kramer's class so I wouldn't have to sit next to you. But I listened every time you spoke about the way you saw beauty in Shakespeare's language and imagery—even in the ugliest scenes.

"'Alas!'" you read aloud, "'a crimson river of warm blood, / Like to a bubbling fountain stirr'd with wind, / Doth rise and fall between thy rosed lips.'" All I could think about was *your* lips and how they felt pressed against mine.

I tried to forget that day, but it was impossible. I couldn't forget what happened to New York, to America, to the people in the towers. And I couldn't forget what happened between us. Even now, whenever anyone asks, "Were you in

New York when the towers fell?" or "Where were you that day?" or "What was it like here?" the first thing I think of is you.

THERE ARE MOMENTS that shift the trajectory of people's lives. For so many of us who lived in New York City then, September 11th was that moment. Anything I did that day would have been important, would have been burned into my mind and branded on my heart. I don't know why I met you that day, but I do know that because I did, you would have been a part of my personal history forever.

V

IT WAS MAY AND WE'D JUST GRADUATED. WE'D handed back our caps and gowns, trading them for diplomas written in Latin, emblazoned with our names, first, middle, and last. I walked into Le Monde with my family—my mother, my father, my brother Jason, two grandparents, and an uncle. They seated us next to another family, a much smaller family—yours.

You looked up as we filed by and you reached out, touching my arm. "Lucy!" you said. "Congratulations!"

I shivered. All those months later, feeling your skin against mine did that to me, but I still managed to say, "You too."

"What are you up to?" you asked. "Are you staying in the city?"

I nodded. "I got a job working in program development

at a new TV production company—kids' shows." I couldn't help grinning. It was a job I'd been crossing my fingers over for almost two months before I got it. The kind of job that I'd started thinking about soon after the towers fell, after I admitted that I wanted to do something more meaningful than advertising. A job that could reach the next generation and had the potential to change the future.

"Kids' shows?" you said, a smile playing across your lips. "Like *Alvin and the Chipmunks*? Will they have helium voices?"

"Not quite," I said, laughing a little, wanting to tell you that it was our conversation that led me there, that the moment we shared in your kitchen meant so much. "How about you?"

"McKinsey," you said. "Consulting. No chipmunks for me."

I was surprised. I hadn't expected that, after our talk, after hearing your analyses in Kramer's class.

But what I said was, "That's great. Congratulations on the job. Maybe I'll see you around the city sometime."

"That would be nice," you answered.

And I went to sit down at the table with my family.

"Who was that?" I heard someone ask. I looked up. There was a girl next to you with long wheat-colored hair almost to the middle of her back and her hand on your thigh. She'd barely registered, I was so focused on you.

"Just a girl I know from class, Stephanie," I heard you say. Which, of course, was all I was. But somehow it stung.

vi

NEW YORK IS A FUNNY CITY. YOU CAN LIVE there for years and never see your next-door neighbor, and then you can run into your best friend while getting into a subway car on your way to work. Fate versus free will. Maybe it's both.

It was March, almost a year after graduation, and New York City had swallowed us up. I was living with Kate on the Upper East Side in that huge apartment that had once belonged to her grandparents. It was something she and I had talked about doing ever since we were in middle school. Our childhood dreams had become a reality.

I'd had a six-month fling with a coworker, a couple of one-night stands, and a handful of dates with men I'd deemed not smart enough or not handsome enough or not exciting enough, though in hindsight there probably wasn't much wrong with them at all. Actually if I'd met Darren then, I might have thought the same thing about him.

Without the constant reminder of Philosophy Hall or the East Campus dorms, I'd stopped thinking about you—mostly. We hadn't seen each other in close to a year. But you did pop into my mind at work when I was skimming storyboards with my boss, when we were reviewing episodes focused on acceptance and respect. I thought about your kitchen and felt good about the decision I made.

Before long it was Thursday, March 20th, and I was turning twenty-three. I had a party planned for the weekend, but my two closest friends at work, Writers' Room Alexis and Art Department Julia as you called them later, insisted that we have a drink on my birthday.

The three of us had become obsessed with Faces & Names that winter because of the fireplace and the couches. The temperature was hovering around forty, but we thought the bar might turn the fireplace on if we asked. We'd been there enough during the past few months, and the bartender liked us.

Julia had made me a paper birthday crown that she insisted I wear, and Alexis ordered all of us apple martinis. We sat on the couch in front of the fire, coming up with things to toast before each sip.

"To birthdays!" Alexis started.

"To Lucy!" Julia said.

"To friends!" I added.

Which devolved into: "To the photocopy machine not jamming today!" and "To bosses who call in sick!" and "To free lunches scrounged after fancy meetings!" and "To bars with fireplaces!" and "To apple martinis!"

The waitress came over to our couch with a tray that had three more martinis on it.

"Oh, we didn't order those," Julia said.

The waitress smiled. "You girls have a secret admirer." She nodded toward the bar.

There you were.

For a moment I thought I was hallucinating.

You gave us a small wave.

"He said to say happy birthday to Lucy."

Alexis's jaw dropped. "You *know* him?" she said. "He's hot!" Then she picked up one of the new martinis that the waitress had placed on the table in front of us. "To cute boys in bars who know your name and send over free drinks!" she toasted. After we all took a sip, she added, "Go thank him, birthday girl."

I put the martini down, but changed my mind, taking it with me as I walked toward you, wobbling only slightly on my high heels.

"Thanks," I said, sliding onto the stool on your left.

"Happy birthday," you answered. "Nice crown."

I laughed and slipped it off. "It might look better on you," I said. "Want to try?"

You did, crushing your curls with the paper.

"Stunning," I told you.

You smiled and put the crown on the bar in front of us.

"I almost didn't recognize you," you said. "You did something new to your hair."

"Bangs," I told you, pushing them to the side.

You stared at me like you did in your kitchen, seeing me from all angles. "Beautiful with or without bangs." You slurred your words a little, and I realized that you were even drunker than I was. Which made me wonder why you were alone, lit at seven p.m. on a Thursday night.

"How are you?" I asked. "Is everything okay?"

You propped your elbow on the bar and leaned your cheek into your hand. "I don't know," you said. "Stephanie and I broke up again. I hate my job. And the U.S. invaded Iraq. Every time I see you, the world is falling apart."

I didn't know how to respond to that, the information about Stephanie or your assertion that the world was falling apart, so I took another sip of my martini.

You kept going. "Maybe the universe knew I needed to find you tonight. You're like . . . Pegasus."

"I'm a winged horse, like in *The Iliad*?" I asked you. "A male winged horse?"

"No," you said. "You're definitely female."

I smiled. You continued talking.

"But Bellerophon never would have defeated the Chimera without Pegasus. Pegasus made him better," you said. "He got to fly above everything—all of the pain, all of the hurt. And he became a great hero."

I hadn't understood that myth the same way. I'd read it as one about teamwork, about cooperation and partnership; I'd always liked how Pegasus had to give Bellerophon permission to ride him. But I could tell your interpretation was important to you. "Well, thank you for the compliment, I think. Though I might have preferred a comparison to Athena. Hera. Even a Gorgon."

The corners of your mouth quirked up. "Not a Gorgon. No snakes on your head."

I touched my hair. "You haven't seen how I look first thing in the morning," I said.

You looked at me like you wanted to.

"Did I ever tell you I was sorry?" you asked. "For what happened. With us. I'm not sorry that I kissed you, I mean. But"—you shrugged—"I'm sorry about what happened after. I was trying to do the right thing. With Stephanie. Life is—"

"Complicated," I finished for you. "It's okay. It's forever ago now. And you did apologize. Twice."

"I still think about you, Lucy," you said, looking into your empty glass of whiskey. I wondered how many you'd had. "I think about that fork in the road, what would have happened if we'd taken it. Two roads diverged."

Now I would laugh if you called us a road, but then it felt so romantic, you quoting Robert Frost to me.

I looked over at Alexis and Julia. They were watching us as they drank their martinis. *You okay?* Julia mouthed to me. I nodded. She tapped her watch and shrugged. I shrugged back. She nodded.

I looked at you. Gorgeous, fragile, wanting me. My birthday present from the universe, perhaps.

"The thing about roads," I said, "is sometimes you happen upon them again. Sometimes you get another chance to travel down the same path."

God, we were lame. Or maybe just young. So, so young.

You looked at me, then, right at me, your blue eyes glassy but still magnetic. "I'm going to kiss you," you said, as you tipped toward me. And then you did, and it felt like a birthday wish come true.

"Will you come to my apartment tonight, Lucy?" you asked, as you tucked a rogue lock of hair behind my ear. "I don't want to go home alone."

I saw the sorrow in your eyes, the loneliness. And I wanted to make it better, to be your salve, your bandage, your antidote. I've always wanted to fix things for you. I still do. It's my Achilles' heel. Or perhaps my pomegranate seed. Like Persephone, it's what keeps drawing me back.

I lifted your fingers to my lips and kissed them. "Yes," I said, "I will."

vii

LATER WE WERE LYING IN YOUR BED, OUR BODIES IL-luminated only by the city lights leaking in around your blinds. You were the outer spoon, your arm wrapped around me, your hand resting on my bare stomach. We were tired, satiated, and still a little drunk.

"I want to quit my job," you whispered, as if the darkness made it safe to say it out loud.

"Okay," I whispered back, sleepily. "You can quit your job."

You rubbed your thumb along the underside of my breast.

"I want to do something meaningful," you said, your breath warm against my neck. "Like you talked about."

"Mm-hm," I answered, half asleep.

"But I didn't get it then."

"Get what?" I mumbled.

"It's not only about finding beauty," you said, your words keeping me awake. "I want to photograph all of it—happiness, sadness, joy, destruction. I want to tell stories with my camera. You understand, right, Lucy? Stephanie didn't. But you were there. You know how that changes your view of the world."

I rolled over so we were facing each other and gave you a soft kiss. "Of course I understand," I whispered, before sleep pulled me under.

But I didn't really get what you meant or know how far it would take you. That it would bring you to here, to this moment. I was drunk and tired and finally in your arms, the way I'd imagined so many times. I would have agreed to anything you asked just then.

viii

YOU DID QUIT YOUR JOB, OF COURSE, TO TAKE PHOTOG-raphy classes. And we kept seeing each other, our physical connection getting even stronger the more time we spent together, finding solace, hope, strength, in each other's embraces. We undressed in restaurant bathrooms because we couldn't wait until we were home. We crushed each other against the sides of buildings, bricks digging into shoulders as our lips met. We took picnics to the park, complete with apple juice bottles full of white wine, and then lay together breathing in the scent of the dirt and the fresh-cut grass and each other.

"I want to know more about your dad," I said, a few months after we reconnected, walking eyes-open into a fault line, willing to risk the earthquake.

"Not much to tell," you answered, shifting so my head

rested on your chest instead of your arm. Your voice was still light, but I could feel your muscles tense. "He's an asshole."

"An asshole how?" I asked, turning so I could wrap an arm around your stomach, holding you closer. Sometimes I got this feeling that we'd never be close enough. I wanted to climb inside your skin, inside your mind, so I could know all there was to know about you.

"My dad was . . . unpredictable," you said slowly, as if choosing that word with the utmost care. "Once I was big enough, I protected my mom."

I picked my head up off your chest and looked at you. I wasn't sure what to say, how much I should ask. I wanted to know what your definition was of "big enough." Four? Ten? Thirteen?

"Oh, Gabe," was all I could think of. I'm sorry it wasn't more.

"He and my mom met at art school. She said he was a beautiful sculptor, but I never saw any of his work." You swallowed hard. "He smashed it all—every single piece— right after I was born. He wanted to design monuments, huge installations. But no one was commissioning anything from him, no one was buying his art."

You turned to look at me. "I know it must've been hard for him. I can't imagine . . ." Then you shook your head. "He gave up," you said. "He tried to run a gallery. But he wasn't much of a businessman. Or a salesman. He was angry all the time, volatile. I . . . I didn't understand what giving up did to him. The power it had. One time, he took a knife to my mother's canvas—a painting she'd been working on for months—because he said she needed to spend her time painting sunsets instead. She cried like it was her body he'd stabbed, not just her art. That's when he left."

I slipped my hand into yours and held it tight. "How old were you?"

"Nine," you said, your voice soft. "I called the cops."

My childhood had been so different from yours, so idyllically Connecticut suburban. I wasn't sure how to respond. If we were having that conversation now, I would acknowledge the pain—both his and yours. Say that your father clearly had a hard time, that he was fighting demons, and that I'm sorry his demons became yours. Because they did, didn't they? You've lived so much of your life in response to his, trying not to become him, that you ended up battling both his demons and your own.

But that day, I couldn't process what you were saying quickly enough and I just wanted to comfort you. After a breath, what I said was, "You did the right thing."

"I know," you answered. Your eyes were hard. "I'll never be like him. I'll never hurt you like that. I'll never act like your dreams are disposable."

"Me neither. I'll never act like your dreams are disposable either, Gabe," I told you, resting my head back on your chest, kissing you through your T-shirt, trying to convey the depth of my admiration and sympathy.

"I know you won't." You stroked my hair. "It's one of the many, many things I love about you."

I sat up so I was looking at you again.

"I love you, Luce," you said.

It was the first time you said that to me. The first time any man had. "I love you too," I answered.

I hope you remember that day. It's something I'll never forget.

A FEW WEEKS AFTER WE SAID *I LOVE YOU* FOR THE first time, you and I had my place to ourselves. We'd decided to celebrate that fact by walking around in our underwear. It was sweltering out, the kind of muggy July heat that makes me wish I could spend the whole day submerged in a swimming pool, and even though the air conditioner was on full blast, the apartment was still warm. It was so big that we probably needed more than one.

"Kate's grandparents were real estate geniuses," you said, as we scrambled eggs half naked. "When did they buy this place?"

"No idea," I said, sticking some English muffins in the toaster. "Before her dad was born. So . . . 1940s?"

You whistled.

I know we didn't stay there often, but I bet you remember

that apartment. It was hard to forget. The two huge bedrooms and bathrooms, that breakfast nook we used as a library. And the ceilings that were about twelve feet high. I didn't appreciate those details then, but I did appreciate the apartment. Kate was in law school, and her dad said it was cheaper for her to live there than for him to pay for housing down by NYU. It worked well for me, too.

"We visited Kate's grandma here when we were in middle school," I told you, as we sat on the couch with our breakfast plates on our bare knees. "She was a docent at the Met until she got sick. She'd studied art history at Smith back before most women even thought about college."

"I wish I'd met her," you said, after a sip of coffee.

"You would've loved her."

We chewed quietly, our thighs against each other as we ate, my shoulder grazing your arm. It was impossible for us to be in a room together without touching.

"When does Kate come back?" you asked, after you'd finished swallowing.

I shrugged. She'd met Tom about a month before, and that night was maybe the second time she'd stayed at his place. "We should probably get dressed soon."

I felt your eyes on my breasts.

You put your plate down, done with breakfast.

"You have no idea what you do to me, Lucy," you said, as you watched me rest my fork on my plate. "All morning, you without any clothes on. It's like being dropped into one of my fantasies." Your hand strayed to your lap and then you were touching yourself slowly through cotton.

I'd never watched you touch yourself, never seen what you did when you were alone. I couldn't stop looking.

"Now you," you said, tugging yourself free of your boxers.

I put my plate down and reached for you, already turned on.

You shook your head and smiled. "That's not what I meant."

I raised my eyebrows, and then I understood what you wanted. I slid my fingers down my stomach. You'd never watched me touch myself either. But the idea of it thrilled me. I closed my eyes, thinking about you, thinking about you looking at me, thinking about sharing this personal moment with you, and I felt my body shudder.

"Lucy," you whispered.

My eyes fluttered open and I saw you stroking yourself faster.

It felt more intimate than sex, the two of us performing this act for each other, an act that was usually private. The lines that separated "you" and "me" were blurring even more into an "us."

While I kept touching myself, you leaned against the couch, taking your boxers off completely, your eyes on me

39

the whole time. Our hands sped up. So did our breathing. You bit your lip. Then I watched your grip tighten. I watched your muscles clench. I watched you come.

"Oh, God," you said. "Oh, Lucy."

I moved my fingers more insistently, to join you, but you clasped your hand around my wrist.

"May I?" you asked.

I shivered at the sound of your voice.

Then I nodded and you shifted so I could lie down along the length of the couch, so you could slide off my underwear. You moved closer and the anticipation made me squirm.

As you slipped your fingers inside me you said, "I have a secret."

"Oh, yeah?" I asked, arching to meet your hand.

"Oh, yeah," you said, stretching out next to me, your mouth against mine. "Whenever I touch myself, I think about you."

A shudder rippled through my body. "Me too," I whispered between breaths.

I came thirty seconds later.

X

IN THOSE FIRST SIX MONTHS, I WAS ALWAYS LEARNING new things about you—things I found sexy, surprising, endearing.

Like that day I came over to your place after work, and you were sitting cross-legged on the floor, piles of paper squares around you, each the size of a small Post-it note.

I dropped my bag on the kitchen table and shut the door behind me. "What's going on?" I asked.

"It's my mom's birthday in two weeks, September nineteenth," you told me, looking up from your paper sorting. "Since I can't fly home for it this year, I wanted to come up with something meaningful to send her."

"So you're making . . . a paper mosaic?" I asked, walking closer.

"In a sense," you said. "They're all pictures of my mom

and me." You lifted up the squares of paper to show me. I looked closer and saw you and your mom at your high school graduation. The two of you in shorts, your feet dangling in a pool. You giving her bunny ears on your front porch.

"Wow," I said.

"I spent most of the day printing them," you told me, "and now I'm organizing them by color. I want to make it look like a kaleidoscope."

I sat down on the floor next to you, and you gave me a quick kiss.

"Why a kaleidoscope?" I asked, picking up a picture of you and your mom, back to back, you a smidge taller. Your hair was the same curly blond—it was hard to tell where she ended and you began.

"I was fourteen," you said, looking at the picture over my shoulder.

"You were cute," I said. "My fourteen-year-old self would have had a crush on your fourteen-year-old self."

You smiled and squeezed my leg. "Without even seeing a picture of you at fourteen, I'll go out on a limb and say the same would be true in reverse."

Now it was my turn to smile. I put the photo down. "But why a kaleidoscope?" I asked again.

You rubbed a hand across your forehead, pushing your curls out of your eyes. "I've never told anyone this story before," you said quietly.

I picked up a couple more pictures. You and your mom blowing out candles on her birthday cake. Your mom holding your hand as the two of you stood in front of a Mexican restaurant. "You don't have to tell me," I said, wondering if your dad had taken the pictures of the two of you from before you were nine—and who had taken them afterward.

"I know," you said. "But I want to." You moved so we were facing each other, knee to knee. "The year after my parents split, money was really tight. I would come home from school to find my mom crying more often than painting. That year, I was pretty sure if we did anything for my birthday at all, it would suck. I told her I didn't want a party with my friends. I didn't want her to worry about paying for it."

I was struck again by how different our childhoods were. There wasn't a time I ever worried that my parents wouldn't be able to pay for a birthday party.

"But my mom . . ." you said. "I had this kaleidoscope that I loved. I would look through it for hours, turning and turning the disc at the end, watching the shapes shift and change, focusing on that instead of how sad my mom was, how sad I was that I couldn't make her happier, how mad I was at my dad."

You couldn't look at me while you were talking; all your focus was on getting the words out. I rested my hand on your knee and squeezed. You gave me a brief smile. "And?" I asked.

You took a breath. "She turned the whole house into a kaleidoscope," you said. "It was . . . it was incredible. She hung pieces of colored glass from the ceiling and turned a fan on low so they'd twirl. It was stunning."

I tried to imagine it, a house transformed into a kaleidoscope.

"My mom and I lay there on the floor, staring up at the colored glass. Even though I thought of myself as a big kid since I'd just turned ten, since I was taking care of my mom as best I could, I started to cry. She asked what was wrong, and I told her that I didn't know why I was crying, that I was happy. She said, 'It's the art, angel.' And I think in some sense she was right, it was the art, but in another sense . . . I don't know."

"What don't you know?" I asked, unconsciously rubbing circles on your knee with my thumb.

"I wonder now if it was relief. If I was crying because my mom was acting more like my mom again. She was taking care of me. And even though she was in this dark and broken place, she was still able to create beauty. I wonder if that art proved to me that she was going to be okay. That we were going to be okay."

You put your hand on my knee now.

"She was strong," I said. "She loved you."

You smiled, as if you were feeling her love right there, in that room. And then you kept talking. "My mom and I lay there, both of us crying, and I couldn't help thinking about my dad. How if he were there, we wouldn't have done this. Living with him . . . I told you, it was unpredictable. It was like I imagine it must have been in London during World War Two, knowing the air-raid sirens would go off and bombs would fall at some point, but never having any idea where or when they would hit. I whispered to my mom then, 'We're better off without him,' and she said, 'I know.' I was only ten, but I felt like a grown-up when I said that."

There were tears in my eyes as you finished talking. I was imagining your ten-year-old self on the floor with your mom, thinking about your dad, feeling like an adult, feeling loved, surrounded by art that she created just for you.

"So I want to make her something special for her birthday, since I won't be there," you said. "Something meaningful. Something that shows her how much I love her—how much I'll always love her, no matter how far away I am. And this mosaic, the idea popped into my head this morning."

My eyes flickered over the tiny photographs. "I think it's perfect," I said.

The apartment felt charged with emotion, from everything you told me, from the fact that you shared it, that fragile part of you. I leaned in to give you a hug, but it turned into a kiss. Our lips met briefly, then more insistently.

"Thank you for telling me," I said softly.

You kissed me again. "Thank you for being someone I wanted to tell."

LATER THAT NIGHT, you started gluing the kaleidoscope together. You seemed so happy in that moment, so content, that I put down my computer and quietly picked up your camera. It's the only photograph I ever took of you. I wonder if you still have it.

As comfortable as we were together alone, as intimate as our relationship was, it took a while to get used to going to parties with you. I always felt like I was floating in your wake. It was like you had this magical spell that brought people's attention to you, your face, your words, your stories. Our world of two became your world of one, and then expanded into a world of many in which I wasn't as important as I'd been before. Midstory I'd slip away to get a drink or go to find someone else to talk to.

Once in a while I'd cast my eyes in your direction and see you holding court. You'd find me, eventually, when you were drunk and drained; it was like working that charm sapped all your energy. When we were alone together, you could recharge, and then we'd go out and mingle again. In those moments, it made me feel special that you chose me to recharge with.

The epitome of Gabe at a Party was that night we went to Gideon's birthday at his parents' apartment on Park Avenue. There was that formal library that we weren't supposed to enter, at least not with drinks in our hands. With our balance impaired by a few too many cocktails, Gideon was worried we'd ruin the first-edition Hemingway or the signed Nabokov. And seeing the way people were drinking at the party, he probably wasn't wrong to worry.

I'd been talking to Gideon's girlfriend, who worked in advertising. I was interested in hearing about the life I'd once contemplated living. We were comparing methods of storytelling when I turned my head sideways to check for you—and you were gone. I assumed you went to the bathroom or to refill your drink, but then it was five minutes, ten minutes, twenty minutes and you hadn't come back.

"I'm so sorry," I said to her, when I became too distracted to participate in the conversation any longer. "But I seem to have lost my boyfriend."

She laughed. "I imagine that happens often with him."

I didn't laugh with her. "Why do you say that?" I asked.

She shrugged apologetically, realizing she'd said the wrong thing. "Oh, I just meant that he's charming. I imagine people like talking to him."

"Well, I can't speak for everyone, but I sure do," I said. She was right, though—that was your magic. Everyone loved talking to you. You made them feel heard, cared about, listened to. I always figured that was part of why people who wouldn't allow anyone else to take their photograph often agreed to let you do it. You made them feel seen. You made *me* feel seen.

I wandered through the apartment and couldn't find you anywhere, until I heard your voice coming from the forbidden library. I poked my head in and you were talking to a woman I didn't know. She had red hair that curled like a lion's mane around a delicate catlike face. My stomach dropped when I saw you leaning against the bookcase, absorbed in whatever she'd been telling you.

"There you are!" I said.

You looked up, and there was no guilt on your face. Just a smile, as if you were expecting me to join, but I was late to the appointment.

"Me?" you said. "There *you* are! Rachel was just telling me about the restaurant she hostesses at. She said she can get us a deal—a discount on the prix fixe menu."

I looked over at Rachel, who was clearly less happy to see me than you were. She'd fallen under your spell. "That's really nice of you," I said.

Rachel smiled a tight little smile. "Nice to meet you, Gabe," she told you. Then she lifted up her empty glass.

"Going to head back to the bar for a refill. But you have my number . . . for the reservations."

"Thanks again," you said to her, your smile beaming her way now, instead of mine. Then she walked out of the room.

I didn't quite know what to say. I hadn't caught you doing anything other than talking to someone about restaurant discounts. But why were you in the library with her? Why hadn't you come to find *me*?

"Whatcha doing in here?" I asked, keeping my voice light.

You crossed the room and pushed the door shut, a grin on your face. "Scouting for someplace we could do this," you said. Then you grabbed my wrists and held them above my head as you leaned me into the bookcase and kissed me hard. "I'm going to make love to you in this library," you told me, "while the whole party is going on outside. And I'm not going to lock the door."

"But—" I said.

You kissed me again, and my protests stopped. I didn't care about finding you in the library with Rachel anymore. All I cared about was your fingers tugging down the waistband of my tights and the sound of you unzipping your fly.

I wouldn't put up with that now, and I shouldn't have put up with it then—you placating me with a kiss, erasing my concerns with an orgasm. I should've made you explain yourself. I should've called you out for flirting with someone else, for not coming to find me. But you were like a drug. When I was high on you, nothing else mattered.

"Shh," you said, as you lifted up my skirt. I didn't even realize I was making any noise.

I bit my lip so hard to keep from calling out as I came that when I kissed you afterward there was a smear of blood on both of our mouths.

I loved you so much—and didn't doubt your love for me—but I'd never forgotten about Stephanie, and I think deep down I was worried that it could happen again, that you'd leave me for someone like her or like Rachel or a million other women you ran into on the subway or at Starbucks or in the grocery store. The seesaw of our relationship wasn't always balanced. Usually we were even, usually we were equal, but once in a while I'd find myself down at the bottom, trying to spring back up, afraid that you'd jump off to be with someone else, and I'd be stuck without any chance of reaching equilibrium. But even if I'd said something in that library, I don't think it would have changed anything.

Because it wasn't another woman that I should've been worrying about.

THOSE DOUBTS DIDN'T APPEAR OFTEN, THOUGH. THERE was so much more to us, so much about us that fit together perfectly. We both cared about each other's passions—about the careers we dreamed we'd have one day. You watched every single episode of *It Takes a Galaxy*, the TV show I was working on then, and gave me your thoughts on how the different aliens modeled social situations for kids. You seemed so into it that I started asking what you thought even before the shows went into production.

I didn't have any real power, then. Not yet. But I got to review scripts and storyboards and pass along feedback to my boss. I took that responsibility more seriously than I probably needed to. When I brought scripts home, you'd act them out with me so we could talk through them together. You always asked to play Galacto, the little green guy who looks kind of like a frog. My favorite was Electra, the dark purple one with sparkly antennae. It seems fitting, somehow, that reading an *It Takes a Galaxy* script is what helped you tell me your dreams. The show is supposed to help children communicate their feelings, but I guess it works on adults too. I remember the episode we were working on when our conversation happened. It was the beginning of November, and we were about a third of the way through the newest season.

Galacto sits in his front yard with his head in his hands. Electra enters.

Electra: *What's wrong, Galacto? You look sad.*

Galacto: *My dad wants me to play on the starball team, but I hate starball!*

Electra: *Does he know that?*

Galacto: *I'm afraid to tell him. I'm afraid he won't want to be my dad anymore if I don't like starball as much as he does.*

Electra: *My dad likes starball, but I don't, so we do other things together. Maybe you could make a list of things you and your dad* both *like.*

Galacto: *Do you think that would work? And then I wouldn't have to play starball anymore?*

Electra: *I think it's worth a try.*

Galacto: *Me too!*

"Do you think maybe Electra should like starball and her dad shouldn't?" I asked, when we finished reading. "You know, flip the gender stereotype a little? Maybe I should suggest that."

"I think that's a great idea," you said, looking at me a beat longer than usual. In that moment it felt like you loved not only my idea, but every aspect of who I was.

I made some notes on my script, then reread the scene silently. "Do you think Electra should name some things that she and her dad like doing together? Would that strengthen the dialogue?"

You didn't respond to my questions this time, so I turned to look at you. Your focus was on a pigeon cooing on your fire escape. "I'm afraid I'll turn into him," you said.

I put the script down. "Turn into who?" Absurdly, my first thought was the pigeon.

You rubbed your hand against the stubble on your chin. "My dad. That I'll have all these dreams and I'll never achieve them. That it'll make me angry and bruised and broken inside, and I'll hurt everyone around me."

"What dreams do you have?" I asked. "New dreams?"

"Do you know who Steve McCurry is?"

I shook my head, so you grabbed my laptop off the floor and put in some search terms, then turned the screen to me. I saw a *National Geographic* cover with a girl on it. She was wearing a headscarf and had stop-you-in-your-tracks green eyes. Her expression looked haunted, hunted.

"This," you said, "is one of his photographs. We were looking at his work today in my photography class, and I felt it. In my heart, in my soul, in wherever you feel things deepest. This is what I want to do. This is what I *have* to do."

There was a fire in your eyes I'd never seen before.

"I realized that if I want to make a difference, truly make a difference, like you're trying to do with this show, I'm going to have to leave New York. My camera and I can do more somewhere else."

"Leave?" I echoed. Of everything you said, it was the one word that lodged in my brain, glowing there like a neon *Emergency Room* sign. "What do you mean? What about us?"

Your face went blank for a moment and I realized my response wasn't the one you were expecting. But really, what *were* you expecting?

"I . . . I wasn't thinking about us . . . It's my dream, Lucy," you said, your voice pleading. "I've figured out my dream. Can't you be happy for me?"

"How can I be happy about a dream that doesn't include me?" I asked.

"It doesn't *not* include you," you said.

I remembered what you'd told me a few months before at

the park, about your parents. I tried to turn off that neon sign and ignore what the word *leave* would do to my universe, ignore the questions you'd just left unanswered. "You figured out your dream," I repeated. "Your dream is not disposable."

I could see tears gathering on your lashes. "I want to make everyone here understand that people all over have the same kinds of dreams, that we're not that different. If I can do that, if I can create a connection . . ." You shook your head; you couldn't find the words. "But I need to take more photographs, sign up for more classes; I need to be the best before I go."

So there was time. We had time. And maybe it would be like you and your mom—you could love me from a distance while you were gone, and then come back when you'd finished an assignment. That didn't seem terrible. That could work.

I grabbed your hand with both of mine. "You will be," I said. "If that's what you want, you will be."

We held each other on the couch after that, breathing in each other's air, lost in our own thoughts.

"Can I tell you something?" I asked.

I felt you nod.

"I'm afraid that I'm going to become my mom one day."

You turned to face me. "But you love your mom."

You were right. I did. I still do. "Did you know that she

and my dad met in law school?" I asked you. "Have I ever mentioned that?"

You shook your head. "She's a lawyer?"

"She was," I said, tucking my head under your chin. "She worked for the Manhattan DA before Jason and I were born. And then she had Jay and quit. And the whole rest of her life she's been defined by her relationship to other people—she's Don's wife or Jason and Lucy's mom. That happens to so many women. I don't want it to happen to me."

You looked me right in the eye. "That doesn't have to happen to you, Lucy. You're passionate, you know what you want, you work harder than anyone." Then you kissed me.

I kissed you back, but inside I was thinking that my mother was probably all of those things too, and it didn't matter. She lost herself anyway. I wonder if she wanted to.

SOMETIMES WE MAKE DECISIONS THAT SEEM RIGHT AT the time, but later, looking back, were clearly a mistake. Some decisions are right even in hindsight. Even though everyone told me not to, and even knowing what happened afterward, I'm still glad I moved in with you that snowy day in January.

"He told you he wants to leave," Kate said, as we sat on the overstuffed chairs in our breakfast nook, coffee cups on the table in front of us.

"But there's no date," I argued with her. "He doesn't have a job yet. It could take a long time for him to get one. And even if he gets one, who knows how long it'll last? He could be gone for a little while, and then come back."

Kate gave me the look I imagine she now uses on the associates in her law firm, the one that says without words:

Are you listening to yourself? Do you expect anyone to believe that?

"Even if he gets a job next month," I told her, "even if he's gone for years, I want to spend as much time as I can with him before he goes. I mean, the world could end tomorrow. Or I could get hit by a truck and die a week from Thursday. I want to live in the now."

"Lu," Kate said. She ran her fingers along the silver beaded Tiffany necklace Tom had given her. She'd taken to wearing it every day. "The problem with living in the now is it means, by definition, you're not making plans for the future. And the probability that the world will end tomorrow or you'll be hit by a truck is incredibly slim. The probability that Gabe will find a job as a photojournalist overseas and break your heart in the process is incredibly high. I'm just trying to help you manage your risk here. It's less risky if you stay."

It was tedious defending my choice to everyone. I'd had a similar conversation with my mother the night before. And my brother Jason a few days before that. Alexis was on board with my decision, but even I knew that she had the most questionable judgment of all of my friends. I'd lost track of the number of men she'd slept with because of her personal "why the hell not" motto.

"The thing is, Kate," I said, "I'm already all in, whether

I live with Gabe or not. So I might as well enjoy myself while he's still here."

Kate was silent for a moment, then leaned over and hugged me. "Oh, Lu," she said. "I love you no matter what, but . . . see if you can figure out a way to Bubble Wrap your heart. I have a bad feeling about this."

Kate was, of course, right. But at that point, there was nothing I could have done to change our trajectory—yours, mine, ours. I stand by that decision. Even now, I stand by it. I've never felt as alive as I did those five months we lived together. You were life-changing, Gabe. I'm glad we made that choice. Free will, despite our fate.

xiv

Soon after we moved in together, you signed up for a photography class where your assignment was to capture different feelings or concepts on film. "Capture beauty" was one week—you aced that one, no problem—then "capture sorrow." Happiness and decay and rebirth were definitely in there. I don't remember the order, but I remember you traveling Manhattan with your camera, bundled up in your scarf and hat. Sometimes I tagged along, zipping my coat up to my chin and wearing my warmest earmuffs. A lot of your assignments ended up being pictures of me, like that one you took of me sleeping, my hair dark and tangled against the white pillowcase. It was for serenity, I think. I still have that picture, framed, wrapped in brown paper in a box under my bed. When I moved in with Darren I couldn't bring myself to get rid of it. Not even when I married him.

Maybe I should unwrap it now, hang it in my office at last. Would you like that?

The assignment you had that day was to capture pain.

"I know where we have to go," you said on that Saturday morning, making sure your camera battery was charged. "Ground Zero."

I shook my head as I ate the last bite of waffle on my plate. Your mom had sent you a waffle maker, remember? She bought it on a whim when she found it on a clearance rack, and we'd made that pact to use it as much as possible. Do you still have it? Did you keep mementos like I did, objects to remind you of our life together? Or did you outgrow us as you traveled, tossing memories out with matchboxes and coffee mugs? I still think about that waffle maker. It was a good waffle maker.

"You can go," I said. "I'm not."

"It's for pain," you said. "For class."

I shook my head again, scraping my fork across the plate to capture the last bit of syrup. "Your class, not mine," I told you.

"I don't understand," you said. "Why don't you want to go?"

I shuddered. "I just . . . I don't need to see it."

"But you do! We need to remember—the people, the ones who died and the ones they left behind, the reasons it happened. All of it. We can't forget."

"I don't need to look at the remains to remember," I said. "That day, it's a part of me. It always will be."

"Then to pay your respects," you said. "Like visiting a grave."

I put my fork down. "Do you really think that the only way to pay your respects to something—or someone—is by visiting the site of the event? The place they're buried? You can't mean that."

You were upset now, but trying not to show it. "No," you said. "I don't. But—I just feel like we're not doing enough. To remember. To understand."

I bit my lip. "Us?" I said.

"Everyone," you answered. Your hands were in fists, thumbs clenched around fingers. "How can people walk around like everything's normal when America's at war in Iraq? When bombs are going off in hotels in Indonesia? When they were here in New York and saw what happened? How come they don't feel it like I do? Why don't they want to do more?" Your voice cracked on the last word, and I could see you struggling so hard to keep your emotions in check.

You were right, though. Most people didn't feel it like you did. I didn't. At least not all the time, not every minute. It didn't engulf my mind or capture my heart the way it did yours.

"Maybe they don't need to force themselves to feel pain

to know it's there. Just because they're not doing it your way doesn't mean they're not doing it at all. And not wanting to go to Ground Zero doesn't mean I don't care."

I didn't wait for your response. I walked toward the kitchen, bringing the dishes, sticky with maple syrup, with me. The plates were yours, the forks mine—the kitchen was a jumble of us.

I turned on the sink and started washing the dishes, not able to stop the tears that overflowed onto my cheeks. I knew then, really knew in my heart, that you would leave me one day soon. This dream you had wasn't a someday dream, it was a right-now dream. You would never be happy in New York. You would never be happy with just me. You needed to confront your disappointment in the world, to work through it, if you were going to end up okay. Even then, I understood that. I just hoped you'd come back.

You walked over so quietly I didn't notice you until I heard your camera click. I looked up and you captured me with my eyes full of tears, the instant one started to slip down my cheek. "Gabe!" I said, wiping my eyes with my forearm. I couldn't believe you were taking my picture then. That you were turning our argument into art.

"I know," you said, putting your camera on the counter. You kissed the top of my head, then my eyelids, then my nose, and finally my lips. "I'm sorry. And I know you care. I love you, Lucy."

I put the plates down and wrapped my sudsy hands around your T-shirt. "You, too, Gabe," I said. "I love you, too."

You went to Ground Zero that day without me and took dozens and dozens of pictures. Because I knew how much it meant to you, I agreed to look through them and help you choose the best shot, even though I kept thinking I smelled that acrid, charred air that floated uptown on September 12th. But in the end, you didn't choose any of them. The picture you handed in for pain was the one of me, washing dishes with tears in my eyes. I never liked that picture.

How would you like it if I took a picture of you now?

XV

AFTER THAT STORY ABOUT YOU AND YOUR MOM
and your birthday kaleidoscope, I understood your desire
for grand gestures, for thoughtful, heartfelt celebration.
And I matched it. That year we went on a helicopter ride
for your birthday at the end of February—and then ate the
twenty-course tasting menu at that restaurant next to
Parm. I'm blanking now on the name, but you know the
place. The one where after about eleven of the courses I
was so full that you ate a couple of mine—so you ended up
with twenty-two courses and I ended up with eighteen,
which was still too many for me. I felt like a snake who'd
eaten an alligator for the whole rest of the weekend, but
you were happy. You said that your birthday had been
properly celebrated. Especially after I went down on you
during the taxi ride home.

And the day before my birthday that year you sent me flowers at work—a dozen stargazer lilies. I still have the note that came with them, hidden away with the wrapped-up photograph of serenity. *Stargazers for my girl filled with starlight. Happy birthday. Happy anniversary. Can't wait until tonight. Love you. Gabe.*

When I got home, there was a big box on the bed.

"Open it," you said, a huge grin taking over your face.

Inside was an outfit from my favorite store back then— BCBG—the one that I shopped in only when they were having their seventy-percent-off sales. The top was turquoise silk, sleeveless with a deep V in the front and in the back. And the skirt was short and tight and black.

"I thought this would look great on you," you said. "It's perfect for seeing *Apollo* at the ballet, and then I thought . . . we could go back to Faces & Names. You'll be the sexiest girl in the room."

I threw my arms around you in a thank-you hug. Your gift was so thoughtful, tailored just for me. I pictured you combing through *Time Out New York* for the perfect night out, walking into BCBG, feeling slightly out of place, touching silk and satin and imagining it on my body. Choosing a color that would make me glow.

"I'm so lucky," I said. "Really and truly the luckiest girl in the world to be with you."

"I think you've got it backward," you said. "I'm the lucky

one. I wish I could do more to show you how incredible it is to be here, right now, with you."

"Well," I said, grabbing your belt and tugging you toward me. "I might be able to come up with some things you could do."

We didn't even make it to the bed that day. And we had the rug burns to prove it.

Lying next to each other, our clothing strewn across the floor, you said, "Did you ever imagine that loving someone would feel like this?"

I snuggled closer to you. Your arm tightened around my shoulder. "Never in my wildest dreams," I said.

"It's like you're my star, Lucy, my sun. Your light, your gravitational pull . . . I don't even know how to say what you mean to me."

"I'd call us a binary star," I said, slowly running my fingers up your thigh. I couldn't keep my hands off you. No self-control. "We're orbiting around each other."

"God, Lucy," you said. "Your mind is as beautiful as your body." You propped your head up on your elbow and faced me. "Do you believe in karma?" you asked.

"Like Hindu karma? Or like, if I steal someone's taxicab, I'll be cursed to suffer the same fate?" I asked back.

You smiled. "There's definitely cab karma in this city, but that's not quite what I'm talking about. It's not Hindu karma either. I guess it's not really karma at all. It's more like . . . do you think we get to love each other like this—so much, so strongly—because my dad was an asshole? Is it my reward for living through that? Getting this?" You gestured at both of our naked bodies. "Or does having this now mean that I'll suffer later to make up for it? Do we all get a finite amount of goodness in this world?"

I sat up then and shook my head. "I don't think the world works that way," I said. "I think life is just life. We're put in situations and we make choices and that's why things happen the way they do. Taking the current when it serves. It's that old question. The one from Kramer's class."

You were quiet.

"But you know what I'd like to think?" I continued, to fill the silence. "I'd like to think that it *is* karma. Hindu karma. That maybe in a past life I did something wonderful for someone and my reward is you in this life. I like that kind of karma better than your idea of a finite amount of goodness."

You smiled again, but this time it was rueful. I could tell you didn't believe me. "I like that idea too," you said. "I just . . . I worry that it's impossible to have it all, for all parts of a life to be wonderful."

I thought about it. "I think they can be," I said. "Maybe not everything all at once, but I think people can end their lives having gotten all that they wanted out of it." And I do believe that, Gabe, I still do.

"I hope you're right," you said.

We never talked about it after that, but I got the feeling you still thought that no one person could ever have everything. I wish I could've figured out a way to shift your perspective on that—because what I think you were saying, what you believed, is that you have to sacrifice. This love for that love. This piece of happiness for that one. It was a theory that shaped your decisions, whether consciously or unconsciously. It was part of what pointed you down the road you traveled, what brought us here.

But I really would like to think that's not the case. That you can have a father who loves you and a girlfriend who does the same. A career that's rewarding, and a personal life that is too. But maybe you'd say that if you have those things, maybe it's your health that will go. Or your finances. Or God knows what else.

Did you ever change your mind, Gabe?

I wish you could answer me.

XVI

SOON AFTER MY BIRTHDAY YOU SIGNED UP FOR THAT class with Pete. I always wondered how long you kept in touch with him after you left New York. I know he meant a lot to you. Clearly. He's the one who jump-started your career. I always wondered if, in him, you'd finally found the support and guidance you'd always wanted from your father. You were the happiest I'd seen you while you were taking his class, selling photographs, with his help, to the *Village Voice*. It made me think briefly that maybe I was wrong, maybe you were wrong, maybe you *could* be happy staying in New York.

You'd taken on dinner responsibilities, too, because I made it a point to stay at the office until Phil left, and he was working later and later then, trying to come up with a new season's worth of ideas for *It Takes a Galaxy*. Do you remember the night I came home even later than usual—close to nine—and you'd made pasta with homemade pesto sauce? There was a bottle of wine open, and you'd already had a glass. When I walked in, you were setting the table. Ella Fitzgerald was playing through the speakers attached to your laptop.

"Well, hello," you said. Your kiss tasted like Malbec.

"You're in a good mood tonight," I answered, shrugging off my denim jacket.

"Guess who's going to have his photograph printed in the *New York Times*?" you asked.

I gasped. "You?"

"Me!" you said, giddy. "Pete connected me with the right people over there, and they're printing the one I took down our block, when the water pipe burst in the middle of the street. It's for a feature article on the crumbling city infrastructure."

I dropped my bags on the floor and threw my arms around you. "Congratulations—to my talented, brilliant boyfriend."

As you lifted me up off the ground and lowered me onto the couch, I thought that maybe, just maybe, this could work long term. Maybe you wouldn't leave after all.

We ate dinner that night half dressed, and afterward I shared some news of my own. Phil had asked me to help him come up with some ideas for next season's shows.

"This is it," I told you. "My chance to really influence what kids in our country see and learn and understand."

You sat up with me late that night as I brainstormed ideas in bed, acting as my incredibly supportive sounding board. But I wasn't happy with my list. Out of the corner of my eye, I saw your camera.

"Hey," I said. "Any ideas in there? What's on your memory card?"

You brought your camera into bed with us, and we clicked through your photos one by one until I made you stop at a little girl in the window of a first-floor apartment, her hands gripping the window bars.

"What's her story, do you think?" I asked.

"Loneliness?" you said. "Parents who left her while they went to work? A dreamer who's yearning for something else?"

"Dreams! We should do an episode on dreams."

It was episode one of our second season.

And I got promoted at the start of the next quarter. But you were gone before both of those things happened.

xvii

Not long after your photograph was in the Times, *It Takes a Galaxy* was nominated for a Daytime Emmy, and I was invited to the ceremony with a date.

I dragged you to Bloomingdale's with me when I tried on gowns. Though I guess *dragged* isn't really the right word, because you enjoyed it. Do you remember? You sat on a couch near the dressing rooms, an audience of one for a private fashion show. I came out in a strapless lace sheath first, with a slit up the front of my right leg.

"Sexy," you said. "Really hot."

"Not quite what I'm going for, at least not for work."

Then I came out in a pink ball gown.

"Sweet," you told me. "Like Cinderella."

That wasn't right either.

I put on a navy blue dress, all angles and corners.

"Severe," you said. "Beautiful and sharp."

I could see the other women at the store noticing us. The older ones smiled indulgently. Some of the younger ones looked jealous. When I saw their stares, I tried to tone down my smile, tamp down the feeling inside me that said, *All is right in the world*. That day happiness felt like our destiny, yours and mine together.

I tried on a few more dresses until I got to a red silk dress, halter, with a low back, tight on top and then looser on the bottom, so it swayed when I moved. Do you remember what you said? I do. I can see you saying it right now, your eyes smoldering as they traveled the length of my body.

"That," you said, "is stunning. You are stunning."

You stood up from the couch and took my hand, twirling me in the middle of the Bloomingdale's formal-wear section. Then you dipped me, and kissed me. "This one," you whispered as you righted us. "And buy it as quickly as possible. Is there a bathroom we can sneak into around here? Or should we just take a cab home?"

I laughed and whispered back, "Cab," as you helped me undo the zipper.

xviii

When we got home that day, you gathered me and my bags into your arms and raced up the two flights to our apartment, fumbling one-handed for your key while I hung on to your neck, laughing.

"What are you doing?" I asked. "You're nuts."

"Couldn't wait any longer," you said, pushing the door open and tossing me onto the bed. You threw my bags on the couch and then came back, already pulling your shirt over your head. "Seeing you in those gowns, knowing you were naked in that dressing room . . . excruciating."

I pulled my T-shirt off, too, and unhooked my bra. When I slipped it over my shoulders, you moaned. "Luce," you said. "Lucy."

And then you climbed onto the bed with me and your lips and fingers were everywhere and I was moaning too, my back arching, and then you were inside me and I felt complete, like I always did the moment you slid into me.

"Gabriel," I said between breaths, "you make me feel infinite."

You bent your head down and kissed me hard. "You make me feel invincible," you whispered.

Love does that. It makes you feel infinite and invincible, like the whole world is open to you, anything is achievable, and each day will be filled with wonder. Maybe it's the act of opening yourself up, letting someone else in—or maybe it's the act of caring so deeply about another person that it expands your heart. I've heard so many people say some version of *I never knew how much I could love another human being until . . .* And after the *until* is usually something like *my niece was born* or *I gave birth to a child* or *I adopted a baby.* I never knew how much I could love another human being until I met you, Gabe.

I'll never forget that.

xix

I THINK I GLOWED THAT DAY. I LOVED A MAN WHO loved me back just as fiercely. Who helped me pick out a dress for an award ceremony that would celebrate my accomplishments. I forgot about the fact that you wanted to leave, the fact that underneath the patina of joy I knew you weren't truly happy. Because that day everything seemed perfect.

XX

THE MORNING OF THE CEREMONY, I HAD MY HAIR blown loose and wavy. I'd had my makeup done, too, with tons of eyeliner and mascara and red lipstick that almost matched my dress. When I slipped on the silk sheath, I felt enchanting. And excited. And like everything I'd been working for since college had truly been worth it.

"Brains and beauty," you said with a half smile when you saw me.

"You're not so bad yourself," I responded. You were in a single-breasted tuxedo with a vest and a tie, your curls tamed with some kind of gel that you used only on important occasions. It made you smell like you'd just left a hair salon. Sometimes I'll walk by someone and catch that same scent, and it'll throw me back to that day, even now. Has that ever happened to you? Have you ever been rocketed back in time by a scent that made you think of me?

As we made our way to Rockefeller Center that day, as we met up with my colleagues and took our seats, I could tell that your mind was elsewhere. You kept clapping a second after everyone else. You kept looking at me with your bottom lip between your teeth—the face you made when you were thinking about something hard, turning it over and over in your mind. What exactly was going through your head then?

And then our award was up, and we won! I could barely breathe. The air was filled with joy. I imagined my parents watching, both of them crying, my dad pretending he wasn't. I imagined Jason whooping, Kate cheering. Phil pulled me up onstage with him and the rest of the team, and I got to stand next to him while he spoke. My smile was so wide I could feel my cheeks stretch. I kept looking right at you in the audience, wanting you to share my happiness, but your eyes were glazed over. You weren't even looking back. For a moment, I wondered what was going on, but then we were all turning and walking off the stage, and when I got back to my seat, right next to yours, you kissed me softly. "I love you," you whispered.

We all partied afterward, high on the rush of the adrenaline that comes from winning. We danced and drank and laughed and you made small talk with my colleagues' wives and boyfriends and fiancés. But the whole time I could tell you weren't really there.

xxi

WHEN WE GOT HOME, I SLIPPED OFF MY HEELS AND collapsed on the couch. You sat down next to me and took my foot in your hands, massaging away the pain of eight hours in stilettos.

"Oh, God," I moaned. "Gabe, this might be better than sex."

You didn't laugh, though, the way I was expecting you to.

"Luce," you said, your fingers still kneading the arch of my left foot, "we have to talk."

I sat up and pulled my feet from your hands, tucked them under me.

"What is it?" I asked. "Are you okay? Are *we* okay? I thought things were great, but if there's anything—"

"Lucy," you said, my whole name. "Stop." Then you took a deep breath. "I don't know how to say this, so I'm just going to say it straight out. I got offered a job with the Associated Press. They want me to go to Iraq, embed with troops there for a feature piece, to start. With the possibility of a salaried position after that. Pete made a few calls, pulled a few strings. He knew I wanted to go abroad."

For a moment I couldn't breathe.

"When?" I whispered. "For how long?"

"They want me to leave in three weeks. The job is for two months at least. Maybe a lot longer."

"When do you have to give them an answer?" I asked. I was thinking: *We could handle two months. Maybe even longer. We could make it work.*

"I already gave it," you said, looking down at your fingers. "I told them yes."

"You what?" I asked. I felt like someone had pulled the plug in a bathtub drain, like our life together was rushing away in a twirling tornado. My mind flashed to Kate, to what she said about the probability of you leaving and breaking my heart.

You still weren't looking at me.

"It's been in the works for a while," you said, "but today all the paperwork went through. I didn't know if it would. It seemed so tenuous. I didn't want to say anything unless it was definite. I didn't want to hurt you if I didn't have to."

I felt every beat of my heart, every pulse of blood as it

moved through my body. I opened my mouth, but I couldn't, for the life of me, figure out what to say.

"A few months ago, when I saw that first article on Abu Ghraib that the AP put out, I just knew I had to go. Images can shift perspectives. They can change opinions and minds. I can't stand back and trust that other people will do this work, not when I think it's so important. I told you I was going to leave, Luce. You knew that was my plan eventually."

And I did. But I don't think I understood you meant forever. That it wasn't negotiable. That we wouldn't work to figure it out together. And even more than that, I wasn't prepared. On that night especially. It was supposed to be a night of celebration, of happiness, of success. I was flying higher than I ever had in my life. The work I'd done had won an Emmy. And I'd let down my guard. I'd allowed myself to be completely happy.

How could you not have told me what Pete was trying to do? The phone calls you must've had? The plans you must have been making? How could you have made that decision without me? It still makes me angry, Gabe, that you didn't include me. We were a binary star. We orbited around each other. When you decided not to tell me, you changed that, you weren't orbiting around me anymore, you were circling someone else, something else. As soon as you started keeping secrets, we had no chance.

All at once, tears rushed to my eyes—tears of anger and sadness and confusion and hurt. "Gabe, Gabe," I said over and over. "How could you?" I finally managed. "How could you not tell me? How could you tell me tonight?"

You reached out to me, and I fought you, pushing your arms away with more strength than I thought I had.

"It would've hurt less if I'd known," I said, "if we'd talked about it. Don't you understand? We were a team. You cut me out. How could you make plans without me? How could you make plans like *that* without me?"

You were crying too, snot dripping from your nose to your lip. "I'm sorry," you said. "I was trying to do the right thing. I didn't want to hurt you, I'm sorry."

"But you did," I choked out. "More than you would have. More than you needed to. It's like I don't matter to you at all."

"That's not true." You wiped your nose and then reached for me again.

"Don't," I said. "Don't touch me."

"Please," you said. "Lucy, please." Now you were crying harder than I was. "I need you to understand. I wish I didn't want this—I wish I didn't feel like this is the thing I have to do, the only way I'll feel whole. I never wanted to hurt you. This isn't about you."

"No," I said. "It's not about me. But it's not only about you either. It's about us. It's about you destroying us."

You looked as if I'd slapped you. And I wanted to.

"I'm not—" you said. "It's not about us, Lucy. It's really not. It *is* about me. I need to do this for me. There's something inside me that's broken, and this is the only thing that will fix it. I thought you'd understand. You always under—"

But I didn't understand this time.

"Why can't you stay?" I interrupted. "What about photographing New York City? There are so many stories here to tell. You were so happy when the *New York Times* printed your picture."

You shook your head. "I can do more somewhere else. I can do better work. I can make more of a difference. I wish it weren't true, but it is. You know what that means to me."

"I do, but there has to be another way."

"There isn't," you said.

"What about taking trips, but coming back home when they're done?" I was begging. I knew it, and I didn't care.

"That's not how it works," you said. "Pete said if I want to do this, I have to be all in."

"Oh, Pete says." I was furious now. "So you talked to Pete all about this, but not to me."

"Lucy—" you started.

"You know what?" I said. "Fuck you." Anger spread to the far reaches of my fingers and toes. I walked to our bed and threw your pillow and the extra blanket onto the couch. "You're sleeping there tonight."

"Lucy, we're not done talking." The blanket dangled from your fingertips.

"We are," I said, unzipping my dress and turning out the light.

OF COURSE, neither one of us slept. I relived the conversation we'd just had over and over in my mind. As much as I hated you just then, I still wanted to walk across the studio and slide in next to you on the couch, to feel the solidity of your body next to mine. You were my comfort and my pain all at once.

At some point later you got up and stood beside the bed. "I have an idea," you said.

I didn't respond.

"I know you're awake," you said. "I can see your eyes."

We hadn't closed the blinds. You were backlit, illuminated by the city lights. It gave you a halo. *Fallen angel*, I thought.

"What?" I finally asked.

"Maybe . . . maybe you can come with me." You reached out your hand tentatively in the semidarkness. "Maybe we could figure that out."

I met your fingers with mine. For a brief moment it made sense. But then my mind focused on what you were asking. It focused on Baghdad. On visas. On apartments. On jobs. "But . . . how?" I asked.

You sat down on the bed, still holding my hand, and shrugged. "We could find a way."

"But where would I live? What would I do? What about *my* career, Gabe?" I felt the anger flooding my body again. You were asking me to give up my dreams for you, when you would never do the same for me, wouldn't even consider compromise, hadn't even talked to me about it.

You shook your head. "I don't know," you said. "But I'm sure people do this. Maybe you could have a different career. You could get a job writing articles and make a difference that way. We could create the words and the pictures together. I should've thought of this earlier. It'd be perfect."

"I thought my dreams weren't disposable, Gabe," I said. I loved you. I did. I do. So much. But what you were asking wasn't fair. And it hurt then—it still hurts now—that you'd made this decision to leave without my input and weren't willing to think about any alternatives.

"That's not what I meant," you said.

I sighed. It was all too much. "Let's talk about it in the morning," I told you.

"But—" you started. Then you closed your mouth. "Okay," you said. But you didn't move. You stayed put, sitting on the bed. You kept your hand on mine.

"Gabe?" I asked.

You turned to face me. A police car sped by, its flashing

lights reflected in your eyes. "I can't sleep without you, Lucy."

I felt my tears pool again. "That's not fair," I said. "You don't get to say that. You have no right."

"But it's true," you said. "That's why you should come to Iraq."

"Because you're having trouble sleeping without me next to you in bed?" I pulled my hand out of yours.

"I didn't mean it literally," you said. "I meant I love you. I meant I'm sorry. I meant I want you to come with me." You didn't get it.

I sat up and turned on the bedside lamp. We both squinted in its harsh light. I saw the pain etched onto your face. You looked raw and vulnerable. Miserable. Lost. Like you did that night at Faces & Names, the night we reconnected. And there it was, my pomegranate seed, that part of you that still makes it so hard for me to turn away. When you show me that vulnerable piece of yourself, it makes me feel responsible. Because we only reveal our true selves to the people we care about most. I think that's why our relationship jump-started so quickly. We had no barriers on September 11th—we revealed our secret selves to each other right away. And you can't ever take that back. But that night it wasn't enough. I needed more from you. I needed understanding and honesty and compromise. I needed commitment. It wasn't even worth fighting anymore.

I reached for your hand. "I love you, too," I said, "but I can't come with you. You know that. Your dreams are there, but mine are here."

"You were right before," you said, your voice sounding strangled. "Let's talk about it in the morning."

I watched you pad across the apartment, fold your long body onto the couch. I turned out the light and thought of all the reasons it made no sense for me to go with you to Iraq—and the one reason it did: because I couldn't imagine my life without you.

WHEN I WOKE UP bleary-eyed, with a pounding headache, you were sitting on the couch watching me.

"I know you can't come," you said quietly, the moment my eyes were open. "But I promise, we'll stay in touch. I'll see you when I come to visit the city. I'll always love you." Your voice caught in your throat. "But I need to do this. And the fact that I was ready to throw away your dream—I'm my father all over again, Lucy. I think . . . I think you'll be better off without me."

My head throbbed. My eyes burned. And I truly fell apart then; I couldn't stop the sobs, the shaking, the sounds coming out of my mouth that seemed prehistoric. Expressions of pain coded into our DNA from our preverbal ancestors. You were really leaving. You were really leaving *me.* I had known this would happen, at some point, but I never let myself imagine what it would be like when it did. And it felt like a nightmare. Like my heart was made of blown glass and someone had thrown it to the floor, shattered it into a million pieces, and then ground their heels into the shards.

The fact that you invited me to go with you, it meant a lot. It always has. But it wasn't a real offer, not a fully thought-out one. It was a middle-of-the-night apology, an attempt to fix your mistake in not telling me sooner, in keeping secrets, in leaving me out of the process. Though a part of me has always wondered what would've happened if I'd said yes. Would it have changed both of our lives completely, or would we still have ended up here, with me in this too-bright room, wishing I were anywhere else, and wishing at the same time that I never had to leave? I guess we'll never know.

You packed up your stuff that week and left to spend time with your mom before you took off for good. And I sat in what used to be our apartment and cried.

xxii

WE NEVER TALKED ABOUT WHAT IT WAS LIKE AFTER-
ward. I never told you how broken I was. How I looked at
the spaces your books left on the bookshelves and couldn't
bring myself to fill them. How I couldn't eat waffles without crying. Or wear the wooden bracelet you bought me at
the street fair on Columbus Avenue—the one we stumbled
upon and then stayed at all afternoon, eating mozzarepas
and crepes and pretending that we needed a new carpet for
our imaginary ski house.

One night, two weeks after you left, I took a bottle of
your favorite whiskey down from the shelf above the kitchen
sink. You'd left it behind too. I poured myself glass after
glass, first over ice, and then when the ice tray was empty,
straight. It burned my lips when I drank it, but it tasted like
kissing you. And it dulled the pain. For the first time since

you left, I slept through the night. I felt like hell the next morning and called in sick to work. But I did it again the next week. And the week after. Making myself go to work, learning how to live with the pain.

There were stores I couldn't pass and restaurants I couldn't eat in. I spent a month sleeping on the floor, because all I felt was your absence when I tried sleeping in our bed—and the couch was worse. It reminded me of the night after the Emmys. I donated half my clothing to Goodwill and threw away the posters we had on the walls.

Six weeks after you left, I sat in the almost-empty apartment and called Kate. "I can't stay here," I said.

"You shouldn't," she answered. "Come stay with me."

So I packed up the rest of the apartment and I did, for two weeks. Kate helped me sublet the studio and then I moved to Brooklyn. I couldn't take it anymore. I needed a new borough, a fresh start. And even there I had to avoid Bubby's, where we went to Kevin and Sara's wedding, and the Red Hook Lobster Pound, where we went to celebrate July Fourth. You were everywhere. We'd only been together for fourteen months, but it was fourteen months that changed my world.

I e-mailed you—do you remember? I didn't tell you how I was feeling, how I was falling apart. *I'm getting a share in the Hamptons with Alexis! Totally last-minute, but it should be fun,* I wrote with false cheer. *Just saw Ben Folds play on Sum-*

merStage—you'd have loved the show. How's everything going? And then I waited and waited and waited for a response that never came. I kept thinking about how you said we'd keep in touch. How you said you'd always love me. Every time I checked my e-mail, I'd feel a combination of rage and sadness, disappointment deeper than anything I'd ever experienced before. I started letters to you. Diatribes, really. But I threw them all out before I sent them. I was afraid that if I yelled at you across continents, you'd write me off completely, and I'd never hear from you again. I didn't think I'd be able to handle that.

Looking back now, I know you were hurting, too, trying to move on, find your own path. My note from New York must've felt like it had been beamed in from another planet. SummerStage? The Hamptons? I can't even imagine what you thought when you read that. But then? Then I couldn't understand how you could ignore me. How one minute you could spin me and kiss me and tell me I made you feel invincible, and then all of a sudden you could disappear.

Two months after you left I got an e-mail from you. The first one since you landed in Iraq. *Glad you're doing well! Things here are crazy. Sorry I didn't write sooner. It was a hard adjustment, but I love the work. The feature's done and they're keeping me on here for a while. Hope you're enjoying New York!*

I read that e-mail over a hundred times, maybe. It could have been two hundred. I analyzed every word. Every punctuation mark. I looked for the hidden meanings, any insight I could glean into how you were feeling or what you were thinking. Trying to figure out whether you missed me, whether you'd found someone new.

But here's the thing: There was no subtext, no hidden messages, no secret codes. It was just a quick response sent in a hurry. I'd been waiting two months for nothing. I created a Gmail folder called Disaster and put all your e-mails in there, including that one. I didn't write back. I knew I wouldn't be able to bear it if you ignored me again.

xxiii

SOMETIMES I'M TOLD THINGS THAT I DON'T REALIZE are important until much later. That's how it always seems to be when I talk to my brother—whenever we have any kind of serious discussion, anything more than the everyday *How are you* and *How's work*, it takes me years to understand what he was trying to tell me. A few weeks after you left, Jason called. He was twenty-eight at the time and had been dating Vanessa for about a year. They'd met at the lab—she was working in communications for the pharmaceutical company, and he was trying to develop some kind of targeted cancer therapy that I still only half understand.

"Hey, Lulu," he said, when I picked up my cell. "I—uh—I wanted to see how you were doing. Mom said things have been pretty rough."

"Yeah," I said, my eyes already filling with tears at his

concern. "I miss him so much, Jay. I love him and I hate him and it's just . . . it's awful." My voice wobbled on the phone. I wasn't questioning my decision not to go with you, I felt secure in that, but I'd been replaying the conversations we had over and over in my head, trying to figure out if there was anything I could've said that would've made you stay. And what it was about me that made you keep secrets. I wondered if you would have acted differently if you were dating someone else. Kate said you probably would have left sooner. I didn't believe her then, but now I wonder if she was right.

"Oh, Lu," Jason said, "I didn't mean to make you cry. I just . . . well . . . I know we haven't talked about relationships before, but remember when Jocelyn and I broke up for the last time?"

I don't know if you and I ever talked about Jocelyn, but she was Jay's girlfriend in college and right afterward. They met their sophomore year at Princeton and kept getting together and breaking up over and over for five years—until finally she decided to go to medical school at Stanford, and after a brief attempt at long distance they broke up for good. I guess their five years has nothing on our . . . how should I calculate it now . . . thirteen? Eleven?

"I remember," I said to Jay, even though I only half did. I was in college at the time and so wrapped up in my own world that I hadn't really been all that involved in my brother's.

"The reason I was able to end things for good is that I

realized that we were like the gummy bear experiment. Do you remember that one? I think I showed it to you in the lab when you came to visit me at college my freshman year. You put potassium chlorate in a test tube and then add a gummy bear, and these two items that are perfectly fine on their own explode. Every single time. Jocelyn and I were like that experiment. Every time we were together we would explode, and it was exciting and wonderful in some ways, but who wants to live with constant explosions?"

"Mm-hm," I answered, thinking of you and me. We didn't break up and get back together over and over, but our relationship back then did feel exciting and wonderful. We were better together than each of us was on our own.

"Anyway, when I met Vanessa, it was different. It was like . . . it was like the Old Nassau experiment. Do you remember that one? It starts out with three clear solutions, but you mix two together first, so I imagine I'm those two mixed solutions, and then when you add the third, nothing happens at first, but then the solution turns orange because of the potassium iodate and then a little while later, it turns color again, this time to black, which you know is my favorite color, because it's the one that contains all the pigment there is, and then it stays that way."

He stopped. I was silent. I had no clue how to respond.

"Basically, what I'm saying, Lu, is that the relationship got better the longer it lasted. Instead of that gummy bear explosion, it's a clock reaction. Do you understand what I mean?"

I didn't understand then, though I do now. Darren showed me that. Though he'd probably say love is like a fine wine, where flavors deepen and change over time. All I said to Jason then was, "But I love him so much, Jay."

"I know," he said. "I loved Jocelyn too. I still do. Probably I always will a little bit. But I love Vanessa—differently. What I wanted to tell you is that there are lots of ways to love people and I know that you'll love someone else again. Even if it's not the same, some of it might be better."

"I don't want to," I whispered. I wanted to love only you. And I couldn't imagine anything could be better than that.

Jason was quiet for a moment. "Maybe it was too soon for me to say that," he said. "I'm sorry. I'm not that good at this sort of thing. But maybe . . . what I said will make its way into your neurons and you'll remember it when you need it most."

"Yeah," I said. "Okay. Thanks for calling."

"I love you, Lucy, like hydrogen loves oxygen. A totally different kind of love. An elemental kind."

And when he said that, I laughed through my tears because only my brother could explain love using the periodic table.

xxiv

ALEXIS DRAGGED ME ALL OVER THAT SUMMER. To bars, to concerts, to parties, to movie screenings. We dressed up every night, in Brooklyn, Manhattan, Southampton, and with enough martinis, I could forget for a little bit.

Kate took me to her parents' place on Cape Cod for a week, leaving Tom back in Manhattan. She pampered me with spa treatments and took me to a salon for a brand-new haircut she'd found in a French fashion magazine her sister sent. That's when I cut off my braid and donated my hair.

Julia told me she was on Team Lucy and that she'd be there whenever I needed her. We spent a lot of nights together eating macaroni and cheese, since you hated it, and watching the most violent action films we could find.

My friends were actually pretty amazing, considering how much they hated you at that point. I don't know if Kate or Alexis has ever forgiven you for leaving me. Julia has, but it took her a while to understand what you and I had together—until your gallery show.

My mom sent me text messages all day long. And inspirational articles in the mail.

Jason came to visit, treating me to a Brooklyn Cyclones game, and hot dogs, and an explosion using Diet Coke and Mentos.

Practically everyone I knew tried to cheer me up in every way they knew how. And I tried as hard as I could to get over you, but really the only thing I needed was time.

XXV

AT THE END OF THAT SUMMER, ABOUT TWO WEEKS
after I got your e-mail and created my Disaster folder, I met
Darren.

Does it bother you that I'm talking about him? I'm sorry
if it does, but he's part of our story too. As much as you
might not like it—might not like him—our road wouldn't
be the same without Darren.

I woke up to make coffee the last weekend of my Hamptons share, Labor Day weekend, and he was sleeping on the
couch in the middle of our living room. I'd never seen him
before. He certainly hadn't been there when I'd gone to bed.
Still, Alexis's friend Sabrina tended to bring groups of people back to the house, and it wasn't a surprise to find them
sleeping on couches or chairs or sometimes even on the
floor in the living room.

I tiptoed around him and headed into the kitchen to make some coffee for the house. After you left, my whole sleep pattern changed. The minute I woke up, no matter how early, no matter how hungover, I got out of bed, because lying there without you was an exercise in misery. So coffee had become my job that summer.

The house was always full of people, and I tried not to look too much like I'd just rolled out of bed. That morning I'd thrown on a bikini—my favorite that summer was a red bandeau—with a pair of cutoff shorts. And I'd tied a bandana around my hair, letting the side-swept bangs hang over my left eye. I was tan from all those Hamptons weekends, and the bike rides to the beach had toned my body more than I'd expected them to. I liked what I saw when I looked in the mirror that summer. I had to stop myself often from wondering what you'd think if you saw me—if you'd like it too.

By the time the coffee machine started percolating, Darren had woken up. He walked into the kitchen and greeted me with the worst attempt at a pickup line I'd ever heard. Or maybe it wasn't even supposed to be a pickup line. He's never admitted one way or the other. Regardless, it was the sort of ridiculous thing that you would never say.

"Have I died and gone to caffeine heaven?" he asked. "Because you seem like a coffee angel."

It did make me smile, though.

His hair was pin-straight, but it was sticking up on one side, where it had been crushed against the arm of the couch. And he was wearing boxer briefs and a T-shirt that said *New Jersey: Only the Strong Survive*. I couldn't help but wonder where the rest of his clothing had gone.

I handed him the first cup of coffee and he took a sip.

"I'm no angel," I told him. "I promise. I'm Lucy."

"Darren," he said, holding out his hand. "This coffee is fantastic."

"I ground the beans yesterday," I told him. "They're from that new fair-trade coffee place in town."

He took another sip. "Your boyfriend is one lucky guy," he said, "dating a girl who can make coffee like this."

I couldn't help it, tears pricked my eyes as I said, "No boyfriend."

"Really," he said, drinking more coffee, his eyes finding mine over the rim of the mug.

I compared him to you then. His straight hair to your curly. His short, muscular frame to your long, lean one. His brown eyes to your blue. I knew he wanted to flirt, but I couldn't do it.

"I'm gonna go get my stuff together for the beach," I told him. "If you leave before I come out of my room again, it was nice to meet you."

He nodded and lifted his mug. "Thanks for the coffee, Lucy," he said.

XXVI

He left before I came out of my room again. Or rather, I didn't come out of my room until I heard him and his friend leave. But he must have asked Sabrina about me, because I got a Friendster request from him the next day. And a message asking for the name of the fair-trade coffee bean store.

We bantered a little through messages, and he invited me to a coffee-and-chocolate pairing event he'd read about in Park Slope. It was a Sunday afternoon, which somehow felt safe and non-date-y, and I had nothing else to do, so I went.

It would be a lie to say I didn't think about you at all. In fact, I thought about you a lot. But interspersed, there were moments of fun. Of jokes. Of coffee almost coming out of Darren's nose because he was laughing so hard at one of the descriptions of the pairings. It was the best time I'd had in months. Well, the best time I'd had in months sober.

So when he asked me out for dinner a week later, I said yes. He wasn't you, but he was clever, he was handsome, he made me laugh . . . he wanted me. And he made me forget about you, at least for a little while.

xxvii

Darren insisted on picking me up at my apartment for our date. He was wearing a suit and his hair was combed back, away from his face. I'd worn a summer dress to work that day—it was new, yellow-and-white seersucker—and I was still wearing it, with a pair of sandals, but he seemed much dressier than I was.

He must've seen me looking at his suit, because he said, "I-banker's uniform. I didn't have time to change."

I smiled. "You look nice in a suit." As I said it, I realized he did. His shoulders were broader than his waist, and the suit was perfectly tailored to accentuate that fact.

I almost offered to change into something fancier, but before I had the chance he said, "You look nicer in that dress. In fact, I'd bet if we took a poll of completely objective humans about the niceness factor of our respective outfits, you'd win."

I couldn't help but laugh. "Niceness factor of our respective outfits?" I repeated.

"That's the technical term," he said.

He wasn't you. He absolutely wasn't you. He was older, for one thing, twenty-nine. And he was calmer, grounded. Solid, Julia called him. And he was the only one who'd been able to make me laugh since you left. That counted for a lot.

When he crooked his elbow and said, "Mademoiselle?" I linked my arm with his and closed my apartment door behind me. I was actually looking forward to dinner with him.

xxviii

AFTER DINNER THAT NIGHT, DARREN SAID HE would walk me home, that it was the gentlemanly thing to do. He even walked on the street side of the sidewalk, so he would block me in the event that a car came zooming down the street and splashed through a puddle. It would drench him and not me, he explained.

"I see," I told him. "What about ladies? What are we supposed to do?"

"Nothing you're not already doing," he said, which made me smile again.

Then he cleared his throat. "You know, I was a tour guide at Penn and happen to be qualified to give tours of Prospect Heights as well."

"Oh really?" I asked, not quite sure if he was joking.

He began talking in an upper-crust accent, like maybe

he was someone who had donated a building to a university. I immediately started laughing. He sounded like I imagined the Schermerhorns or the Havermeyers or the Hartleys did, those families that had buildings named after them on campus. I always wondered about them when we were at school. I pictured them living in huge mansions in someplace like Armonk and summering on Martha's Vineyard. Mr. Schermerhorn wore those red pants that everyone wears on Nantucket and had a perma-tan and an underbite. And Mrs. Havermeyer never left the house without three-carat diamonds in each ear. She had three children who were raised by three different nannies, who shaped each of their personalities quite differently. She was oddly obsessed with the number three. And the Hartleys had show dogs. Corgis, like the queen of England.

I guess I could probably find out about them online now, if I wanted, but that would ruin the stories I made up in my head. I haven't thought about those stories in years.

So Darren turned to me and, in a voice like a Schermerhorn, said, "That large brownstone is the home of Ashton Cranston Wellington Leeds the Fourth, of the Kensington Leedses. The nobler side of the family. Everyone knows the Glasgow Leedses are gamblers and crooks. And horse thieves. They use teaspoons for their soup and dinner forks for dessert. Utter blasphemy. In fact, there's been a movement to hyphenate the family name to Kensington-Leeds. You know, for the sake of disambiguation."

I laughed so hard at that one I almost snorted, which made me laugh even more.

He kept going in his Schermerhorn voice. "I've heard that's why Julia Louis-Dreyfus hyphenated. Those other Dreyfuses were terrible. Same with Wal-Mart. Those other Marts? Forget about it. Disambiguation is very important."

Every time I tried to respond, my words were broken up with giggles. Then Darren and I rounded the corner toward my apartment. He stopped in front of my building. I stopped too. The laughter died in my throat when I saw the way he looked at me. He was going to kiss me. Panic constricted my lungs.

I hadn't kissed anyone since you left.

I hadn't wanted to kiss anyone since you left.

"I . . ." I started, but I didn't quite know where to go with that.

Darren must've seen the look on my face, though, and instead of kissing my lips, he leaned forward and kissed my forehead.

"Thanks for a really fun night," he said. "I hope we can do it again."

I nodded, and he smiled.

"I'll call you," he said.

I could breathe again.

"I'd like that," I answered. Because I did have a fun night with him. And because it was better to spend time with him than to sit home, alone, or get trashed with Alexis.

And as he walked away, I realized I was disappointed that he was leaving. My world seemed a little brighter while he shared it with me, and I liked that. A lot.

Then I turned to walk into my apartment and thought again about you.

xxix

THE NEXT DAY I SPOKE TO ALEXIS. "WHAT DID YOU
tell Darren about me?" I asked her.

"Me?" she said. "Nothing."

I sighed. I'd been going over the forehead kiss in my
mind all morning, and I realized that someone must've said
something. Someone must've told him not to move too fast.

"Okay, not you," I said. "Sabrina? What did she tell
him?"

Alexis took a deep breath. I could imagine her running
her hand through her hair on the other side of the phone. I
haven't seen her in about a year, since my last work trip to
LA. She was such a huge part of my world back then, and
just . . . isn't anymore. It's kind of sad that I don't really miss
her. I guess people change, lives change. We know that better than anybody.

"She told him you just got out of something serious," Alexis said over the phone. "She told him to be patient. Not to break you."

I cringed, even though Sabrina was probably right in saying all those things.

"And what did he say?" I asked.

"He said not only would he not break you, that he'd help put you back together."

I leaned my head against the back of my couch. "Well," I said. "That's bold. What's his deal? Does he have some sort of savior complex? A need to be a hero?"

"He's really a good guy," Alexis told me. "His friends are pretty much asshats, but he's really decent. Not that Gabe wasn't, but . . . I guess I'm just saying . . . give him a shot, Lu."

I felt tears welling up in my eyes again at the mention of your name. I needed to stop that from happening, but I had no idea how.

"I don't know if I can," I said, wiping my nose with the back of my hand.

"It takes a guy to get over a guy," Alexis said then. "And believe me, I should know."

I let out a short burst of sound that was caught somewhere between a laugh and a sob.

"Seriously," Alexis said, "give him a chance. If nothing else, he'll show you that there are other good, smart people out there who think you're pretty great."

I nodded, even though she couldn't see me. "I'll give him a chance," I told her.

"Nothing more I can ask for," she said. "Except maybe plans for next Friday night? You know that hot guy I met on the L train? He's in a piece of performance art on the Lower East Side. Can you go with me?"

"Is this the one with the green hair?" I asked.

"Ew, no," Alexis said. "Did I not tell you? He picked his nose at dinner. Done. This is the one with the Buddy Holly glasses and the beard."

"Got it," I said. "Count me in." Even though really the last thing I wanted to do was go to see performance art starring some wacko Alexis met on the subway. But it was better than missing you.

XXX

DARREN DIDN'T TRY TO KISS ME AGAIN. NOT THE next time we hung out, not the time after that, not the time after that either. And then it was almost Halloween.

"Want to come with me to a Halloween party this weekend?" he asked, when he called me a few days after our last date. "I promise it'll be fun."

And that was the thing: with Darren it always was fun. Being with him was easy. It was relaxed—and relaxing. It was comfortable. And I found that I was looking forward more and more to seeing him. And thinking less and less about you. Which was good, because I hadn't heard from you again—or tried to contact you myself. I felt saner when I wasn't waiting for a message from you. You weren't out of my life completely, though. Once in a while I'd see your published photographs in the *New York Times*—your name would jump out at me as I rode on the subway. Every time it happened, my heart raced and I felt vaguely ill and off for the rest of the day. But I never felt that way around Darren.

"Halloween party?" I asked. "Okay, sounds good. Do we need costumes?"

"Do we need costumes, she asks!" he said, as if he were telling someone else about our conversation, even though he lived alone. We both did. "We absolutely need costumes," he said. "I was thinking . . . *Prisoner of Azkaban*? We could be Harry and Hermione? Or maybe I could be Spider-Man and you could be MJ?"

I couldn't help but think, in that brief moment, that those were two costumes you would never, in your whole life, ever suggest. The year before you and I had gone as a plug and a socket, remember? That was more your style. More both of our styles, actually.

"So you're going for pop culture?" I asked Darren.

"Okay, can I confess something?" he said.

My heart lurched. "Okay . . ." I answered, really having no idea what was coming next. Already regretting that I hadn't kissed him, that I hadn't tried harder.

"I was drawing a blank with Halloween costumes, so I Googled 'popular Halloween costumes.' If you have any more original ideas, I'm all ears. Well, actually, I'm not. I'm eyes and a nose and a mouth and . . . well . . . other body parts too."

I laughed, so incredibly relieved. "Other body parts?" I asked, realizing for the first time that I really wanted to flirt with him. That I was enjoying it. "Really?"

He was silent on the other end of the line. I could imagine his face, eyes opening wider, cheeks turning pink. "I didn't mean . . ." he said.

"How about a Freudian slip?" I asked. "For Halloween? I can wear a slip with the word *Freudian* on it. And you can be Dr. Freud himself. I'll find you a cigar."

He laughed. "I like it!" he said. "Better than Spider-Man and MJ for sure."

"What time's the party?" I asked.

"Starts at nine," he said, "at Gavin and Arjit's place. Do you remember Arjit from the Hamptons?"

"I don't think I do."

"Well, you'll meet them both at the party, then. How about I come over at eight with pizza? I have no idea what those guys think is appropriate party food, so we should be fortified before we leave."

"Sounds good to me. I think I have a slip somewhere around here. And I'll look for some fabric markers tomorrow."

"And my cigar?" Darren said. "Actually, I think I'll bring my own cigar."

"Oh, will you?" I asked.

I could tell I'd flustered him again. "Um . . ." he said.

"Just teasing. I'll see you Saturday night."

SATURDAY NIGHT CAME and Darren arrived at my apartment wearing a white beard, fake glasses, a gray three-piece suit, and a sedately striped tie. He was carrying a pizza box in one hand and a cigar in the other.

"Do I look Freud-ish?" he asked.

"Remarkably so," I answered. "Do I look like a Freudian slip?"

My hair was down and loose, and I was wearing a knee-length white lacy slip with the word *Freudian* written on it in red fabric marker. I hadn't been quite sure which shoes were appropriate, so I went with silver ballet flats. I matched my lipstick to the fabric marker, so it was bright red.

Darren smiled behind his fake beard. "You do," he said. "You absolutely do."

SOMETHING BETWEEN US changed palpably that night. Instead of doing his goofy gentlemanly arm crook, he held my hand as we walked to his friends' apartment. We were quickly roped into a game of flip cup and another and another, which left him tipsy and me one level past that.

Wherever he was at the party, his eyes kept coming back to me, as if he was making sure I was okay, making sure I was still there. I remembered going to parties with you, my eyes roaming the room for you the way Darren's were for me. It was nice, the change in roles.

When the party started winding down, Darren drifted back toward me. I was chatting with some other girlfriends about I have no idea what. "I'm getting a little tired," he said.

I turned toward him. "Me too. Shall we?"

He nodded. "I'll grab our coats and meet you by the door."

I said good-bye to the girlfriends and headed to where Darren was talking with Gavin. He'd been pointed out to me earlier, but we hadn't met yet.

"This is Lucy," Darren said, when I got closer.

"So you're the paper doll," Gavin said.

"I'm the what?" I asked.

I saw Darren give Gavin a look. "You're beautiful," he said quickly. "Just like a doll."

"Thanks," I said, smiling.

I knew there was something I was missing, but it didn't matter. That night, as we left the Halloween party, I felt adored. And happy. And completely thrilled that Darren took my hand as we walked out into the crisp fall night together.

"Walk you home?" he asked.

"Sure," I answered. My gaze lingered on his lips, where they peeked out of his Freud beard. If he'd tried to kiss me three weeks before then, I would've freaked. Maybe never seen him again. But at that point, I wanted it. I wanted him. He wasn't you, he'd never be you, but he was sweet and kind and funny and smart and endearing. And there was something wonderful about that.

We got to my door, and Darren stopped. I stopped. We faced each other. He'd taken off his fake beard and my eyes went to his lips again.

"Lucy," he said, "I don't want to go too fast, but I want to . . ."

"Kiss me," I said.

His eyebrows popped.

"You want to kiss me," I repeated. "It's okay. Kiss me."

Darren leaned in, and our lips met, soft and warm in the night air. Our bodies pressed together. I smelled that Kenneth Cole Reaction cologne that half the men at work seemed to have started wearing that year.

He smelled so different than you did. He tasted different and felt different. I blinked tears away from the corners of my eyes.

Then our lips separated and Darren looked at me and smiled.

I wondered if I should invite him inside, if that was the right thing to do. I didn't really want to, but didn't want to send him a message that I wasn't interested. Before I could puzzle through it, Darren said, "I should go . . . but tonight was a lot of fun. Are you free on Thursday?"

I smiled. "I am."

Darren leaned in and kissed me once more. "I'll call you," he said, as he walked away and I headed inside.

For the first time since you left, I dreamed about someone else.

xxxi

IT'S FUNNY TO EXPERIENCE THE SAME THING WITH different people. You see how they react, and how they meet or subvert your expectations. It happened with Darren a lot. I had assumed that you were the male standard, that you acted the way all men acted. But really, there is no standard.

The first morning Darren and I went running together was the second morning he'd stayed at my apartment. He'd come from work with a gym bag that he'd never actually brought to the gym. He said he'd meant to go before he got to the office, but there was trouble on the subway. I believed him. But that next morning, while we were running, he admitted the truth: he'd packed it in the hope that I'd invite him over, and this way he'd have more to wear than just his work suit.

"What if I didn't invite you over?" I asked him.

"Then I'd carry my gym bag back home and drown my sorrows in pretzels dipped in peanut butter."

"Pretzels dipped in peanut butter?" I asked. "Really?"

"It's a delicacy," Darren said. "I swear. After we finish running, we can buy some."

Darren can run faster than me, but he didn't make a big deal of it. He waited until I started running, and then paced himself next to me. That way, we could talk without any trouble. It was a pleasant surprise. Did you notice that I hardly ever agreed to go running with you? We never talked about it. We probably should have. When we ran together I always felt like I was reining you in when you wanted to fly.

I started lagging a little bit.

"You okay?" Darren asked.

I nodded, gathering strength. "I can keep up a little longer," I said.

"You don't have to," he answered, slowing down to a walk.

"You can keep running," I told him, as I slowed down too. "Get your workout in." That was what you did, after I tired out.

He shook his head. "I'd rather walk with you than run alone. And, you know, walking is a good workout too. You burn the exact same number of calories walking a mile as you do running a mile. It just takes less time when you run."

I looked sideways at him, wondering if he was really

being honest. It seemed like he was. "You don't get the cardio, though," I said.

He shrugged. "But I get to spend time with you."

I HAD SEX WITH HIM for the first time that afternoon. That felt different than it did with you, too. Not worse, just different. He was slower, thoughtful, and checked in to see if I liked what he was doing, if there was anything else I wanted. At the beginning, I thought it was a little weird, but toward the end, he'd started to win me over. I began to give directions, which I'd never done with you.

"Put my legs on your shoulders," I told him. He did and slid further inside me.

"Oh my God," he whispered, thrusting faster.

"I know," I said. My eyes were closed and I could feel him hitting the spot deep inside that would make me orgasm. "If you keep doing that, I'm going to come," I told him.

"Me too," he said. "We'll come together."

I opened my eyes and saw him looking at me. His eyes were dark normally, but now they looked almost black.

My breathing changed pitch and so did his. We were both so close, and both waiting for each other.

"Now?" he asked

"Now," I said.

And we both let go. I felt tears in my eyes as I came, and they slipped down the sides of my face into my ears.

"Are you okay?" he asked, after he'd slid off the condom and rolled next to me on the bed.

"More than okay," I told him. "I'm great."

"Me too," he said. "More than great."

He wrapped his arm around me, and we lay in bed together for a while, not talking, just breathing.

I thought about you, then, for a little. Thought about how everything was different with Darren. But I didn't fall apart. I didn't break.

Maybe it takes a man to get over a man—or maybe he *was* helping put me back together.

xxxii

It's always telling to see unmarried couples together at weddings. There are the ones who act extra loving, wrapping their arms around each other while they watch their friends speak their vows. And then there are the ones who stare straight ahead during the ceremony, not acknowledging their other half, and then proceed to get far too drunk on the dance floor. They look like they're having a good time, but I think on the inside they're probably miserable. Sometimes weddings are too much to handle when you're not secure in your own relationship.

Darren and I hadn't been dating that long—about three months—when I got Jason and Vanessa's wedding invitation in the mail. Jay had told me that I could bring a guest if I wanted, or not, if I wanted. A guy, if I wanted, or Kate or Alexis or Julia if I wanted. Whatever would make me the happiest.

I talked to Kate for hours about this. She offered to come, of course. But the idea of being at my brother's wedding with my childhood best friend instead of a boyfriend made my insides flip. I could imagine my parents' friends' looks of pity, and I didn't want to be on the receiving end of those.

I contemplated going alone, but I wasn't sure if I'd be able to hold it together the whole night without someone next to me. You and I had been broken up for seven months at that point, but I still couldn't talk about you without my voice catching. I still avoided eating waffles.

"Take Darren," Kate kept saying.

I wasn't sure. "It's only been three months," I told her. "I don't know how long this is going to last."

"Only three months?" she parroted back at me. "How long did you date Gabe before you two moved in together?"

"That was different," I said. "We'd known each other before." *And we loved each other like crazy*, I finished in my head. Darren was great, but it wasn't the same.

"Hmph," she said over the phone, sounding like someone's old conservative aunt. "Do you have fun with Darren?" she asked.

"Yes."

"Do you think you'd have fun at your brother's wedding with him?"

I thought about it. "Yeah," I said. "I do."

"Okay," she said. "Case closed. Invite him."

I waited another month, until the day before my brother and Vanessa needed the head count for the venue. Then I asked him.

"Really?" he said. "Your brother's wedding?"

I felt my face turn hot. In all my conversations with Kate, I'd always assumed that Darren would want to go. "You don't want to?" I asked.

"No, no!" he said. "I absolutely want to. Yes, I'd love to go to your brother's wedding. Thank you for inviting me." Then he smiled his most genuinely happy smile. The one that looks almost exactly like someone drew a perfect half circle and filled it with two rows of teeth.

"You're welcome," I said. "I think we'll have fun."

He tapped his finger against his lips. "You said one month, right?"

I nodded.

"I know this sounds ridiculous," he said, "but I think it's a sign."

"For what?" I asked.

He poked his hand into his briefcase and pulled out a colorful flyer. "For this!" he said, handing it over. "Someone was giving them out today at the subway stop near my office, and something in me said not to throw it away. It must be providence."

The paper he'd handed me was a coupon for fifty percent off four weeks' worth of couples dance classes. *Learn to Fox-trot, Cha-Cha, Tango, and Jive!*

I started to laugh. "You really want to do this?" I asked him. Never in a million years would you suggest something like this.

"To be honest," he said, "I'm not the very best dancer, but I think this could be hilarious. And fifty percent off! Who can pass up a deal like that?"

He shrugged, and something about the way his shoulders went up to his ears touched my heart. I kissed him. Then I slid my arm around his shoulders and leaned my head against his head. And it felt so good.

AFTER OUR FOUR WEEKS of dance classes we weren't much better than when we started. We might have actually been the worst students in the class, but we also might have been the two people having the best time. We cracked up so often that the teacher shushed us all class long, and during the tango lesson she told us we'd have to leave if we couldn't take dancing seriously.

AT THE WEDDING I stood in a line with the rest of the bridesmaids and kept an eye on Darren as the ceremony progressed. He kept looking at his program and at me and once in a while at Jason and Vanessa.

As soon as the reception started, Darren pulled me onto the dance floor and we attempted to foxtrot and tango and cha-cha, tripping over each other's feet and laughing. Mid-cha-cha, my heel caught on the back of my gown and I pitched forward, tumbling into Darren's arms.

"Well," he said, "that's one way to get dipped." And then after he helped me back to a standing position, he knelt down and freed my skirt from my heel.

"Thanks," I said to him, as I gathered the fabric in one hand and pulled it up so I wouldn't trip over it again.

"An honor, milady," he said. I couldn't stop the giggle that escaped through my nose.

"So," my uncle George said from where he was standing next to us, taking pictures with one of the disposable cameras Vanessa had placed around the room, "are you two next?"

I felt my face flush and looked over at Darren, hoping that talk like that five months in wasn't going to freak him out, because it absolutely freaked me out. But he just smiled and said, "If I'm lucky."

I stilled the panic in my heart. I wasn't ready to think about the future yet. But I couldn't help thinking that whatever woman ended up with Darren would be lucky. I just wasn't sure if I wanted it to be me.

xxxiii

VALENTINE'S DAY HAS ALWAYS STRUCK ME AS ODD. Even in elementary school, when we had to write cards for everyone in the class and leave them in heart-shaped construction-paper mailboxes we'd put together with staples and glue. I'd painstakingly decide which Peanuts valentine to give each person in the class—Snoopy or Charlie Brown or, my favorite, Lucy, because we shared a name and a hairstyle back then. Only my closest friends got the Lucy cards.

Then as an adult it became one of those holidays like New Year's Eve and July Fourth that felt like it was supposed to be so fantastic that the expectation always ruined whatever it was you did that night. And you stood there in a too-crowded bar or lay on a blanket staring up at a cloudy night sky thinking: *I'm supposed to be having more fun than this.*

The first Valentine's Day after college, a month before you and I reconnected, I went out with Alexis and Julia and Sabrina and we got stupidly drunk on cosmos and apple martinis. Julia didn't get out of bed until two in the afternoon, and Alexis BlackBerry-messaged all of us each time she vomited, which I think was six times that day. I just had a headache for about eleven hours straight. Sabrina, of course, was fine.

Then there was you—and your epic celebrations. The Valentine's Day we spent together was incredible, the kind of thing only you would do. By the time I got home from work you'd cut photographs of both of us into tiny stars and tacked them to the ceiling.

"'And he will make the face of heaven so fine / That all the world will be in love with night / And pay no worship to the garish sun,'" I said, when I saw what you'd done.

You answered by wrapping your arms around me. "God, I love you," you said.

"I love you right back," I answered. You kissed the top of my head as I looked around.

You'd moved the furniture so there was space for an enormous picnic blanket in the middle of the studio. A plate of truffle-grilled-cheese sandwiches rested on one corner of the blanket, and a bottle of champagne sat in a small garbage pail full of ice on another. When I took my coat off, you pressed play on an album of Shakespeare's sonnets set to music.

"Wow, Gabe," I said, once I'd hung my coat in the closet. Everything you had done floored me but also somehow made me feel a bit unworthy. I hadn't done close to this amount of planning for Valentine's Day.

"I figured it was too cold out for a picnic under the stars, so I brought the stars to us. Shakespeare's stars."

I kissed you, hard, then slipped off my heels and sat down with you on the blanket.

"This was the best way I could think of to celebrate you and me," you said, as you picked up a triangle of grilled cheese. "Hungry?" you asked.

I nodded and you held the sandwich while I took a bite. Then you took a bite yourself.

After I'd chewed and swallowed, I looked up at you. "My present for you isn't quite as . . . extravagant," I said. I walked across the studio and pulled a wrapped bundle from underneath my side of the bed. It was a cashmere scarf that I'd knitted during a month of lunchtimes at work—the same exact blue as your eyes.

"Happy Valentine's Day," I said, as I handed the gift to you.

You opened it, and your smile lit up your face. "Did you make this?" you asked.

I nodded, feeling less insecure about my gift.

"It's so soft." You wrapped the scarf around your neck and left it there the whole rest of the night. "I love it," you said, "almost as much as I love you."

I saw you pack the scarf when you left for Iraq. Did you wear it there? Did it make you think of me? If I head back to your apartment now, will it be tucked in the bottom of one of your boxes?

ALMOST TWO WEEKS after Jason and Vanessa's wedding, it was Valentine's Day 2005. Darren isn't the kind of guy who would create an elaborate romantic Valentine's Day picnic like you, but he's sweet and generous and I knew he would do something to celebrate. I wasn't sure I wanted him to. I wasn't sure if I should break up with him, since I didn't know if I felt as strongly for him as he did for me.

I called Kate and told her what I was thinking. "I just don't feel like I did with Gabe," I said.

I heard her take a deep breath. "You do need to be fair to him," she said. "Because I think he was serious when he responded to your uncle at Jason's wedding."

"I know," I told her. "That's what got me thinking about all of this. And because it's almost Valentine's Day."

"Do you like spending time with him?" Kate asked.

"I do," I said.

"Does being with him make you happy?" she asked.

"It does," I said.

"Okay. That's good. Could you see yourself falling in love with him?"

I thought about it. I thought about *him*, about his sweetness and generosity and sense of humor. I thought about running with him and going to parties with him and cooking at home with him. I thought about his body, naked next to mine.

"I think I could love him," I said.

"Do you think you could marry him?" she asked. "Because, you know, he *is* almost thirty. He's going to be thinking about that for real pretty soon, if he's not already."

I tried to picture it—me, Darren, a wedding, a baby, coming home to him every night.

"Maybe," I said. "I don't know. Maybe."

Kate was silent for a moment. "Then I don't think you should break up with him," she said. "If you'd said no you couldn't love him or no you couldn't see yourself marrying him, then I'd say you have to. I'd say it isn't fair otherwise. But since you can, I think you owe it to both of you to see if that's where this goes. Just take things one step at a time."

"Okay," I said. "That makes sense. I'll see where it goes."

"Also," Kate said. "Tom and I are planning a Valentine's Day dinner party. Would you and Darren like to come?"

I wondered for a split second if the reason she didn't want me to break up with Darren was so we could come to her

Valentine's Day dinner party as a couple. "I'll ask Darren and let you know," I said.

I asked him, and he said yes. Then added, "But can we spend the day before together? Sunday?"

"Sure," I told him. "Should we come up with something fun to do?"

"I have some ideas," he said.

Valentine's Day with Darren meant a trip to a bike shop in Chelsea.

"So," he said, "I was trying to think of the perfect gift to get you for Valentine's Day; I wanted it to be something that felt . . . couple-y. And I was walking by this shop and I saw that sign." He pointed to one that said: *Sweetheart Special! Bike with Your Baby!* "I went in to see what the deal is, and basically we can get a set of matching bicycles for Valentine's Day for the price of one!"

I blinked at him. "You want to buy me a bike?"

He shrugged. "Well," he said, "I want to buy us both bikes. And then maybe this summer we can ride them together. Either here, or if we get a share in the Hamptons. Biking to the beach together could be a lot of fun."

I blinked again. After I got over the fact that Darren wanted to buy me a bike, which I admit is a weird gift, I realized what a thoughtful gift it actually was. He wanted to get me something that showed me he planned to be together throughout the spring and summer too. If I accepted it, was I agreeing to the same thing? Did I want to agree to the same thing? I thought about bike riding with him—it would probably be a lot of fun. And the idea of going into a share house with Darren instead of just by myself was really appealing. I liked my life with Darren in it, and I was pretty sure I'd continue to like it. More and more, in fact.

"This is a huge gift," I said.

"Well, your bike will be a little smaller than mine," he answered.

I laughed. "Do the colors have to match?"

He scratched his head. "I don't think so," he said. "But let's go ask?" He said it like a question, like he wasn't a hundred percent sure I'd accept this gift, or his suggestion to go into the bike shop.

I took his gloved hand in mine. "Yes, let's," I said. "And if I forget to say it later, thank you."

I'd planned to give him a bottle of his favorite bourbon for Valentine's Day, but I quickly changed my mind.

"By the way," I told him, spotting a sign as we walked in the door. "I'm returning the Valentine's Day gift I was going to give you."

He looked at me with questions in his eyes.

"I'm getting us matching helmets instead." I pointed to the sign that said: *Cold Weather Sale: Two for the price of one!*

He smiled and then leaned over and kissed my cheek. "I knew you were my kind of girl," he said.

And I was starting to think he was right.

XXXIV

A WEEK AFTER VALENTINE'S DAY, MY CELL PHONE rang with a long-distance number on it. I didn't recognize the country code, and—amazingly—you weren't the first person I thought it could be. I'd figured maybe someone from one of the stations in Europe that was licensing our show was trying to get Phil and couldn't find him at the office so was trying my cell. (I know, not likely.) I picked up the way I did at work.

"Hello, this is Lucy Carter," I said.

The line was quiet.

"Hello?" I said again.

"Luce?" It was you. It was your voice. I felt it deep in my stomach. My name on your lips vibrated through my whole body, and I was glad I was sitting in my desk chair already because I didn't think my legs would've been able to support me.

"Gabe?" I said.

I heard you sniffle over the phone.

"Are you okay, Gabe? What's going on?"

"I have a black eye," you said. "And a gash in my cheek. My lip is split. And my ribs are bruised."

My heartbeat was speeding up now. "Where are you? What happened?"

"They tried to take my camera, and I wouldn't give it to them, so they beat me up until some U.S. soldiers stopped them."

"Are you in Baghdad?" I asked.

"Yeah," you said. "I'm in the green zone now. I'm safe, I'm okay. I just . . . I just needed to hear your voice. I hope it's okay that I called."

"Of course it's okay," I said. My eyes were welling with tears at the thought of you broken and bleeding and wanting to talk to me. I wondered, if I were hurt and shaken, who would make me feel better—you or Darren. Or maybe it would be Kate. Or my parents. "Is there anything I can do?" I asked.

"You're doing it," you said. "You're there, you're talking to me. When those guys were on top of me, all I kept thinking was: What if I never hear Lucy's voice again? And I'm okay, and I'm hearing your voice. So it's good. The universe is good."

I didn't know how to respond to that. What to say. After all those months of silence, here you were, hurting and missing me too.

"Will you be back in New York any time soon?" I asked.

"I think this summer," you said. "The Associated Press is making me take next week off, and I think I'm going to go see my mom. Then I have vacation time coming this summer. I was thinking about visiting then. I miss everyone. I miss you the most."

I wanted to ask if you were coming home to stay. If you missed everyone enough to give up on the idea of living in Iraq. If you missed me enough. But instead I said, "I miss you too, Gabe."

Then Phil was standing in the opening of my cube and saying, "Lucy? Do you have the notes from that budget meeting yesterday?"

And then I was nodding at Phil and telling you that I had to go, and you were saying you'd get in touch soon, and I was saying okay, we'd talk more then.

But I didn't hear from you again until the last day of your trip to visit your mom when you wrote me a quick e-mail saying that you were feeling better and looking forward to your return to Baghdad. And then all the worry for you, the concern I'd felt when I heard your voice—it hardened back into anger. How could you have called me like that, brought those feelings back to the surface, if you weren't planning on following through? It wasn't fair, Gabe. So much of what you've done, what you've asked of me—if I were a referee, if life were some sport, I'd stand up and shout, *Foul!* or *Do-over!* like we did when I was in summer camp. But there are no referees in real life, no true do-overs.

I kissed Darren extra hard that night.

BUT I COULDN'T GET YOU out of my mind—I kept thinking about how you were trying to show people everywhere how similar we all are in the hope it would combat violence, and instead you got hurt.

There had to be a message there. Wisdom I could share with the next generation. I wanted to turn something awful into something helpful, carry on your mission, in a way.

A few weeks later, I proposed a new storyline for an episode of *It Takes a Galaxy*. The story was about Roxie, the gray alien, going to another planet and taking pictures for her Book of Caring, the pamphlet she'd been putting together and sharing with her friends and neighbors in earlier episodes. When she got there and started to take pictures, some of the people on that planet didn't understand what she was doing, why she was taking their picture. And they beat her up because of it. There was a huge debate about it at the office, but violence among children was on the rise, and Phil decided we should go ahead and make it.

I don't know if you read any of the coverage it got, but that remains the most-talked-about episode of *It Takes a Galaxy* in the show's history. It was the first time physical violence was depicted in a cartoon kids' show on network television. There were debates on the Internet, pundits speaking about it on the news. It raised the profile of our show and opened up a channel for us to tackle other difficult issues. That episode took *It Takes a Galaxy* in a whole different direction. And it got me another promotion.

I should have thanked you for that. For the inspiration. I'm sorry I didn't do it before. But I'm thanking you now.

XXXV

It's funny, when you and I were together I sometimes daydreamed about the future—but not in a concrete way. Thoughts would come in snaps and flashes. I'd imagine meeting your mom—which I'm sorry I never got to do in person. Or I'd imagine us moving into a bigger apartment so you could have an office that wasn't the coffee table. Or I'd imagine us going on a long vacation together—another thing I'm sorry we never did.

With Darren, the future didn't come in flashes like that, it was discussed over and over. Darren has a plan, always. He plays chess, and I've come to realize that he treats life a bit like a chess game, thinking six or eight or ten steps ahead so that he's sure to reach whatever goal he's set for himself. Close the deal. Capture the queen. Check. Mate.

That first year he and I were dating, a couple of weeks before my birthday, he asked me if I had a bucket list.

"A what?" I asked.

"You know," he said, "a list of things you want to make sure you do before you kick the bucket." He pulled his wallet out of his pocket and unfolded a list that was tucked inside. "I started mine—wow—almost five years ago. When I turned twenty-five. I've been crossing things off and adding to it ever since."

There was something nice about being with a guy who was almost five years older than I was—seeing that careers move along, people pair off, things end up okay—but once in a while the gap between us felt even wider, like he'd done so much more living than I had. This was one of those times.

He spread the paper out in front of us on the dinner table at Teresa's on Montague—his favorite Sunday night dinner place. I looked down and saw:

Bucket List
1. *Ride a Segway*
2. ~~*Run a marathon*~~
3. ~~*Go island hopping in Greece*~~
4. ~~*Learn to scuba dive*~~
5. ~~*Go on a cruise*~~
6. *Get a rescue pet*
7. ~~*Learn to speak Chinese*~~

8. *Drive a racecar*
9. *Get married*
10. *Become a dad*
11. *Visit Australia*
12. *Race in a triathlon*
13. *Buy a beach house*
14. *Ride a bike from Brooklyn to Montauk Point*

"That's an impressive list. And an impressive bunch of things you've crossed off. How was Greece?"

"Beautiful," he said. "I went with my cousin Frank. He lives in Silicon Valley. Good guy. We drank a lot of ouzo and went snorkeling and sailing. Ate a lot of fantastic food, too."

"So what's next?" I asked, hoping he wasn't going to say "get married," hoping this didn't mean he was going to propose to me right then, right there.

He studied the list. "I think either the Segway or the bike ride," he said. "Or maybe the triathlon, but that's a lot of training to commit to if I decide to do it."

"How far is it from Brooklyn to Montauk Point?" I asked.

"About a hundred twenty-five miles," he said. "I've mapped it, but I'm not sure I'm ready."

"But now that we have our new bikes . . ." I said, smiling.

He cocked an eyebrow at me. "Would you ride that with me?"

I shrugged. "How about for your birthday?" I suggested. "That gives us from now until June to build up our stamina. We can train in three months."

He leaned across the table and kissed me. "That sounds like the best way to spend my thirtieth birthday I can think of. But I was really asking about your bucket list because of *your* birthday. Is there anything that you want to do?"

I couldn't think of anything off the top of my head. "Maybe I should start a list and see what comes to me," I told him, pulling a pen and an old Duane Reade receipt out of my bag. My bucket list is still written on the back of that receipt. I don't think I ever showed it to you. I should add that to my list right now: *Share this list with Gabe.* And maybe: *Ask Gabe to make his own bucket list.* But if I add those items, I don't think I'll ever get to cross them off. Prove me wrong, Gabe. Please.

I wrote *Bucket List* at the top of my receipt and then cribbed a few points off Darren's—even though numbers 2 and 3 seemed more to me like eventualities than desires.

1. *Go to Australia*
2. *Get married*
3. *Become a mom*
4. *Go to the top of the Empire State Building*
5. *Drive a boat*
6. *Go to Paris for a long weekend just because*
7. *Become an executive producer on a kids' TV show*

8. *Get a pair of Manolo Blahnik pumps*
9. *Own a dog*
10.

"I ran out of things," I told Darren.

"You'll think of more," he said. "I think of more all the time. But that's a great start." He pulled my list toward him. "Oh, some of these are easy! You know what we're doing for your birthday? Top of the Empire State Building. Then you'll get something crossed off right away."

"Yeah?" I said.

"Oh, absolutely," he answered.

It was like I could see the wheels turning in his head, trying to figure out what else we could do. I wonder if that's when he decided he was going to fly us to Paris so he could propose. Or if he was already planning my thirtieth-birthday trip to Australia. Or plotting to buy me a pair of Manolo Blahniks. He really is a planner. And he's not afraid to wait, if he thinks his plan will work out. It's actually something I admire about him.

But then he looked at my number 7.

"You want to be an executive producer on a kids' TV show?" he asked.

"Yeah." I nodded.

He smiled. "That's cute," he said.

I was taken aback. "What?" I asked.

"Your job is adorable," he said. "Just like you."

I blinked. It seemed so . . . demeaning . . . but I knew he didn't mean it that way. At least, I hoped he didn't. I couldn't help but think about how seriously you took my dreams. How important they were to you.

"My job's not cute," I said. "It's not adorable."

Darren seemed at a loss for words. I'd surprised him. He had no idea he'd said anything wrong. Which almost made it worse.

"Would you tell a man who was an executive producer on . . . *Law & Order* that his job was cute?" I asked. "What is it, exactly, that makes my career aspirations cute?"

Darren recovered his voice. "Whoa, whoa," he said. "I didn't mean anything by it. I'm sorry. That was the wrong word. You know how adorable I think you are—everything is adorable when it has to do with you. Your shoes, your hairbrush, the pack of gum in your purse. All of it—because it's yours."

I put down the pen and picked up my fork, taking another bite of the pasta I'd thought I was finished eating, just so I didn't have to respond right away. What I wanted to say was: *I'm more than adorable.* What I wanted to say was: *I need you to understand how important my career is to me.* What I wanted to say was: *I need you to love me because of that, not in spite of it.* But so much about Darren was wonderful, and he was apologizing—he didn't mean to hurt me. Besides, he was a smart guy. I figured in time he'd understand.

I swallowed my mouthful of pasta. "I hope you think I'm more than adorable," I said.

"Of course!" he answered. "You're beautiful, too, and sweet and funny and smart. Do you want me to keep going? There's no shortage of adjectives that describe you."

I laughed. "Well, I wouldn't mind a few more . . ."

Darren smiled—relieved. "Hmm, how about sexy? How about thoughtful?"

"Those are good ones," I said.

I wonder, sometimes, if I should've taken that conversation more seriously. If I should have pushed it further and said all the things I was thinking but kept inside. Because he still doesn't understand. Not truly.

XXXVI

IN PREPARATION FOR DARREN'S BIRTHDAY WE GOT
saddlebags for our bikes and three pairs of bike shorts each,
and made reservations at bed-and-breakfasts in Sayville and
Southampton. We decided to celebrate a little early and do
the ride over Memorial Day weekend. Since we'd gotten a
share in a house in Montauk that summer, we figured we
could spend the final night of our trip there and then take
the train home. Everything was coming together perfectly,
which was exactly how Darren liked things.

We'd gone on training rides starting at the end of
March, biking up to Westchester, or over the George
Washington Bridge, or out to Coney Island. Darren
insisted on packing our saddlebags with snacks and blankets and water so we could have impromptu picnics wherever we went—and so we could practice biking with the

proper amount of weight on our bikes. For our last training ride, we biked over the Brooklyn Bridge into Manhattan, then up to the Cloisters. The day was gorgeous—sunny and cool—and we ended up laughing about a million different things that if I told you about now wouldn't even seem funny. But we were in one of those moods where humor was everywhere.

"I'm so lucky to have found you," Darren said, when we got home that day.

"We're both lucky," I answered. "To have found each other." And it felt that way, at that moment. It really did.

ON THE MORNING we were set to head out, I got up extra early. With images of our last long ride together in my mind, I was excited about the trip, but also a tiny bit worried. This was going to be the longest Darren and I had spent together alone. It felt like a trial run for the future. What would it mean if we got sick of each other? Or more than that, what would it mean if we didn't?

But then Darren woke up and rolled over so both of our heads were on the same pillow. "Thank you so much for doing this with me. It's gonna be great. And I just want you to know that if we have to stop and rest or take the train part of the way, it's completely fine. No pressure on either of us, okay?"

The nervous part of me relaxed. I kissed him and said, "But we'll make it."

The first day was fun, though about thirty miles in, it started to get a little boring. We couldn't talk much, and all we were doing was pedaling. Darren went first since he knew the route, and I followed along, memorizing his back and his T-shirt and the speed at which he moved his legs. I sang some songs in my head until he said, "Sandwich break!"

Before we left, he'd made ten peanut-butter-and-jelly sandwiches, getting smooth peanut butter especially for me and crunchy for himself. We both preferred strawberry jelly.

"Milady," he said, when we'd pulled to the side of the road and rested our bikes in the grass, "can I interest you in one sandwich or two?"

I stretched my muscles and laughed. "One for now."

We took off our helmets and our biking gloves, then rinsed our hands and sat down to eat.

"Digestion break?" he asked, as he leaned backward, lying on the grass, resting his head against his saddlebag.

"Digestion break," I agreed, leaning my head on his chest.

"This is amazing," he said. "Did I ever tell you that last year, on my birthday, I wished that in the coming year I'd find an awesome girl who was beautiful and daring and funny and smart . . . and then there you were not even three months later in that beach house?"

I sat up so I was looking at him. "You might want to be careful what you wish for this year, then, if your wishes are so powerful," I told him.

"Oh, I already have that wish planned."

I smiled. "Of course you do."

He laughed. "But you know I can't tell, because once you tell a wish, it won't come true."

"That's right. Gotta keep it secret."

He brushed my bangs to the side.

"We're going to be sore tonight," he said. "But I brought mineral ice and Advil. And Vaseline for our butts. You know, in case they get chafed."

"What?" I said.

"I wouldn't want to ride with a chafed butt," he answered, with a bashful look on his face that made me understand exactly what he looked like when he was six and eight and thirteen. I saw his whole life in that look. He seemed so sweet just then, and my heart filled.

"I love you," I said. It was the first time either one of us had said it.

He looked at me, still for a moment, and then smiled. "Me too," he said. "I love you too."

Then he sat up and kissed me. "Can I tell you a secret?" he asked.

I nodded, not at all sure what he was going to say.

"I've loved you for months. Ever since we took those hilarious dance classes. I loved you then."

"Why didn't you say anything?" I asked.

"Because I didn't want to scare you off," he said.

His honesty was refreshing. And disarming. I kissed him again because he was right. He would have scared me off.

Darren understands so much about me. He has, right from the start. Though he's definitely never understood my connection to you—but I don't blame him for that.

xxxvii

THERE ARE PEOPLE WE COME ACROSS DURING OUR LIVES who, after they drift out of our worlds, drift out for good. Even if we see them again, it's a quick, meaningless *hi and how are you?* There are other people, though, with whom things pick up right where the relationship left off, whenever we run into them. The level of comfort—it feels like no time has passed.

That's what it was like when I saw you again. It was a little more than a year after you left. A few months after your phone call. You e-mailed me saying:

Hey Lucy,

I just landed at JFK. Are you around this week? I'd love to see you. Maybe a drink on Wednesday or Thursday?

Gabe

PS. Watched *It Takes a Galaxy* on the plane.
Loved the way the dream episode came out.

I was at Darren's apartment when the e-mail came
through. It was a Sunday and we'd just returned from Montauk. I wanted to get back to my place that night, but Darren had food in his refrigerator and I didn't, so we were
going to have a quick bite together before I went home to do
laundry and get things ready for work the next day. Darren
was unpacking his bag of damp beach stuff and dropping it
in the bathtub so it wouldn't mildew, and I was scanning
the contents of his kitchen cabinets for extra items to add to
our sandwich dinner. I'd pulled my BlackBerry out of my
bag to see if any crazy work things had gone on while we
were on the train. Nothing from work, but that e-mail from
you. I was glad Darren was in the other room.

My body reacts so physically to you that it's almost
bizarre. It's been like that ever since I met you, and I always
assumed—perhaps hoped—that would change at some
point. But it never has.

I saw your name, and my stomach flipped. I clicked on
the e-mail. Even though part of me thought, *This is not a
good idea*, I knew I would meet up with you. I wanted to see
you, to hear how you were doing. I also knew I had to bring

it up with Darren. Not to ask his permission, but because it would feel wrong not to tell him.

His face was completely calm when I said that I'd just gotten an e-mail from my ex. It cracked slightly when I told him I was planning to meet you for a drink but then went back to normal.

"Will you tell me when?" he asked.

"Of course," I answered.

"Will you come here afterward?"

I wasn't planning on sleeping with you. I wasn't planning on staying out late either. But I had a feeling I'd want to be alone that night. Still, I knew I had to compromise a little. For Darren. Because I loved him.

"Absolutely," I told him.

He seemed happy with that, and our conversation moved on. To the new guy Alexis was dating, the surfer she met at Ditch Plains the weekend before. To the three weddings we were going to that summer—all his friends—and whether we'd rather rent a car and drive to Philly for Brad and Tracey's wedding, or take the train and cab it around the city once we got there. I was totally normal on the outside, having these conversations with Darren, but inside all I wanted to do was check my BlackBerry to see if you'd responded. To know when exactly I was going to see you again. This is why it was better when we weren't in touch. Waiting is always excruciating.

ON THURSDAY MORNING I changed my outfit four times. First I had on a dress that was loose and flowing and made my body look shapeless. I thought maybe that would be a good way to keep things platonic. But then I looked in the mirror again. I hadn't seen you in over a year, and didn't want you to think I'd let myself go. So I put on something tight. But then thought maybe it looked like I was trying too hard. So I changed into a pair of summer pants and a tank top. But then remembered that you liked how I looked in skirts. So I put on a pencil skirt and a sleeveless silk blouse and peep-toe heels. It was an outfit that made me feel confident and successful and in charge. I wore something like it when I had to make presentations at the office. I flat-ironed my hair and spent extra time on my bangs.

I could barely concentrate at work all day. I was supposed to be reviewing the scripts for the newest episodes of *It Takes a Galaxy* and had to read one of them four times before I actually knew what was happening in the show.

After work, I walked slowly to Pazza Notte. I was a few minutes early and contemplated walking around the block, but went inside instead and got us two seats at the bar. You BlackBerry-messaged me to say you were running late, which was rare for you, so I ordered myself a glass of wine. I'd drunk about half of it by the time you got there, in a whirlwind of dimples and apologies.

"It's good to see you, Luce," you said, wrapping me in a hug.

I hugged you back just as hard, and realized that you smelled exactly the same. Scientists say that scent is one of the strongest memory triggers we have. I totally believe it. With my face against your shirt, I was catapulted back in time.

After we separated from our hug, you looked at me for a long moment. "Just drinking you in," you said. "You look . . . great. I like the haircut."

I could feel myself blush. "Thanks," I said. "You too." And you did. In the time you were away, you'd lost a little weight and the structure of your face became more pronounced. Your hair still sprung up in curls, but they were shorter and tighter. You were tan, and the hair on your forearms had gotten blonder.

I was so caught up in the fog of you that I can't even remember what we talked about that night. Can you? I'm sure it was my show, your work, our families. I just remember feeling wholly and completely alive. Like every molecule of my body was awake and alert and excited. Any other feelings were pushed aside, smashed down because you were there, in front of me, smiling like I was the only person who existed in the world.

I didn't want to cheat on Darren, and I don't think I would have, but I did find myself slightly disappointed that you didn't try. A kiss sliding from my cheek to my lips, a hand on my thigh. Sometimes I wonder what would have happened if you had. Would it have changed anything? Would it have changed everything?

Darren texted once to say hello, and I realized that knowing I was out with you wasn't easy for him. That he was probably home and worried. What's ironic is that he shouldn't have been worried then. It was later he should have worried—but by then I think that me sleeping with you was probably the furthest thing from his mind. He thought I was fully and completely his. But he's never had all of me.

xxxviii

A FEW DAYS AFTER I SAW YOU, I WENT SHOPPING WITH Kate. She'd messaged me saying that she and Tom were going away—really away—together for the first time, for ten days to Spain—and she wanted to spruce up her wardrobe.

"What do you need?" I asked her, when I got to her apartment, the one I'd once shared with her. She and Tom weren't living together. She'd told him that she wouldn't live with anyone unless there was an engagement ring on her finger. I couldn't help feeling defensive about you and me when she told me she'd said that. I'd known that had always been her plan, but I'd thought she'd change her mind when she met someone wonderful. And Tom truly was wonderful—calm and caring and generous. But she hadn't.

Kate pulled a list up on her BlackBerry. "Two bathing

suits, a cover-up, and a maxidress for our time in San Sebastián and Barcelona. And maybe a pair of wedge heels I can walk in for Madrid. And I wouldn't mind a big straw hat. Don't you think those are glamorous?"

I smiled at Kate. "I think you'd look like a movie star in one of those hats," I told her. "Very, um, Greta Garbo?"

She looked at me out of the corner of her eye and then we both laughed.

"You don't have any idea what Greta Garbo's style was, do you?" she said, slinging her arm across my shoulder.

"None whatsoever," I told her. "But isn't she supposed to be glamorous?"

Kate sighed. "Very. But I think you mean Hedy Lamarr. She looked stunning in big, broad-brimmed hats."

"Oh yes, absolutely Hedy Lamarr," I said, wrapping my arm around Kate's waist. "So where to? Are we taking on each challenge one by one, or department store?"

"Department store," she said, without a moment's hesitation. "I was thinking Bloomingdale's is closest, and then we can get that yogurt for lunch."

Bloomingdale's, of course, made me think of you. I'd actually avoided the store for the last year-plus, which was pretty easy since I was living in Brooklyn. But I'd decided it was time to integrate Gabe-things back into my life, so I didn't say anything except, "Love that yogurt."

We got there and searched through the racks for bathing suits. Kate wanted ones that would go with the Hedy Lamarr hat she had yet to purchase, so we looked for vintage styles and conservative colors. With six or seven options, we headed into a dressing room.

I sat down on a chair with the bathing suits on my lap and told Kate—actually for the first time—that I'd seen you for a drink.

"How was that?" she asked, carefully.

"Weird," I told her. "I love Darren, I really do, and don't doubt that. But it feels so different than it does with Gabe. I can't tell if I just love Darren less. Or love him differently . . . Does Tom make you feel more alive when you're with him than you do without him?"

Kate looked at me very seriously, like she was contemplating the question and how best to respond. I love that about Kate. Her words have always been fully considered, even when we were kids.

"No," she finally said. "I feel just as alive right now, here in this dressing room with you, as I do when I'm with Tom."

I handed her one of the bathing suits.

"I feel more alive when I'm with Gabe than I do with anyone else on the planet," I told her. "Not to take anything away from how much I love you," I added.

"Or Darren?" she asked.

"It's just . . . it's different," I said. "And I'm worried that it won't be enough. That what I feel for Gabe is just so monumental that nothing else will ever be enough."

Kate pulled the bathing suit up and stuck her arms through the straps. "What do you think?" she asked, looking at herself in the mirror.

"Honestly?" I answered.

"Always," she said.

"Honestly, I think it cuts your butt in a funny place."

She turned around and then twisted her head to look at her back in the mirror. "Oh wow. You're right. How strange."

Kate started pulling the bathing suit off and said, "I was talking to my sister about relationships earlier this year, and she said something interesting."

Did you ever meet Kate's sister? I must've told you about Liz, even if you hadn't met her. She went to Brown and is pretty much the opposite of Kate in every way someone could be an opposite—she's incredibly creative and artistic and moved to Paris after college to work for *Vogue* when Kate and I were sixteen. She's had a string of romances with men and with women, and she remains, to this day, one of the most interesting people I know.

"What did Liz say?" I asked.

"She said that she thinks of every romance she's in as if it's a type of fire. That some relationships feel like a wildfire—they're powerful and compelling and majestic and dangerous and have the capability to burn you before you even realize you've been consumed. And that some relation-ships feel like a hearth fire—they're solid and stable and cozy and nourishing. She had other examples—a bonfire relationship, a sparkler—that one was for a one-night stand, I think—but the wildfire and the hearth fire are the two that I remember most."

"Are you and Tom a hearth fire?" I asked.

Kate nodded. "I think so. And I think that's what I want. Safety and stability and warmth."

"I think Darren and I are a hearth fire," I told her, ruminating on what she'd just said. "But Gabe and I were a wildfire."

"Yeah, I think that's true," Kate said.

She had a bikini on. It was red-and-white polka-dot, with a high-waisted bottom. "Oh, that looks great on you," I told her.

She checked herself out in the mirror. "I like it!" she said, nodding at her reflection. "One down, one to go."

"So did Liz say which is better?" I asked.

Kate shook her head as she unclasped the bikini top. "She said it depends on who you are. On what you want. She said that hearth-fire relationships bore her after a while. That she prefers wildfires, but that she's starting to think she might want something in between. Oh, I think that's what the bonfire was—where the relationship is always on the verge of being all-consuming but doesn't quite go that far. She said she hasn't had any of those but wants to find one."

"Can you tame a wildfire or grow a hearth fire?" I asked.

"I don't know," Kate said, stepping out of the bikini bottom. "Liz said she hasn't had any luck transforming a relationship from one to the other. But, I mean, if you extend the metaphor, firefighters can tame wildfires, so maybe people can, too. I guess the question is if you can tame them without putting them out completely."

I handed Kate another bikini, wondering if I should look for a bonfire too. If I should experience all of the different kinds of relationships before I decided which one I wanted.

"The thing I worry about," Kate said, "is what if you give up a wonderful hearth fire to try out a bonfire, and discover that it's not what you wanted after all. And then you lost the hearth fire."

"Are you talking about you and Tom now?" I asked.

She shrugged. "Maybe. I don't know."

"I guess it's complicated," I said. "And that bikini top gives you side boob."

Kate looked down. "Oh, that's terrible," she said, pulling the halter straps over her head. "I think you have to do a kind of risk analysis in a relationship. How happy you are factored in with whether losing that happiness is worth potentially finding more of it with someone else. I don't know if I'm willing to take that risk. Like, what's the threshold? If I'm eighty-five percent happy with Tom, do I risk it for the possibility of being ninety-five percent happy with someone else? And what's the maximum happiness you can achieve with someone? I don't think it's a hundred percent."

"No, definitely not a hundred percent," I said. "Nothing's ever perfect." I wondered what my happiness percentage had been with you. And what it was with Darren.

And then I wondered how you or Darren would answer that question—about your happiness percentage with me. What do you think? Was our percentage the same back then? Were we eighty percent happy? Eighty-five percent? I have a feeling I was happier than you, because you were the one who left, who wanted to go. Even if you didn't think about it in those same terms, clearly you were willing to take that risk—to see if you would be happier without me in your life, pursuing the career that you wanted.

Did it work? Even for a little while?

I know it didn't in the end.

xxxix

SOMETIMES A YEAR FEELS LIKE AN ETERNITY, BROKEN UP into tiny capsules of time. Each chunk is so monumental that it seems like its own lifetime within a life. That was my 2004. There was the chunk of time we were living together, the chunk of time after we broke up, the chunk of time after I met Darren. That year had three discrete sections to it. But the twelve months after Darren and I met felt like one solid unit. It almost came as a surprise when Darren said one Saturday, the minute I walked in his door after meeting Julia for brunch, "So, our anniversary is in two weeks. Were you thinking about doing anything in particular?"

I had the urge to double-check the calendar on my BlackBerry, but I knew he was right. He wouldn't ever forget a date. Besides, the summer was ending, and that was when we met last year—the end of the saddest summer I'd ever had.

"Is that a Montauk weekend for us?" I asked, grabbing myself a glass of water. He'd put in the bids for our weekends and was in charge of keeping track of when we went out to the house.

"But of course," he replied.

I should've known better. He'd probably had the date marked when he gave in our requests.

"Maybe a clambake dinner?" I said, as I added ice to my cup. "At that fancy place on the docks? You know, where it's mostly grown-ups and everybody gets dressed up?"

Darren crossed the kitchen to kiss me. "We're grown-ups," he said.

I laughed. "You know what I mean."

He kissed me on the nose this time. "I think that sounds great. I had one other thought, too," he said. "And it's about gifts."

I wondered if he was going to talk about an engagement ring. Sabrina had gotten engaged the month before—mostly because she'd gotten pregnant—but still, the idea of it seemed nice. Satisfying, like finding the right piece of a jigsaw puzzle, one you'd been hunting for for a long time and never would have to hunt for again. Not right then, but one day.

"What about gifts?" I asked.

"Well," he said, "I was thinking about our bucket lists, and on mine it says 'rescue a pet,' and on yours it says 'own a dog.' And I've been thinking about doing this for years, so . . . I have a surprise for you. I know it's a little early, but once I thought of the idea, I couldn't wait another minute!"

He walked toward his bedroom door, which was uncharacteristically closed, went inside, and came out with a small, wriggling, white, furry bundle in his arms. The bundle barked. A puppy. There was a puppy in his arms. I froze.

"Look what I got you!" he said. "I figured she could live at my place, and then maybe one day you'll come live with me and the dog."

"A dog?" I said. "You got me a dog?" I was stunned.

"I'm hoping you'll share her with me," Darren said. "That she can be our dog."

He handed me the puppy, and I automatically took her. She licked my neck and chin and nose.

"She was the sweetest dog at the whole North Shore Animal League," he said. "I met every single one."

I looked at the dog and she barked a hello. I said hello right back and she smiled a big doggy grin.

Here was the thing: The idea of getting me a dog was thoughtful, in a very Darren way. But what he didn't realize about me then, and still doesn't understand, is that *I* wanted to meet all the dogs at the North Shore Animal League. *I* wanted to be part of the decision about which dog to get—

or even whether we got a dog. I think he thinks there's something gallant about presenting these grand gestures to me fait accompli, but it's just . . . it feels . . . infantilizing. Or . . . patronizing. Like my opinions aren't worthy of his consideration. You'd never do something like that.

"I wish I'd met every single one of them," I told Darren. "This is a great gift, but . . . I feel like I missed the fun part."

He looked confused, eyebrow askew. "The fun part is now! When we get to have a dog!"

I sighed. "I know . . . but it would've been nice if we chose a dog together. So it was *our* dog. One that we both agreed on. I want us to be partners, Darren."

"Lucy," he said, closing the space between us. "Of course we're partners. I just wanted to surprise you with something special. Aren't I allowed to surprise my beautiful girlfriend with an amazing present every once in a while?"

Once he said that, I didn't know how to respond. Because in that context, it sounded like I was being silly. I couldn't tell him never to surprise me, that he wasn't allowed. And how could I fight with someone who'd just done this incredible thing, who had just gotten me a dog?

The dog tried to lick inside my nostril, like she was hoping to get me to laugh. Maybe she understood.

"Of course you're allowed," I said, finally. "So did she come with a name?"

"They found her without any identification," Darren said. "One of the workers there started calling her Annie, because of her curly hair, but I was thinking we could lengthen that."

"Angel?" I asked.

"Anniversary!" he said.

And then I did laugh. Because that was an absolutely absurd name for a dog, but also somehow perfect. And she really was a perfect dog—loving and smart and not yappy at all. She wasn't an engagement ring, thank goodness, but sharing responsibility for another living being seemed like a pretty solid commitment. Once I said yes to Annie, I could see how it would be easy to say yes to other things down the line.

xl

I ALWAYS FIGURED THERE WERE TWO KINDS OF PEOPLE in the world—some who loved giving gifts and others who loved receiving them. I've always loved getting gifts, and still do. But the second Christmas I spent with Darren I realized that I loved giving gifts as well.

We were supposed to go with Darren's family to Colorado that Christmas. I'd met them before—the youngest of his three older sisters first, along with her husband. Then the other two sisters with their husbands and kids. Then his parents. Then various permutations and combinations of them at different events. But this was the first holiday I'd be spending with his family, and the first time I'd be confronted with all of them at once. They were nice individually, especially his dad, who was quiet—the eye of the hurricane that was the Maxwell clan—but I was a little worried about what it would be like to spend so much time with them, and about how much I'd miss my own family.

Darren's parents had rented a huge place in Vail and his mom promised a big Christmas tree in the chalet. His family had shipped out two big boxes of gifts to arrive in advance. We'd been a little late with ours, so we'd gotten small ones—things we could pack in our suitcases. We contemplated bringing Annie, but my brother had offered to watch her and take her with him to my parents' place, and somehow having her there felt a little bit like being there myself, so I said fine.

"This is big, Lulu," Jay had said to me, when I told him my plan to spend Christmas with Darren's family instead of ours. "Is he your clock reaction, for real?"

I remembered that conversation he and I had more than a year and a half before, when I told him I didn't want to love anyone but you. My feelings had clearly changed.

"I think he might be," I told Jay.

I could hear the smile in my brother's voice when he said, "I'm happy for you, even if I'll miss you at Christmas."

"I'll miss you, too," I said. "A lot. But I'll see you when I get back. How about a New Year's Day brunch? You, Vanessa, me, and Darren?"

"Sounds good," my brother said. "Already looking forward to it."

We'd gone to my parents' house the week before so I

could grab the ski pants, helmet, and goggles I'd stored in their basement.

"Darren's a good man," my father had said to me, as he helped me hunt for my helmet. "I'm sorry we won't see you both for Christmas, but maybe we'll get you next year. And for Easter."

I smiled. "That sounds good to me," I said. My family liked Darren, and he and I spent a lot more time with them than you and I ever did. I'm not sure exactly why. Perhaps it was that when you and I were together we didn't need anyone else, didn't really think of anyone else. Darren's and my world encompassed everyone we both knew—he was more the social secretary than I was, making sure we made time in our calendars to fit everyone in.

And he was so excited about this holiday trip. He made list upon list to be sure we wouldn't forget anything, and after he checked and double-checked our suitcases, he declared us all set to leave the day before Christmas. Then he got the flu.

Darren's nose had been running and he'd had a bit of a cough on the twenty-third, so he went to bed early that night, hoping that would help shake it. The plan was for both of us to stay at his apartment and then head to the airport together, so I ended up watching *It's a Wonderful Life* myself in his living room and slipping into bed a little after midnight, about three hours after he did.

I cuddled up next to him, and let his body heat warm me until I realized that he was really warm. Even warmer than usual. I turned over and pressed my lips against his forehead, the way my mom always did when my brother or I was sick. His head felt hot against my lips.

His eyes fluttered open, and I could see how glassy they were in the semidarkness.

"Darren?" I whispered. "You're burning up. Do you feel okay?"

He coughed a long racking cough. "Not really," he said. "My head hurts. Do you think I have a fever?"

I went and got the thermometer I knew he kept in his medicine cabinet, and he took his temperature. 102.4.

"Maybe it's broken," he said.

I cleaned it with alcohol and took my temperature. 98.6.

"I don't think it's broken," I said. "And I think you might have the flu."

I got him some Tylenol, and we both fell asleep.

He woke up early the next morning with the same high fever, the same body-racking cough, and a headache and runny nose that had intensified.

"I'm really sick," he said, when his coughing woke me up.

"Yeah," I said. "You are."

And then his eyes filled with tears. It was the first time I'd ever seen him cry. "Our plane's taking off in four hours.

I don't think I can go to Colorado today. I don't even know if I can get out of bed."

Even though Darren was the one who usually handled logistics—and still is—I quickly called the airline and, with some pleas and explanations, got our tickets moved to a flight two days later. Then I called his mom and explained the situation. And then threw on some boots and a coat and went to the drugstore to get him whatever I could find—cough suppressants and fever reducers and cold-and-flu medications.

"I'm sorry for ruining your Christmas," he said when I got back.

I kissed his feverish forehead and said, "As long as I get to spend it with you, it's not ruined."

He took some medication and went back to sleep, and I snuck out of the apartment again. I bought a three-foot-tall tree—the biggest I could carry on my own—and lights and tinsel and glitter snowflakes that had already been marked twenty percent off at Duane Reade. I got a box of red and gold ornaments, too, and a ballerina for the top of the tree, because everything else had been sold out. Then, while Darren slept, I turned his living room into Christmas. I even unpacked our gifts for his whole family and put them under the tree, which I'd balanced on the coffee table, to make it look taller. It felt like I was giving him back some of the happiness that he'd given to me over the past year.

"Lucy?" Darren called from the bedroom, just as I was sticking the last sparkly snowflake to the wall behind the couch. "Are you moving furniture?"

I heard him padding slowly to the door, coughing as he walked, and then the bedroom door opened, and he was there, leaning against the door frame, pale and rumpled, with dark circles under his eyes. He looked at the living room and didn't say a word.

"Darren? Is this okay? I wanted to make sure that being sick didn't mean you missed Christmas."

I took a step closer to him and saw tears in his eyes. "Lucy," he said, and started to cough. "Sometimes I love you so much that I don't even know how my heart can stand it."

I walked over to him and hugged him, harder than I ever had, as if I somehow needed to show him how much I loved him with the strength of that hug.

Darren was my Old Nassau experiment. The longer we were together, the more I loved him, and the better it got.

xli

THERE ARE CERTAIN EVENTS IN A PERSON'S LIFE that feel like turning points, even as they're happening. September 11th was a turning point in my life. Your moving away was another. And Christmas with Darren was a third. We'd been together not quite a year and a half at that point, but I knew then that we would get married. Not necessarily right away, but I knew it would happen—unless something unexpected happened instead. Unless you happened, actually. I always imagined you were the only person, the only thing that could stop me from marrying Darren. I wondered if that meant I shouldn't marry him, but I also knew then that I couldn't have you, and I couldn't imagine my life without him. And I loved him—I love him—really and truly. Just not the same way I loved—love—you.

I still dream about you—I've told you this—I have ever since you left. You and I are in Central Park having a picnic, or in a hotel room, or apple picking. Sometimes the dream is about something we actually did together, and sometimes it isn't. But it always ends with you pulling me toward you, our bodies pressed together, our lips meeting—and then I wake up, my heart racing, feeling so guilty for thinking about someone else when I'm in bed with Darren, even all these years later. I've tried so hard to stop them, but they still come.

Do you dream about me? Are you dreaming about me right now?

ONE MORNING, right around my twenty-sixth birthday, I saw a picture you took in the *New York Times*. Pakistanis protesting civilian casualties from a drone strike. Pakistanis, not Iraqis. You had moved. You'd moved to a brand-new country and you hadn't told me.

I dreamed about you that night, but that dream was different. We were walking through Times Square, and a rush of tourists came. My hand was torn out of yours; we got separated and I was looking for you all over. I was panicked in the dream, and I must've called out to you, because the next thing I knew, Darren was shaking my shoulders and saying, "You're having a nightmare. Wake up, Lucy."

I woke up sweaty, the panicked feeling still there.

"What was it?" Darren asked. "You were saying 'gave.' What did you give?"

I shook my head. "I . . . I don't know," I stammered. But, of course, I knew I wasn't saying "gave" at all.

Darren got me a glass of water, then climbed back into bed and held me close to him. "It's okay," he said. "I'm here. I'll keep the bad dreams away."

I wrapped my arms around him but knew that no one could keep that kind of bad dream away. I stayed up a long time after that and finally fell back to sleep as the sun was coming up.

That day at work I e-mailed you. *Haven't heard from you in a while, but saw that you're in Pakistan. Loved the photograph. Are you there for a while?*

The response came quickly. *Hey Luce! So nice to hear from you. Hope you're doing well. Have been in Pakistan for a few months, but they asked if I'd transfer here officially. I'm thinking about saying yes. I'll probably be in the States again this summer. Hope we can get together then. I keep an eye out for* It Takes a Galaxy *whenever I travel. Your team has been doing great work. Still love that Galacto.*

Do you remember sending that? I was so glad you did. Knowing that you hadn't moved without telling me made me feel calmer, as if the world were spinning at the right speed again. But really, I'm not sure why it mattered so much to me. I guess I wanted to still be important to you, to be the person you wanted to share news with, even if you weren't that person for me. Some psychologist would have fun with that one.

What you didn't tell me then was that you'd met a journalist—Raina—who was reporting from Islamabad, and that was why you were thinking about moving. I'm not sure how I would have felt if I'd known that just then. Honestly, I think I'm glad you didn't tell me.

xlii

THAT YEAR DARREN GAVE ME A PAIR OF MANOLO Blahniks for my birthday. And we decided to move in together. We'd been a couple for a little over a year and a half, and both of our leases were up in the summer.

"Let's find a new place," he said. "One that's not yours and not mine—one that will only ever be ours."

I liked that idea. It had felt a little strange moving your clothes out of drawers so that mine could fit in, and you offering to take down a poster or two on the wall so I could put up some of mine. You had shared your space with me, and I didn't want to take more than what was offered or change too much, even if I would've set the apartment up differently.

"What do you think we should look for?" Darren asked, grabbing a piece of paper and a pen off his coffee table. We were at his place. It seemed we were mostly at his place. Probably because it was bigger and easier to get to on the subway and had a particular dog bed that Annie loved that was too big to lug with us and too expensive to buy a duplicate of.

"Dishwasher," I told him, as I put my socked feet up on the table. "Light. As much space as we can afford."

He nodded, writing furiously. "I'm adding close to a subway stop, near good restaurants and shopping, and two bedrooms."

"Two bedrooms?" I asked, my feet back on the floor.

"For guests," he answered, not looking at me.

But my brain went to babies. Moving in with Darren didn't feel like moving in with you. It felt more serious. More like we were making a real commitment to each other. More like the step before getting engaged.

We spent our weekends looking at apartments. Darren wouldn't let us settle for something less than perfect. Our real estate agent was ready to kill us.

"I think this is it," I finally said to Darren one Sunday in late April. It was prewar, put together in a seemingly haphazard way that involved hallways and alcoves and an archway into the kitchen. It was two flights up and had an exposed brick wall in the master bedroom. "I love it."

He smiled at me. "And I love you."

I swatted at him and laughed. "But do you like the apartment?" I asked.

"I do," he said. "And not just because you do."

"Good," I said.

We signed the lease that day, and moved in together three weeks later. We took tons of pictures and I posted our smiles on Facebook. We went to Bed Bath & Beyond and bought anything that made us laugh—a cookie jar in the shape of a muffin, a teapot with a sculpted face, a shower curtain with a picture of a shower curtain that had a picture of a shower curtain on it ad infinitum.

"*Mise en abyme*," I said.

Darren looked at me like I was speaking another language, which I guess I was.

"The Quaker Oats phenomenon," I clarified. "An image with an image of itself on it, over and over again."

"I didn't know that had a name," he said.

You would've known, but I didn't think about you just then. I didn't think about you when Darren paid for everything in our cart, or when we got home and played fetch with Annie. But I couldn't help comparing Darren's and my first night in our place with the one that you and I spent together in your studio that became ours that became mine.

Darren and I cooked dinner together—a fancy affair that involved simmering sauces and Cornish game hens and a bottle of champagne. Then we took Annie for a walk, watched a movie, and made love.

You and I had ordered in pizza and split a bottle of wine and had sex on every surface imaginable. The couch, the floor, the coffee table, and the bed of course. Then we woke up the next morning and did it all again.

But you and I didn't wash each other's hair in the shower, like Darren and I did that first morning. I don't know why we never thought to do that, but it's wonderful, washing the hair of someone you love, having him wash your hair back. It's intimate. Maybe it connects to some part of the genetic material we share with apes; they always groom their mates.

And you and I didn't leave notes for each other in the refrigerator either. Little Post-its stuck to various containers so that the milk read *I love you* and the orange juice said *You're beautiful* and the bag of string cheese had *I'm so happy* and *Me too* next to the image of that Polly-O parrot.

I don't remember how it started, but I do remember thinking: *This is something Gabe would never ever do. He'd probably think this is moronic.* I hope you don't. I hope I'm wrong. Because I loved it.

xliii

WHEN WE MET FOR A CUP OF COFFEE THAT SPRING AS you were passing through the city, I could sense there was something different about you. There was something different about the city, too. They'd started building the Freedom Tower at Ground Zero. It felt like the bandaging of a wound, or like an elaborate tattoo inked to cover a scar. I understood the desire to rebuild, to create something tall and grand, a big fuck-you in the New York City skyline. But the area felt sacred to me, too, still raw. Not quite healed enough to build on.

It had nothing to do with us. It had to do with the people who looked like birds flying out of windows as the towers burned and collapsed. With the new building going up, it made it harder for me to see them. I kept away from that part of Manhattan. Is it awful to admit that I've never gone, even now that it's all completed? Even now that there's a memorial there too? I didn't think I'd be able to handle it alone, and I didn't want to go with Darren.

We didn't talk about the Freedom Tower that day, though, or the memorial, or the morning we met.

You started out by telling me how impressed you were with the *It Takes a Galaxy* episode you saw during your lay-over in London. "The one where Electra proves to her grandfather that she can repair his spaceship, even though he thinks they should ask her brother. Was that one yours?" you asked.

I smiled. "Guilty as charged," I said.

"I thought so," you told me, as you sipped your Ameri-cano. "It felt like taking a little trip into your brain."

Darren never said anything about *It Takes a Galaxy*. He certainly wouldn't have said that. I felt a pang, a wistful-ness. It had been great to be in a relationship with someone who cared so much about my job, who understood that part of me.

"How's Islamabad?" I asked.

"Good," you answered. "It's . . . good."

For you—for us—a nonanswer like that felt off. I took you in, then, trying to see what I was missing. You seemed relaxed. You were leaning back against your chair, holding the cup of coffee in your lap.

I started fishing. "Do you like your apartment?"

"It's nice," you said. "It's a house, really. I share it with some other journalists."

"Oh, that sounds fun. A nice group of guys?"

You looked down at your coffee cup. "Actually," you said, "I share it with Raina. I met her when the AP first sent me to Islamabad. We ended up collaborating on the piece." You shrugged.

"And you collaborated on a lot more?" I supplied for you. I wondered if that kind of work and life collaboration was what you'd imagined for us when you asked me to come away with you.

You shrugged again, as if you were embarrassed to tell me this. "She's a Pegasus," you finally said, "like you."

It felt like a punch in the gut when you said that, which was idiotic because I never agreed with your interpretation of that myth anyway. But I knew what that word meant to you. And even though I'd been with Darren for nearly two years, and you hadn't been with anyone, and it only seemed fair that you find someone too, it still hurt. As long as I'd been with him, Darren had never taken your place in my heart, and I hated the idea that someone else had taken my place in yours.

"That's great," I told you then. "I'm happy for you, Gabe."

You ran your fingers through your hair, like I'd seen you do hundreds of times before. "Thanks," you said. "So how's your boyfriend? Daniel? Derrick?"

"Darren," I said. "He's good."

Did you mess up his name on purpose? I always figured you had, but I didn't say anything about it.

I'm glad we only saw each other for coffee that day. I don't think I could have taken much more than that. The jealousy I felt scared me—it made me question my relationship with Darren, and I didn't want to do that. I loved him. And you loved someone else.

xliv

THERE ARE CERTAIN QUESTIONS THAT CHANGE THE world. Not the big-picture world, but the small, personal world. *Will you marry me*, I think, tops that list.

The last week in May, not long after I saw you, Darren told me to pack a bag, that he was planning an early anniversary trip for us Memorial Day weekend. A surprise four-day weekend away to celebrate the fact that we moved in together, that we'd soon be dating for two years. He still hadn't caught on that big surprises like that weren't my favorite, but I was still trying to be a good sport about it. He clearly liked planning things and surprising me, so I decided to try to let my own feelings about it go and just appreciate how much it meant to him. Even so, I couldn't stop trying to figure out where we were headed. I'd been assuming Cape Cod or someplace on the coast of Maine, since it was just four days, we both liked the beach, and we'd never been to either place as a couple. But when Darren gave me a list of what to put in my bag, I noticed there was no bathing suit on the list.

"Did you forget anything?" I asked as I was packing.

Darren had been getting ready for bed, and came over in a T-shirt and boxer briefs, smelling like face soap and toothpaste. He looked at his list in my hand, reading each item. "Nope," he said. "Not one thing. It's all there."

"No bathing suit?" I asked.

"Nope," he said again. "Everything you need is right there."

I revamped my thoughts for the weekend. Maybe we were going to the Berkshires. Or that spa his oldest sister always talked about in Connecticut. Either of those would be fun.

"You can get out of work tomorrow night right at five?" he said.

I nodded. "I told Phil, he said fine."

Darren had moved over to his own suitcase and was packing too. "I'll pick you up outside the office," he said, "and we'll head off."

"I can meet you at the rental car place," I told him.

"Nah." He folded a pair of pants so the creases stayed creased and placed them in his suitcase. "I think it makes more sense for me to come get you."

I paused in my packing to watch him ball his socks and then tuck them into his shoes—he fit three pairs in each sneaker, his neck curving forward to make sure they were pushed all the way inside.

Sometimes I looked at him, and all I could think was: *Mine. That's my boyfriend, my body to cuddle, my hand to hold.* I never felt you were mine in the same sense that Darren was—is. It always seemed like you belonged to you and lent yourself out to me when you felt like it; I never had complete ownership. With Darren, I did. And the fact that he was so wholly mine made me ignore things that perhaps I shouldn't have.

I snuck up behind him that night, wrapped my arms around his chest, and kissed the back of his neck. "Okay, I get it, it's your surprise trip. I'll stop trying to change your plans."

He turned around and kissed me back and I felt him hard against me.

"Hey," I said, raising my eyebrows.

"Hey," he said back, softly.

I lifted up his shirt and kissed my way down his torso to the elastic of his underwear, and then slipped it off, knelt down and kissed lower.

"Oh, Lucy." He pulled me up off my knees and onto the bed with him.

We didn't go to sleep until far too late that night.

I was groggy the whole next day at work, and was ten minutes late heading out to meet Darren for our trip.

"Where have you been?" he asked, when I finally made it outside.

He was pacing on the sidewalk in front of a limo.

"That's not a rental car," I said.

He laughed and snapped out of whatever funk he'd been in. "It's not. We're going to the airport."

"The airport?" I repeated.

"I'm taking you to Paris!" he said. "Like on your bucket list: *Go to Paris for a long weekend just because.*"

I felt my eyes go wide. "Are you serious?" I asked, completely dumbfounded. A surprise vacation to Paris! This was the sort of thing that happened in movies, not in the real world. But it *was* happening in the real world. And it was happening to me!

It was an incredibly grand and romantic gesture. The kind of thing tons of women dream about. But after the initial shock wore off, it felt odd to me, like when Darren bought us Annie. I wanted to have had a say. What if I wanted to stay in a particular arrondissement? Or visit Biarritz while we were there? Or Giverny?

"Serious as global warming," he said. "Come on, we have to get to the airport!" He opened the car door for me.

"But my passport!" I said, as I got in the car.

"Right here," he answered, sliding in next to me and patting his laptop case.

WHEN WE GOT TO JFK, I found out that he'd booked us seats in business class.

"Are you crazy?" I asked him, as we waited in the American Airlines lounge.

"Miles," he said. "Credit card points. Didn't cost a thing."

I squinted at him suspiciously and he laughed.

"Even if I did pay for it," he said, "it's absolutely worth it for your first trip to Paris."

WE HAD THE MOST DELICIOUS MEAL I'd ever eaten on an airplane, and each had our own tiny bottle of wine. Darren poured mine, narrating in a terrible French accent that made me laugh so hard I had to wipe the tears from my eyes. Along with them, I wiped away the last vestiges of my annoyance that he'd planned this trip without me. We fell asleep holding hands and woke up to the flight attendant bringing us breakfast.

Once we'd gotten out of the airport, Darren led me to the train, which we took into the city, and then we switched to another train underground.

"Where are we going?" I asked.

"Still a surprise," he said.

When we popped out of the metro, we were standing right near Notre Dame Cathedral. "Oh my God!" I said.

"Beautiful, right?" he asked. "But that's not the surprise. Our apartment is close by. I hope it looks as good in real life as it did in the pictures."

Darren had found a place online and rented it for us for three nights, which in the days before Airbnb was incredible. When we got there it wasn't quite like the pictures, but it was still lovely. It had a balcony overlooking the Seine and was decorated exactly like you'd imagine a Parisian apartment would be, all ornate molding and bold colors and quirky accents. It also had a round bed.

"I've never seen anything like this before," Darren said, when he stepped into the bedroom. "This was definitely not in the pictures."

I stood next to him staring at it. "I didn't know they made round sheets. And round blankets. Maybe it's a French thing?"

Darren scratched his head. "I think maybe it's just a whoever-owns-this-apartment thing."

I laughed.

"I hope it's okay," he said, wrapping an arm around my shoulders.

"Of course it's okay," I told him. "It'll be a sleeping adventure."

WE HAD TO SLEEP closer to each other that night than we usually did so neither one of us had our feet hanging off the circle. It was kind of nice, sleeping tangled together, like how you and I used to. Is that how you slept with Raina? Or Alina? Or the women I'm sure were in between, even though you never told me about them?

THE NEXT DAY was a whirlwind of sightseeing—Notre Dame, the Louvre, the Eiffel Tower, Sainte-Chapelle. We sat outside for dinner and could see the Eiffel Tower shimmer with lights every hour on the hour, as if it were shaking fairy dust down on the whole city.

"Are you happy?" Darren asked me, over a dessert of crème brûlée and Vin Santo.

"Incredibly so," I told him. "Thank you for this trip." I looked at the starry night sky, the Parisian buildings, and the cobblestone street. I looked at Darren, smiling at me. And my heart felt full. But then that tiny part of me, the one that would've liked to plan this trip together, wondered how much he was doing this for me, and how much he was doing it because he wanted to be the kind of guy who planned surprise trips to Paris for his girlfriend. Darren does these things, makes these grand gestures, all the time, and so many years later I'm still not sure how much of it is for me and how much is for him.

Right before we went to Paris, after he'd told me about the mystery anniversary trip he was planning, I'd bought him a bracelet. The kind with a metal bar that can get engraved. On one side it said his name, and on the other, the side that sat against his wrist, it said, "I love you. XO, Lucy."

When the last scoop of crème brûlée was eaten, I went to pull the box out of my bag. "I have something for you," I told him. "An anniversary present."

"I have something for you, too," he said.

"I thought this trip was my present," I told him, playing with the wrapped box in my lap.

"It's just part of it," he said. "But I know of a better place to exchange gifts than right here." He checked his watch. "Do you mind running a little?"

I looked down at my feet. "I'm wearing heels," I said.

"Just a little bit of running. I'll keep you balanced."

So he paid the bill, and then we ran, holding hands, across the cobblestoned streets of Paris until we made it to the middle of the Pont Neuf.

"Perfect timing!" Darren said, looking at the Eiffel Tower as it once again shimmered with light.

Then he got down on one knee and pulled a tiny box out of his pants pocket, and before I could even process what was going on, "Lucy," he said, "will you marry me?"

I felt my body flush, my stomach flip. Perhaps I should've

expected this, but I hadn't. And in that moment, I didn't think about you at all. Or about the fact that Darren planned this trip without me. And didn't seem to care about my job. And thought my dreams were cute instead of important. All I thought about was how sweet he was. How much he loved me. How much thought he'd put into this proposal, how much planning. How it felt like he was wholly and completely mine. And how much I loved all of that.

"Of course," I said. "Absolutely. Yes."

He stood up and tried to slip the ring on my finger—any finger—grabbing at my right hand until I offered him my left in its place.

And then we kissed, and the Eiffel Tower was still sparkling and it was the kind of romantic moment that belonged in a book or a movie or a fifteen-year-old's diary.

I've wondered, since then, if you would go through that kind of trouble to propose to someone. How did you ask Alina? I don't think you ever told me how that engagement started, just how it ended.

xlv

A FEW WEEKENDS AFTER WE GOT HOME, DARREN LEFT
to go to Montreal for his friend Arjit's bachelor party and
I got a call from Jay that Friday night.

"Lu?" he said, when I picked up. "Any chance you're free
on Sunday?"

I'd taken Darren's absence as a chance to plan a Saturday
morning boozy brunch with Alexis, a Saturday afternoon
trip to the Met with Kate, and a Saturday night dinner in
Koreatown with Julia, where we planned to cook meat on
sticks while she told me about her string of less-than-stellar
OkCupid dates. I'd made not one plan on Sunday. I wanted
to spend it at home, cuddled on the couch with just Annie
for company. I wanted to eat Cheerios out of the box, which
Darren thought was uncouth, and watch reruns of *90210*,
and stay in my pajamas until at least two p.m.

I sighed. "I am, what's up?" I asked.

I could imagine Jay scratching his scruff of a beard on the other side of the phone. "So . . . would you be able to do me a huge favor?"

Jay wasn't the kind of person who called in favors. Hardly ever. The fact he was asking actually made me a bit nervous.

"For you, Jay?" I said. "Of course. What do you need?"

"Would you come to my lab for family day? Vanessa's coming, of course, but . . . there are going to be lots of kids there and you and I haven't really talked about this, but we've been trying, Vanessa and I, to have kids. And it's been over a year. And I just think it'll be easier for her if you're there too. So, would you?"

Here's what I love about my brother: When he finally asked me for a favor, he didn't ask for himself. He asked for Vanessa.

"Of course," I said.

And so I went out to New Jersey and spent Sunday afternoon touring Jay's lab and watching him and the other researchers perform experiments for the kids. It was clear that family day was really "kids day," perhaps conceived as a way to get children interested in science or give them a chance to visit their parents' workplace, which was usually off-limits. I'm actually not sure why this was a thing, but once I got there I completely understood why it might be hard for someone who had been trying to get pregnant to go alone.

I wasn't sure quite how much I was supposed to know, so I didn't say anything to Vanessa about kids at all. But when we were both standing in the back of a group, watching Jay wow elementary schoolers with a clock reaction—his favorite, the one that went from clear to orange to black—Vanessa said to me, "I've stopped taking walks in the park."

I turned. "You have?" I asked.

She nodded. "It's just so hard to see the strollers and the playgrounds."

"I can imagine," I told her, as the group in front of us *oooh*ed when the mixture turned orange. "Have you gone to the doctor yet?"

"A few weeks ago," she said, looking at the reaction instead of my face. "I'm on medication right now. So hopefully . . ."

I glanced over at her. "I'm sure it'll happen," I said. "There's nothing wrong with needing a little help. A lot of people go through this sort of thing and end up pregnant."

The clock reaction turned black, and Vanessa looked at me. "I know," she said. "I just never imagined I would be one of them."

She excused herself to go to the bathroom after that, and I wandered over to a table that looked like it had been set up for an experiment you could do at home, with bottles of hydrogen peroxide, dish soap, and yeast. I'd never seen Jay do this one, so I wasn't quite sure what would happen when they mixed together. I stared at the ingredients, trying to puzzle it out.

"Foam," a voice said.

I looked next to me, and one of Jay's colleagues was there. I hadn't met him yet, but he was wearing a lab coat and a name tag. *Dr. Christopher Morgan.* He was tall, like you, with curly hair, like you, but that's where the similarities ended. He had dark eyes, dark hair, and a broad nose that was balanced perfectly by a squared-off chin.

"Hi," I said to him. "I'm Lucy Carter, Jason's sister."

He squinted at me. "I see it," he said. "In the eyebrows." Then he smiled. "Don't tell your brother, but they look better on a girl. I'm Chris, by the way."

I laughed. "I won't tell," I said. "Nice to meet you."

Chris walked to the other side of the table and started tightening the cap on the bottle of hydrogen peroxide. "No one seems too interested in my experiment. I thought it would be cool if I showed the kids something they could do at home, but they seem to be more interested in the ones that don't use kitchen ingredients. I guess I don't know kids too well."

He looked about my age. Maybe a year or so older. I figured he probably didn't have kids—maybe not nieces or nephews either.

"I'm interested," I told him. "I'd love to see your foam."

He looked over at me. "Really?" he asked. "You would?"

"Sure," I responded. But as I was saying it, I wondered if I was flirting with him. Or were we just talking? The diamond on my ring finger felt instantly heavy.

"Well, then," he said, unscrewing the top. "Some foam, coming right up."

Chris asked me questions as he poured the ingredients into beakers: where I lived, what I did, how I got to New Jersey that day. I found myself answering without mentioning Darren once. I knew this wasn't good.

"You know," he said, "I happen to visit New York City a lot. Maybe next time I come, we could grab a drink."

"I . . ." I said. And then I lifted up my left hand. "I'm so sorry, but I'm engaged."

"Oh," he said. "Oh, I'm sorry. I didn't—"

"No, no," I said, cutting him off. "Truly, it's my fault if I gave you the wrong impression."

Chris looked at my hand again, then back at the ingredients in front of him. "Do you want to add the yeast?" he asked finally.

I smiled, and I did, and we made foam. But as I drove back with Vanessa and Jay to their house later that day, I couldn't help but wonder what would've happened if I hadn't been engaged. Would I have given Chris my number? Would he and I have met for a drink? Would I have tasted something new and wonderful in his kiss?

Dating Darren for so long, right after dating you, it made me forget that there were other men. Tons of other men. And my mind went back to the conversation Kate and I had about Liz and her fire metaphors. What if I was cutting off all other possibilities too soon? Should I have tried looking for a bonfire and sparkler and whatever else Liz told Kate about?

But then I got home, and Darren was there waiting with presents for me from Montreal, and we made spaghetti carbonara together and walked Annie and laughed at the ridiculous things the guys had done during the bachelor party, and I thought: *This is it. This is what I want.* But I think back on that day sometimes and I wonder if maybe my gut was telling me something that neither my brain nor my heart wanted to acknowledge. Would we still be here now, like this, if I had listened?

xlvi

PEOPLE SAY RAIN ON A WEDDING DAY IS GOOD LUCK. I think someone somewhere just made that up so brides wouldn't feel so bad when they woke up to a gloomy, overcast sky the day they were getting married.

That's what our wedding was like, Darren's and mine. The sun was trying so hard to peek through the clouds, but it never quite made it. We got married six months after Darren proposed—Thanksgiving weekend 2006. He said he couldn't wait a minute longer to be my husband, and I was so swept up by the romance of it all that I agreed wholeheartedly. I was twenty-six years old. Darren was thirty-one. In addition to Darren's three sisters and my sister-in-law Vanessa, I had three more bridesmaids: Kate, Alexis, and Julia.

I had all the girls wearing yellow because it felt like a

happy color, and Darren and I wanted everything to be happy at our wedding. As happy as we were. No one else made me laugh like Darren did. No one else could turn a day of storm clouds and hurricanes into sunshine and clear blue skies. So maybe it was actually fitting that our wedding day was overcast—because marrying him made it seem sunny. He made the future seem sunny.

I even carried a bouquet of sunflowers—not very subtle, I know. I posted pictures on Facebook—so many people did that I'm guessing you already knew about the sunflowers. I didn't invite you, though. It didn't seem right. And I hadn't seen you at all that year. I'd e-mailed you about my engagement and you went silent, didn't let me know when you were in town, but I saw you on Adam's Facebook page, a picture of you, him, Justin, and Scott under a status update that said: *The boys are back in town!* I felt a pang when I saw that photo, but I remember thinking then that it was better we hadn't seen each other, better we'd slipped out of each other's lives.

Darren's and my wedding was at the Boathouse in Central Park. Our borough, I know, yours and mine, but I wasn't thinking about that when we booked it. My mom had been pushing for Connecticut, his parents had suggested Jersey, and Darren had thought Montauk would be nice. But I wanted New York City, and something I learned is that the bride usually gets what she wants. And once we saw the Boathouse, in the park, right near running trails, Darren was happy. He even designed our save-the-date card, a photo of both of us, from the knees down, our feet clad in running shoes with a line that said: *Whether you come by plane, train, car, or your own two feet, we can't wait to have you join us for our wedding!* I know, I know, you would've rolled your eyes if you'd gotten that in the mail. I don't think you and Alina got far enough along in wedding planning to have a save-the-date card. But even if you had gotten that far, I can imagine you ignoring that custom completely.

The night before the wedding, I'd slept at my parents' house in Connecticut, and had just woken up in my childhood bed when my cell phone rang. The number calling was long and clearly from outside the country. It could have been a few different people—Kate's sister Liz, colleagues from the U.K. or Germany, where *It Takes a Galaxy* was doing almost as well as it was in the U.S.—but something told me it was you. I waited another ring, and another, and then decided to pick up. I thought maybe you were going to wish me good luck or something.

But you had no idea what day it was. Or at least not consciously. I've always wondered if somewhere in the back of your mind you knew. Someone must've told you. Or you must've seen it somewhere on Facebook. But perhaps not. Perhaps it was a coincidence.

"Luce?" you said.

"Gabe?" I asked.

"It's me," you said. "I'm sorry if I'm interrupting something. I know we haven't talked in a while. But I . . . I needed you."

I sat up in my Laura Ashley bed, my body reacting to your voice the way it always does, and leaned back against the pillows. "What's wrong?" I asked, imagining explosions and wounds and missing limbs.

"Raina's not a Pegasus," you said.

I let out a breath. You weren't hurt. You weren't in pieces. At least not physically. I hoped not emotionally either. "What happened?" I asked.

"She met an aid worker. She liked him better. Said he was more available than I was. Am I unavailable, Luce?"

At first I wasn't sure how to answer but then figured I might as well be honest. "I don't know," I said. "It's been more than a year since we talked to each other. I don't know you anymore."

"Yes, you do," you told me. "I'm the same. You know me better than anyone. I just . . . I need to know: Is Raina right about me?"

I couldn't believe that I was psychoanalyzing my ex-boyfriend the morning of my wedding. "I think," I said, choosing my words delicately, "that making yourself available means putting the relationship you're in first. Not necessarily always, but often. It means making the decision that's best for the two of you, as a unit, even if it means compromising a little individually. It means sharing everything. The Gabe I knew wasn't interested in doing that."

There was a long pause. "I guess I wasn't," you said, so quietly I almost couldn't hear the disappointment in your voice. "I was hoping you'd say something different."

"I'm sorry," I said. "I think maybe today's not the best day for this."

"Is everything okay?" you said. "I should've asked first. If you want to talk about anything—"

"It's just . . . today's my wedding day." I had trouble saying the words. Had trouble saying them to you.

"Luce," you said, sounding like I'd slapped you. "You're getting married today?"

"I'm getting married today," I echoed.

"Oh," you said. "Shit." I remember that exactly. The way you said it, your intonation. *Oh. Shit.* Like each word was a complete sentence all its own.

I was quiet for a moment.

There was silence on your end too. And I felt bad. "It'll be okay," I said. "You'll find another Pegasus."

"What if—" You never finished the sentence, as if you were afraid to say it, or maybe it was that you were afraid for me to hear it.

"You will," I said. Then quieter, "I should probably go."

"Yeah," you said. "I'm . . . I'm sorry I called."

"No," I told you, "don't worry about it. It's fine."

"Sorry," you said again.

We hung up, but of course I was thinking about you for the rest of the morning.

xlvii

WITHOUT WATERPROOF MASCARA, I DON'T THINK I would've been able to get through my wedding day. As I was getting dressed, as my hair was twisted into a chignon, as a nice woman named Jackie was applying concealer to my face, I kept thinking about you saying *Oh. Shit.* I kept hearing your unfinished sentence: *What if—?* I *was* sure Darren was what I'd wanted. I'd thought I was sure. Up until that moment, I was certain. And then you got me thinking.

When Jackie decided she was going to give up on the undereye liner because my eyes kept overflowing with tears, my mom asked everyone to clear out of the room.

"Just give us a moment," she said, touching the pearls around her neck, as if there were a reservoir of strength in that family heirloom.

Once the room was empty, she leaned against the counter in the bridal suite. "Lucy," she said. "What's wrong?"

I didn't want to admit the truth, that I was thinking about you on my wedding day, that I was questioning my decision.

"I guess I'm just emotional," I said.

She looked at me hard, her icy eyes cutting through my lie, just the way they did when I was a kid. "Lucy," she said, "I'm your mother. Whatever it is, you can tell me."

So I told her something. I told her something I'd been worrying about for months, something I hadn't admitted to anyone. "I think Darren loves me more than I love him," I said.

She hugged me, but carefully, so my damp makeup wouldn't rub off onto her champagne silk dress. "Oh, honey," she said. "Relationships aren't always equal. The balance is forever shifting. Who loves whom more, who needs whom more. Your relationship with Darren today won't be the same even a year from now."

She held me by my shoulders and pulled away so she could look into my eyes. "And I don't think it's so terrible if he loves you just a little more than you love him right now. Then you know he'll treat you like a princess."

I laughed and wiped my eyes. But she was still looking at me with that lie-detector expression. "There's something else," she said.

I looked down at my fingers, at the elegantly painted French manicure on my nails. "Gabe called this morning."

"Gabe Samson?" my mother asked.

I nodded, my eyes welling with tears again. "What if he's the man I'm supposed to be with, not Darren?"

My mom leaned back against the counter again and rubbed her pearls. She was quiet for a while. Then she spoke: "I want you to think, truly think, about the relationship you have with Darren and about the relationship you had with Gabe," she said. "And I want you to think about who would be a better partner—a better father to your children. If you think the answer's not Darren, you don't have to get married today. Even if it's not Gabe. If you think there's someone else out there who would make you happier than Darren does, you can walk away. It won't be easy, but you can do it. Just say the word and I'll tell your father, he'll tell the guests. But you won't get to change your mind again. If you say good-bye to Darren today, that's forever. I've seen how much the two of you care about each other and how much fun you have together. But if this doesn't feel right, no one is making you marry him."

I nodded. My mother walked over to the window. And I thought about you, Gabe. I thought about how wonderful you made me feel, but also how awful. How you cared so much more about yourself than you did about us. How in the end, your life was *The Gabe Show*, and to keep you I would've had to play the supporting actress to the star. I know it might be hard for you to hear this, but I'm just telling you the truth. That's what I thought that day.

I also thought about Darren. About the fact that he wasn't perfect. That he still didn't really take my job seriously. And sometimes I worried that he didn't take *me* seriously. But I figured I could change that, I could work harder to show him what it meant to me. I could help him see that I wanted to be his partner, his equal. And I loved him. I loved his laugh, his sense of humor, his grin. He wasn't dark and complicated—being with him was fun and easy. It felt solid and stable. He made me happy—most of the time. And we'd built the foundation of a beautiful future together. I could never leave him there at the Boathouse on our wedding day.

I wiped my eyes. "Thank you," I said to my mother. "I'm fine now. I'm ready."

My mom let out a huge breath and gave me a hug. "You know I would support you no matter what."

"I know," I said, smelling the Shalimar perfume on her neck.

"Just remember," she added, "there's a difference between infatuation and love."

I nodded.

Was I infatuated with you? Were we infatuated with each other? Can infatuation last this long? Or has it always been love between us? I'd like to think it has.

xlviii

EVEN THOUGH I'D BEEN WORKING ON *IT TAKES A GALAXY* for a while, researching real-life stories, trying to pull conflicts from as many countries and cultures as possible so the writers could use them as the basis of various episodes, I'd never traveled any farther than Europe. So Darren and I decided to go to Turkey on our honeymoon. I wanted to hear the call to prayer. I wanted to see a tiny piece of one of the countries I'd researched. And when we got there I couldn't stop taking notes. I saw women with their heads covered walking down the street, talking to women with hair falling around their shoulders. I pulled out a ticket stub and scribbled a message to myself to suggest a scene like that in our next episode, but with aliens, of course.

"Enough with the writing!" Darren said. "We're here on our honeymoon. Work is back in New York. I haven't checked in with the office once since we've been here, and you haven't stopped scribbling and muttering to yourself."

I stopped midword. "My work is important to me," I said. But then I remembered what I told you when you'd called. "But you and I are more important. I'll stop." And I did.

Still, I couldn't help thinking about what it would've been like if it were you and me on that trip. You wouldn't have asked me to stop—you would have suggested things too. And we both would have been looking out for great opportunities for photographs, just like we did when we walked holes through the soles of our sneakers in Manhattan.

DARREN'S AND MY TRIP took us to Cappadocia, where we toured a landscape that looked like the moon and took off right before dawn in a hot-air balloon that rose up just in time for us to see the sunrise. It was exquisite—a swirl of pinks and oranges and purples—and Darren had his arms wrapped around me, keeping me warm, making me feel loved in the middle of the sky's majesty. But I couldn't stop thinking about those women. I wished I had spoken to them, asked them what their lives were like, what they would want American kids to know about Turkey.

LATER, DARREN AND I were at a spot called Devrent Valley. Darren read from the guidebook, "'Devrent or "Imagination" Valley is filled with rock formations that look like people and animals. Spend time discovering what you see in the rocks.'"

I stood next to him, seeing a camel and a dolphin and a snake in a hat.

"I think that one looks like the Virgin Mary," he said, pointing to a pillar. "What do you think, Mrs. Maxwell?" He'd been calling me Mrs. Maxwell the whole trip, which at first I found sweet and funny but then started to irritate me. I'd told him I'd take his name personally, but I was still going to be Lucy Carter at work. Is that how I'm keyed into your phone? Or did you change my name when Darren and I married? Your boss called me Lucy Carter Maxwell. You did too, actually. I guess that's how you think of me.

I stared at the rock that Darren was facing, looking for a mother and child, looking for a veil. "I just see a man holding a camera," I said.

xlix

I KNOW SO MANY PEOPLE WHO SPENT YEARS TRYING to get pregnant. Vanessa and Jay wound up with triplets after taking Clomid. Kate ended up going through in vitro, twice. Darren jokes that when he sneezes on me, I conceive. I smile when he says that, but I don't find it funny. It makes me think of the Birthmothers in that book *The Giver* I read in high school, where getting pregnant over and over again was their assigned task, their only use in society.

Not long after we got married, Darren started talking about having kids. He thought we were the perfect age to start a family. The same exact age his parents were when they had his oldest sister. Even though Kate had just told me that she was pregnant, I wasn't so sure he was right. The triplets had been born a week earlier, prematurely but remarkably okay. Vanessa and Jay had a nanny and a night nurse—and Vanessa's mom, who stayed with them for the first six months—and even still, when Jay called he sounded like a zombie. That first week, he rang me from the lab while I was still at work.

"Can you talk?" he asked.

"I'm at the office," I answered, cradling my cell phone to my ear. "Is everything okay?"

"Humans weren't meant to have three babies at once," he said. "Am I a terrible person if I don't want to go home to them?"

"You're not a terrible person, Jay, you're just tired," I told him. "It's understandable. Give yourself another thirty minutes, but then you have to go back. Those babies need you. Vanessa needs you."

"I can't even tell them apart," he said. "Unless they're wearing clothes."

That one gave me pause, but not too much. Sometimes I wonder if my brother would recognize me if he saw me on the street, out of context.

"Think about them like you do different viruses," I told him. "Pay close attention. Notice their differences, not their similarities."

I hoped that would help. I felt bad for Jay. Three babies at once was definitely more than he and Vanessa had thought they would get.

He took a big breath and let it out. "Like hydrogen loves oxygen," he said. "I'll let you work now."

"Love you too, Jay," I said, before hanging up.

So after that, after the triplets, I wasn't completely convinced a baby was something I wanted to add to my life just then. But Darren was sure. He reminded me that parenthood was on both of our bucket lists.

"And besides," he said, "it'll probably take at least a year, if we go by Vanessa and Kate."

It took a month.

There were a few weeks of absolute exhaustion, going to sleep before nine p.m. Then way too many weeks of nausea, the kind where I would run out of meetings, sure that if I didn't, I would hurl all over the writers' room and the scenes they were revising. Then, once that mercifully passed, there were months of having to pee approximately once an hour.

It took me about four months of being pregnant to be okay with it. To come to terms with what my life would be like once the baby arrived. But once I did, I was excited. I didn't think I would react this way, but I spent my lunchtimes at the office looking at baby clothes and nursery furniture. I read articles about breastfeeding and water births and when the ideal time was to introduce peanut butter into your child's diet. I became baby obsessed.

I even started wondering if having a successful career really was all that important to me, or if being a mom trumped that. I wondered if I'd come back after maternity leave. I know, after everything I told you about not wanting to be defined by my role as a wife or a mother and hoping to make a difference in the world with my work—how my main complaint about Darren was that he didn't understand that part of me—the fact that I was considering quitting might seem crazy. It felt crazy to me—like I was turning into someone else, an alternate Lucy whose priorities morphed and changed. But it was truly how I felt. Being pregnant did that to me. And Darren really wanted me to stay home too. He said that no one would take care of our baby better than I would, and I was starting to think he was right.

DARREN WAS DOING incredibly well at work. The deals he closed had impressed his bosses so much that they made him a director, and his new salary blew my mind. He was earning more than five times what I was, and I wasn't doing all that badly myself. With all the extra income, he wanted to buy a big apartment in a great neighborhood.

"Let's move to Manhattan," he said, one morning, with the *New York Times* spread across his legs and Annie at his feet. "Maybe the Upper East Side."

But Manhattan was our borough. Yours and mine. And ever since your phone call five months before, I'd felt more aware of that. Even though Darren and I had gotten married in Manhattan, we'd never really claimed it. Brooklyn was our place.

"I like Brooklyn," I told him. "How about Park Slope? Or Brooklyn Heights?"

Even married with a baby on the way, I was thinking about you. I was making life decisions based on us. But I truly thought it would stop—that you'd fade from my mind again, the way you had before. And that turned out to be more or less true. But at that point, you were still there, front of brain, guiding my thoughts.

"Are you sure?" he asked. "P.S. 6 is a great elementary school." Then he shrugged. "I guess we could always send the baby to private school."

"So Brooklyn?" I asked him.

He was already looking at the Brooklyn Heights listings.

"I found one!" he said a few minutes later. "Listen to this: four bedrooms, three and a half bathrooms, two floors of a brownstone on Love Lane. How could we not live on Love Lane?"

Then he pulled me over and kissed my stomach before he kissed my lips. I kissed him back. "Do we need four bedrooms?" I asked him.

"We might one day," he said with a smile.

I knew he wanted a big family, like his. I wasn't quite

sure how I felt about that, but I wasn't ruling it out either. "How about we check it out?" I said.

We went to the open house. I'd never seen an apartment that big in the city before. There was a formal dining room, an eat-in kitchen—what am I saying, you know all these things. Obviously. You've been there.

Once we bought the apartment, once we moved in, once we started decorating the nursery, once all of that happened, I felt like a mom for real. I couldn't wait to meet my baby.

1

I'm not sure why fives and tens are big deals: thirtieth birthdays, twenty-fifth wedding anniversaries, five-year reunions—ours was the summer I was pregnant for the first time, a week after Darren and I had moved to our new Brooklyn Heights apartment. Darren couldn't stop talking about filling all the bedrooms with babies, but I was too busy concentrating on the one growing inside me.

You'd come to town but hadn't let me know. You hadn't contacted me at all since I'd gotten married. That was probably the right choice. I thought about you enough without the real you making appearances in my world.

But I guess you didn't want to catch me off guard at the reunion, or maybe you wanted to prepare yourself, to see what kind of reaction I'd give before we saw each other in person. You texted me that afternoon.

See you tonight? you wrote.

I stared at the message on my phone for a good two minutes. You didn't know I was pregnant. I thought I should tell you before you saw me.

I'll be the pregnant one in the blue dress, I wrote back, half an hour later.

Probably not the most elegant way to give you the news. You didn't write back.

And, of course, for the entire rest of the day I wondered what you were thinking. If you were upset or happy for me. If you were going to avoid me at the reunion, or specifically look for me.

"What's going on with you today?" Darren asked, touching my shoulder. "I just called your name four times, it's like you're in a different world. Do you want me to zip your dress?"

"Sorry," I said, "just thinking about college. And yes, thank you."

Darren has a thing about zipping up my dresses. He thinks there's something especially intimate about the act of dressing someone. More so than undressing. He says it showed love, not just lust.

"Want me to tie your tie?" I asked.

He smiled and said yes.

How did you get ready for the reunion? Were you staying with friends? In a hotel room? I never had a chance to ask you.

The reunion was a little insane—don't you agree? People conspicuously holding on to their husbands or wives. A few of us wearing high-end maternity dresses. The same way I felt those jealous eyes on us in Bloomingdale's years before, I saw women at the reunion looking at me with envy. I'd nabbed the successful husband, I was about to have the baby. It didn't matter that we went to an Ivy League university, that the women there were lawyers and doctors, playwrights and bankers, consultants and academics—they all came up to me and asked about the baby, about the wedding. No one asked where I was working, what I'd been up to since graduation. No one cared that I'd just been promoted to associate producer, that I was developing a new show on my own called *Rocket Through Time* that took kids on an exploration of history and showed how it affected the present. It was just, "When are you due?" "Have you found out the sex?" "How long have you been married?" "Where did you meet him?" I wouldn't be surprised if half the women I spoke to put in for share houses in the Hamptons that summer. I was starting to think that my college roommates had made the right decision in staying away.

Then I saw you. You were on the other side of the tent, and a woman I didn't recognize had her hand on your forearm while the two of you spoke. She smiled at something you said, then responded. You laughed. All of a sudden I felt nauseated.

"I need some air," I whispered to Darren, who had found another investment banker and was talking shop.

"Oh!" he said. "Are you okay?"

I nodded. "Just a little queasy, I'll be fine."

I'd only gotten over the morning sickness phase of the pregnancy a few weeks before. Darren was used to watching me vomit, but it wasn't a pleasant experience for either one of us.

"You sure?" he asked.

"Positive," I answered, and headed out of the tent.

I took a few deep breaths and then turned back around. There were no walls, so I could see straight inside the tent. I couldn't find you anymore, but that woman was talking to someone else, her hand on his arm. That did more for me than the deep breaths. My nausea abated.

I was about to head back to Darren when I felt someone touch my shoulder. It was you, of course.

"Luce," you said.

I turned. "Gabe," I answered. "Hi."

The skin on my shoulder prickled with goose bumps where you'd touched me.

"Nice dress," you said.

Darren told me once that when men say that, they mean, "You look hot in that dress." I've never been completely sure if he was right about that. I should've asked you then what you meant.

"Thanks," I answered. "Nice shirt."

Your dimple appeared. "I can't even tell," you told me. "You look exactly the same."

Then I turned sideways and held the drapey dress close to my body. "How about now?" I asked.

Your eyes grew wide for a moment before you smiled. "Well that's . . ."

"Yeah," I said. "That's a baby." It wasn't much of one, just about a four-month bump. But I couldn't wear my regular clothes anymore. I'd had to buy a new dress.

"Congratulations, Luce," you said. "I'm happy for you."

"Thanks." I let go of my dress. "How's everything been on your end?"

Your smile faded and you shrugged. "Coming back to New York is always strange. It feels like I'm in *Back to the Future* and I've returned to a world that jumped ahead while I wasn't looking." Your eyes wandered back to my stomach.

"Your world's changed too, though," I said.

You shook your head. "I can't explain it. My world's changed, but my New York feels like it should be the same. Everything should be just as I left it, like coming back to a childhood bedroom." You stopped abruptly. "I'm not making any sense."

"No," I said, "you are. Your safe space has changed."

"Yeah," you said. Your gaze lingered on my stomach. "Yeah," you said again. Then, "I should probably go . . . it was great to see you, Lucy. Good luck. I really am happy for you."

You walked quickly toward the bar set up next to the sundial.

I wanted to call out and tell you to wait. I wanted to ask you more questions so I could understand what you were feeling, so I could hear what your world was like. I wanted you to touch me again and give me goose bumps.

But you were right to walk away. Nothing good could have come of prolonging that conversation. So instead I went back to Darren.

"You feeling okay, sweetie?" he asked.

"Much better," I told him, and leaned my head against his shoulder.

Without missing a beat in the conversation he was having, he wrapped his arm around me and dropped a kiss on the top of my head.

It didn't give me goose bumps, but it did feel good.

li

ONE THING I'VE LEARNED—FROM WORK, FROM YOU, from my life with Darren—is that as far as I'm concerned, ninety-nine percent of surprises should be avoided at all cost. When I can prepare for something, I'm much better at handling it. If I could have prepared myself when you were leaving New York, if I'd known you were in talks with the Associated Press for a job, I can't help thinking I would've been better at dealing with it. But the fact that it was a surprise, that . . . that made everything harder. That's why we decided to find out the baby's sex. I wanted to know so I could prepare. We learned we were having a girl a few weeks after the reunion. I didn't bother getting in touch with all the women there who'd asked me. I figured they'd find out on Facebook if they were all that interested.

Because of my distaste for surprises, I read books—I

can't tell you how many books—on different people's birthing experiences, on what to expect, on the choices people had. I thought it might help prepare me—might stop the nightmares I was having about giving birth on the subway or in my office or in a taxicab. Or the ones about the baby tearing me open like that scene in *Alien*. I made a birthing plan, like the doctor suggested, but I knew as I was making it that the baby could have her own birthing plan that I would not be privy to.

I went into labor at night, after dinner at Heights Cafe. I ate a burger—actually, half a burger because there was practically no room in my stomach then for food. The baby was due in two days, on November 21st, and Darren said that we should get in as many date nights as possible before she was born, even if it just meant half a burger at a restaurant within walking distance of our apartment. We'd figured out as much as we could by then. We knew we were going to name her Violet, after Darren's grandmother, who'd passed away when he was sixteen. I loved the name—the sound of it, the way it was a flower and a color, the nickname *Vi*. We'd decided on a middle name, too—Anne—after my great-aunt. Violet Anne Maxwell. I still love her name.

So after dinner, as we walked home, me with a coat that barely closed over my stomach, my underwear started to feel damp. Is this too much information? Do you actually care what it felt like the night Violet was born? If you tell me to stop, I will. Just give me a sign. No? Okay.

I remember thinking: *Really? Now?* One of my modest pregnancy goals was to make it through the whole experience without "making a mistake," as we called it when we were potty-training Violet. Kate had needed to change her underwear almost every time she sneezed while she was pregnant. I'd really hoped that wouldn't happen to me. When we were a block away from our apartment, though, the trickle of wetness turned into more than a trickle, and I realized what was happening.

I turned to Darren. "I think my water broke," I said.

He stopped dead in his tracks. "Really?" he asked. I could see the excitement in his eyes. "Wait, you think or you know?"

"I think I know," I answered.

He laughed and hugged me and kissed me and said, "Can you walk? Are you okay? Should we call the doctor? Right now?"

Even though I was already worrying about what would happen from that point on, and even though my leggings were wet and getting cold, I told him I was pretty sure I could walk the block to our apartment with him, and that we could call the doctor when we got there. He held my hand the whole way, talking much faster than he usually did about who we had to call and what he couldn't forget once we left for the hospital. (The phone chargers! His laptop! His iPod and speakers!) He'd made a few playlists for us to listen to at various parts of the labor and delivery experience. I wasn't sure I'd want to hear any of them, but it gave him something to do, a way to prepare.

We waited at home, trying to watch a made-for-TV movie that I can't remember at all, until my contractions were five minutes apart, just like the doctor said. And then we took a cab to the hospital. Twelve hours later, Violet was born. She was beautiful and perfect with dark hair and dark eyes and the longest eyelashes I'd ever seen on a baby.

Darren has this thing where he thinks all his friends' babies—and Jay and Vanessa's triplets—looked like either Winston Churchill or Mr. Magoo when they were born. He'll still hold up his computer screen every now and then to show me someone's kid on Facebook and say, "Churchill or Magoo?" And truly, they do always look like one of the two options.

When Violet was washed and dressed and wrapped up like a burrito, with a little striped hat on her head, the nurse handed her to me, and I looked up at Darren. "Churchill or Magoo?" I asked him.

"I think she's the first baby in the history of the world who looks like neither. She looks like you," he said. "Lucky little girl."

Then he slid off his shoes and climbed into bed with me,

and the three of us cuddled. At that moment, I truly was in awe—of the way Darren and I had created a person together, of the way genetics made her look like me, of the way biology works to make this moment of happiness possible.

"I love you," I told Darren.

"I love you both," he said back.

I need you to understand that I do really, truly love him. What he and I have isn't perfect, but it is absolutely love.

lii

WHEN I GOT ENGAGED, ALL OF A SUDDEN I FELT LIKE I'd joined a club, one that had a membership that went back decades, centuries, millennia—the Club of Women Who Had Become Engaged. I felt the same way about getting married, like my membership in the Club of Women Who Had Gotten Married was shored up when I put on a white dress and walked down an aisle and said *I do*. But nothing felt more like joining a club than having a child. There was a dividing line between the women who had babies, and the women who didn't. The Moms and the Not Moms.

And even in that club there was a subset—the God Help Me Moms and the Expert Moms, the ones who Facebooked photos of their children dressed in pristine outfits, asleep on satin pillows, with captions like *I Dream of Daddy*.

I was not that kind of mom. I am still not that kind of mom. I will never be that kind of mom.

I joined the Mom Club—had to, there was no way around that—but I counted the day a good one if both Violet and I were clean and fed and had slept more than five hours total in a night. I had three months of maternity leave, but by the end of eight weeks, I felt like I was fraying at the edges. Being a stay-at-home mom was nothing like I imagined it would be.

Kate called at least once a day to check in on me, even if she could only chat for a minute or two. She'd had her daughter, Victoria, six months before and her firm had a really generous maternity plan, so she'd just gone back to the office and was working like crazy, trying to make sure she wasn't mommy-tracked. "It'll get easier," she told me. "I promise." But it didn't feel like it was.

I was nursing, and Violet ate practically all day. Or at least that was what it seemed like. On some days I didn't even bother putting on a shirt. And I came up with what I called the Fecal Incident Levels. Level One was no big deal. Level Two filled a diaper. Level Three leaked out through the leg holes. Level Four oozed up her back. Level Five was the worst—it basically meant there was feces smeared from her shoulders to knees. It required a bath. And often a change of clothes for me too. Between Levels Three, Four, and Five, I threw away so many onesies, it's amazing she had enough to wear.

One day, though, Violet somehow managed to reach Fecal Incident Level Six. We'd had a great morning. She was clean, I was clean, we'd both eaten—though I hadn't really slept more than three hours in succession in days—and since the heat in the apartment was blasting, she was wearing only a diaper and a T-shirt. She had just started to smile, and my heart melted a little each time she did.

We were having such a good day that I'd decided to make a real dinner, something that had happened maybe twice in the last eight weeks. I'd put Violet in a little baby seat that vibrated and turned it on. Then I'd defrosted some chicken and started breading it. The radio was on—a '60s station that reminded me of my dad—and I started singing along to "My Girl." My hands were covered in eggs and bread crumbs, but I felt great. And then Violet started wailing.

I looked over, and froze. The first ever Fecal Incident Level Six. Maybe it was because of the vibrating chair, or the angle she was sitting in, or the lack of clothing other than diaper and T-shirt, but somehow there was poop on her thighs that had gotten onto her hands and into her hair. I took a deep breath, quickly rinsed my hands, and lifted her out of the seat. She flailed her arms, so now there was poop on my cheek, on my shirt, and my wrist. And then she spit up in my hair. She was still screaming, and I started crying too.

That was how Darren found us.

"Lucy?" I heard him yell from the entryway. "What's going on? Why's Violet . . . ?" And then he made it to the kitchen. "Oh," he said. "Oh my God."

He dropped his briefcase on the floor and took off his suit jacket. "I got the poop machine," he said. "You go shower."

I looked at him and took a shaky breath. "Strip first," I said. "You don't want to get this on your suit. And she's not just a poop machine. She's a puke machine too."

"Yikes," he said, working the buttons on his shirt and dropping it on top of his jacket. "What do you think the headline should be for this one? *Naked Man Saves Wife from Soiled Baby?*"

I laughed a little bit. "How about *Naked Man Does What Wife Does All Day Long with Soiled Baby?*" I suggested.

"Really?" he asked. "This happens a lot?" He'd gotten completely naked, except for his boxer briefs, and took Violet. "Oh, gross," he said, once he had her by her armpits.

"Well, not a Level Six," I told him, "but Level Five isn't that rare."

"What are you talking about?" he asked, as the three of us walked to the master bathroom. It had both a tub and a shower, and we'd put the little plastic baby bathtub in the larger one for Violet. Annie joined our parade once we got upstairs, barking her confusion.

Darren started the water for Violet's bath while I stripped and got in the shower and Annie curled herself up on the little rug in front of the sink. Through the steam, I explained to him about Fecal Incident Levels. And while I was at it, I told him that I wanted to go back to work when my maternity leave was over. That I needed to. We'd been having this conversation since late in my pregnancy, but I'd put off making an official decision because it had felt like there were too many variables, there was too much I didn't know. I knew what Darren wanted me to do, though.

"I thought we'd discussed this," he said.

"We did," I said, as I quickly shampooed my puke-stained hair. "And now we're discussing it again."

"But I thought you agreed that Violet would be better off with you than with a stranger. No one will take care of her the way you will."

I leaned my head back into the shower stream. "To be honest," I said, "I think that you're wrong. And that's only part of the issue. I've been thinking about this thing that my grandfather used to say all the time: *Those who can, do.* He meant it as a mantle of responsibility. If you can help someone, if you can do something good, if you can make a difference, you should. And I can. I'm capable of making more of a contribution to the world than I would be making if I stayed home with Violet every day. I made a commitment to myself on September Eleventh to live my life in a way that would give back. And I want to do that. I *need* to do that."

"But don't you love being home with Violet?" Darren asked, as if he hadn't heard a word I said.

I took a deep breath. "There are moments that are wonderful," I said. "But I love being an associate producer, too. I love making television shows. I've worked my ass off for the last five years, and I'm good at what I do. I'm not good at this."

"You just need more time," he said, dropping Violet's T-shirt and soiled diaper into the trash can. "There's no way you can think your job is more important than your daughter."

I was ready to kick something. Or cry. Or both. I gave my hair one final rinse and turned off the shower.

"Of course I don't think that," I said, wrapping myself in a terry-cloth robe. "But I value my own happiness too. And if I stayed home, if this was my life, I'd resent it. I'd resent *her*. And you."

"I think she's peeing?" he said, as he slipped her into the baby bathtub.

"Happens," I answered, kneeling to take over.

"So many women would die for this opportunity," Darren said. "You don't need to work. I make enough money. I have this job so you don't need to work."

"No," I said, shampooing Violet's hair. "You have that job because you love that job. You love making money and having people respect you. You love the high that comes with closing huge deals."

"That's not the only—" Darren said.

I stopped him. "And you like being a provider, too, I get it. You like being able to take care of us. And I appreciate it, I do. But don't pretend you work just so I don't have to. You work because you like how your job makes you feel. Just like I like how *my* job makes me feel."

Darren was quiet. When I looked up at him, he seemed to be evaluating me, assessing me.

"Would you want to give it up?" I asked. "And stay with her every day, all day, alone? I know she's wonderful, and we both love her. But would you want that?"

"It's not financially sustainable," he said, while I washed Violet's back with a washcloth shaped like a duck.

"That wasn't my question."

"It's a ridiculous question," he said. "We couldn't live off your salary alone."

"Pretend," I said, through my teeth. "Pretend it's financially sustainable. Pretend we could live off my salary in a way that would make you happy. Would you want to do it?"

"So many of my colleagues' wives—" he started.

"I am not your colleagues' wives," I said. "I'm me. And you still haven't answered my question: Would you want to stay home with her every day and quit your job? In theory?" Violet seemed clean, so I took her out of the bath. She cried until I'd swaddled her in a hot-pink hooded towel that had bunny rabbit ears attached to it. And a cottontail.

"This isn't what I thought our lives would be like," Darren said. "This isn't what I wanted."

I looked him full in the face while holding our daughter to my chest. I felt tears filling my eyes but was powerless to stop them. "This isn't what I wanted either."

He opened his mouth but seemed at a loss for words.

I didn't look at Darren again. I didn't say anything else. Instead, I rubbed Violet dry and brought her into her room, where I gave her a new diaper and snapped her into a pair of striped pajamas. "All better?" I asked her. She smiled and gurgled at me as I wiped the tears off my cheek with a burp cloth.

I heard Darren walk into the room behind me.

"No," he said. "I wouldn't. I wouldn't want to quit my job and stay home with her every day."

I nodded, pressing my lips to Violet's hair, feeling her warmth against my chest, pulling strength from her, for her. She needed a mother who stood up for herself, who wasn't afraid to go after what she wanted. I needed to be a role model for Violet. "You understand now," I said to Darren.

He came over and wrapped his arm around my shoulders.

"I'm sorry I'm not one of those women," I said, "like your colleagues' wives. I'm sorry staying at home won't make me happy. But this is me. And I need to work."

"Don't say that," he said. "You don't have to apologize for being who you are. I should apologize."

I wanted to ask, *For what?* To make sure he wasn't apologizing just to keep the peace. But instead I said, "Apology accepted." Though looking back I realized he didn't quite apologize. Just acknowledged he should.

THE NEXT DAY we started a search for a nanny. And about a month after that I went back to work. I did miss Violet when I was there—more than I expected, actually. But I was grateful for Darren then. Grateful that we had choices, that we could hire people to help us when we needed it, that in the end, he wanted me to be happy.

liii

THERE ARE SOME MOMENTS OF MY LIFE I CAN PICTURE so clearly, as if I could slip back into the memories and relive them word for word, and then there are long swaths of time—days and weeks—that seem indistinguishable from one another. The months after I went back to work, while Violet was still an infant, are a blur. I was barely sleeping and developing two new shows and pumping breast milk in my office and making sure I spent as much time with Violet as possible. I was barely on Facebook, and when I was it was just to post those obligatory "5 months, 6 months, 7 months" photos. So I missed seeing pictures of you and Alina. I missed the whole development of that relationship. If I hadn't been so busy, I might have noticed that we hadn't spoken at all since the reunion, but it didn't even register. I'd gotten back to a place where you didn't really matter, the place I'd been in before you called the morning of my wedding.

And then when I was posting Violet's "8 months" photograph, and liking photos of Julia's trip to Amsterdam, that little heart emblem popped into my news feed, and there it was. *Gabriel Samson is engaged to Alina Alexandrov.* There was a picture of you underneath it, with your arms around a beautiful woman with auburn hair, wide-set hazel eyes, and an enormous smile. My stomach flipped. *This shouldn't make a difference to you*, I told myself. *You're married, you have a child, you haven't seen him in more than a year, he hasn't been yours in more than four years.* But it did. It made a difference. In that photograph I saw my "might have been." I saw the road not taken.

I spent the next hour clicking on your pictures and looking at the two of you on vacation in Croatia. I'd never been to Croatia. Then there you were in China, on top of the Great Wall. And in Egypt, dancing with Alina, who was wearing a belly-dancing skirt made of bright red chiffon and silver coins. I was surprised by how jealous I was of that life. I wanted to climb the Great Wall of China, I wanted to belly dance in Egypt.

You were based in Baghdad again, and it looked like she was, too, working for *The Guardian*. I clicked on its website and read every article she wrote. And then Googled her name and read her Wikipedia page. Then I discovered you had a Wikipedia page. And your pages were linked, with an update that someone must have recently added mentioning your engagement.

I checked myself. I did not have a Wikipedia page. Neither did Darren. Then Violet started crying, so I shut down the computer. But later that day I e-mailed you a quick note that said: *Congratulations!*

You didn't write back.

liv

THAT SEPTEMBER I WAS STILL IN MY POST-VIOLET FOG, but life was starting to enter a sustainable groove. She was sleeping through the night, finally, and we'd spent the last week of August as a family in a rented house in Westhampton Beach. Violet loved the pool, so we slathered her with sunscreen, dropped her in a little inner tube contraption that had an attached hood to block her from the sun, and let her bob around like a tiny buoy while we floated in the pool ourselves. It felt like a small slice of heaven.

"You like it out here," Darren said later, as Violet bobbed and splashed and the two of us sat on the steps in the shallow end of the pool with cold glasses of Chardonnay.

"You like it out here, too," I answered, leaning my head on his shoulder.

"I do," he said. "We should buy a place."

"Maybe one day," I told him. "But for now, renting for a week or two each summer sounds pretty ideal to me."

He nodded. "One day. It's on my bucket list, remember?"

I hadn't. "Of course," I said. "We've been bucket-list remiss as of late, I'm afraid."

He shook his head. "No, we haven't," he said. "This year we became parents. That was on our lists."

I laughed. "That's right," I said. "I take it back. We are awesome at bucket lists."

"We are," he said, kissing me, while Violet splashed us both.

That's what I was thinking about that morning on the subway—the week in Westhampton, the pool, how relaxing it was. And then I looked up. The man across from me was holding a copy of the *New York Times*. The article facing me said: *More Bodies Pulled from Hotel Rubble in Pakistan*. My mind went straight to you. Were you in Pakistan? Last I'd seen you were in Baghdad, but could you have moved? Or been covering something in Islamabad? Could you have been staying at that hotel?

I couldn't breathe properly until I'd gotten to work, logged into Facebook and seen the Associated Press article you posted about the hotel. You knew people who had been killed in the explosion, but you hadn't been. You were still in Iraq.

"Oh, thank God," I whispered. Then I scrolled down

your page, curious to see what you'd been up to. A little broken heart icon jumped out at me. You and Alina had broken up. I wondered what had happened, and truly, I felt bad. I wanted you to be happy. I thought for a moment about reaching out to you, but I didn't.

My day went on, my week, my month, but you were in my thoughts more than you had been since Violet was born. I kept my eye out for your photographs. I wondered if you were going to make it back to New York any time soon, and if you did, if you'd let me know.

ORDINARY DAYS SOMETIMES TURN INTO EXTRAOR-
dinary days when you least expect them to. It was a Friday
in January. I was working from home, listening to Violet
chatter to the nanny while answering e-mails from the office. Violet was fourteen months old at that point and could
say only a handful of words, but that didn't stop her from
attempting to explain the secrets of the universe to us. At
least that's what Darren and I imagined she was doing as
she monologued with nonsense sounds for minutes on end.

Maria, our nanny, was responding in Spanish—courtesy
of Darren's idea to try to get Violet to grow up bilingual. I
figured trying to get her to speak one language was enough,
but he felt strongly, and I said fine. I asked Maria to read
her books in English, though, and bring her to music classes
and play groups and story time at the local library. It felt
like a fair compromise. And by the way, Violet never learned

much more than *hola*, *adiós*, *por favor*, and *gracias*, until she started watching *Dora the Explorer*. The power of television! Other kids had limits on what they could watch, but Violet watched all my shows, and some of the competition besides. She was my own little focus group of one, and it was interesting to see what caught her attention, which shows she latched on to. I was secretly thrilled when *Rocket Through Time* kept her transfixed. And also when she walked out of the room when *Guillaume* came on. I detest that show. Kate swears it taught Victoria how to whine. She's probably right.

While I was in the middle of typing a response about next season's budget for *It Takes a Galaxy*, my Gmail pinged, and there was a message from you:

Hi Luce,

I know it's been a while. More than a while. An eon, it feels like. But I'll be in New York tomorrow, swinging through en route to the inauguration in D.C. Couldn't miss a moment like that. Can you believe, our first African-American president? Everyone over here is ecstatic. I think Obama's election is going to mean great things for our country—a new, better, kinder direction. Anyway, I'd love to see you. Any chance you're free for coffee tomorrow afternoon?

-Gabe

I couldn't believe it. I didn't respond right away. In fact, I didn't respond until that night, after I'd casually mentioned your visit to Darren.

"You're still in touch with that guy?" he asked, genuinely surprised.

I shook my head. "I haven't seen or spoken to him since my Columbia reunion. He e-mailed me out of the blue."

Darren unbuttoned his collar. "Would you do me a favor?" he asked.

I steeled myself. Was he going to ask me not to see you? "What is it?" I asked back.

"Will you bring Violet with you?"

I sat for a moment, a bit stunned. "You don't trust me?" I asked.

Darren took a deep breath. "I trust you," he said. "But I don't trust him. I don't know why he wants to see you. And I think you should bring Violet."

I nodded. I knew that saying no would send Darren a message I didn't want to send. "Of course," I said. "I'll bring Violet. But I think he's just an old friend who wants to catch up."

I wrote you back that night:

Great to hear from you. How about 3 p.m. tomorrow in Brooklyn Heights? There's a Starbucks on Montague.

I didn't mention Violet.

You shot back: *Sounds good.*

We had a plan.

THE NEXT DAY I dressed Violet up in baby jeans, baby Uggs, and a gray sweater with a pink appliqué heart. I put a pink bow in her hair. I was actually wearing something similar, though my sweater was brown without an appliqué, and I didn't have a bow.

Darren was at the gym when I zipped us both into our winter coats and we left.

I peered through the Starbucks's glass door, and saw you sitting at a table, your head down, reading something on your BlackBerry. Darren and I had just made the switch to iPhones, but it made sense somehow, you still on a Black-Berry. I parked the stroller outside, adjusted Violet on my hip, and opened the door. You looked up.

"Hi, Lucy," you said. "And hi . . ."

"Violet," I supplied. "Violet, this is Mommy's friend Gabe. Gabe, this is my daughter."

"Hihi," Violet said. It was one of her words, always dou-bled, though Darren and I couldn't figure out why.

"She looks just like you," you said, standing up. "Wow."

What were you thinking just then? I've always wondered. Did the fact that she looked like me and not Darren make Violet more . . . exciting? Tolerable? Lovable?

Violet must've sensed something she liked, because she held out her arms, and you took her. "Hihi," she said, and patted your cheeks.

"Hihi," you said back to her.

Then you used your free arm to hug me. "It's been so long; I'm glad you came."

I took Violet back, and we sat down across from each other. I put some board books and a few blocks on the table, and Violet started playing with them.

"I saw you were engaged," I said, "on Facebook."

I didn't know how much time we had, and I wanted to know what was going on. Because Darren was right, there was no obvious motive for this meeting, after so long.

You laughed. "Getting right to it."

I shrugged and retrieved the book Violet had knocked to the floor.

"You want to know what happened," you said.

"Only if you want to tell me," I answered.

So you told me about Alina and the job she was offered in D.C. and how you both realized that your careers were more important than your relationship. She wanted to go to D.C., you wanted to stay abroad, and neither one of you was willing to compromise to stay together. I couldn't help thinking about us, about how you left me for the same reason.

"It was a case of two very nice people not meant for each other," you said.

I wondered if you said that about me.

"I'm sorry," I answered.

"Sorr-eee," Violet echoed, looking up. Another of her words.

You laughed. "Did you clone yourself?" you asked. "Make a Xerox? She's fantastic."

"Are you fantastic?" I asked Violet.

She smiled and clapped.

Then I laughed too.

"You're happy," you said to me. "With Darren, with Violet, you're happy."

"I am," I said. And it was true.

"I'm glad one of us is." It wasn't sarcastic or malicious, the way you said it. Just kind of wistful.

"You're the one who left," I reminded you.

"I know," you said. "I've been thinking a lot about the choices I made. Why I made them. What life would have been like if I hadn't."

You seemed so contemplative, as if you were taking stock of your life, judging it.

"Do you think you would have been happier?" I ventured. "If you'd stayed?"

You sighed. "I don't know," you said. "On some days I think I would have been happier if I'd never tried photography at all. I think I was proud of my pursuit, proud of doing something important. But it's been really hard. It's taken a lot out of me. But . . . I don't know. Maybe I'm not the kind of person who will ever be happy. Maybe I'm not the man I hoped I was."

"Mama!" Violet said.

"Violet!" I answered her. She turned back to the toys in front of her.

"I just want so many conflicting things," you said, your eyes on my daughter, watching her flip the pages of her book. "I don't know if they're compatible."

"You're just in a bad spot right now," I said. "You'll figure it out."

"I haven't so far," you said into your coffee cup. "And I miss us, you, what we had." You looked up at me. "I watch your shows whenever I find them on the air. Whenever I'm afraid, I dream about you. Whenever I'm sad, I wish I hadn't left."

My heartbeat sped up slightly. "Please don't do this," I said, holding tight to Violet.

You ran your fingers through your hair. "I'm sorry," you said. "Forget I said that."

I flipped Violet around so I could pick her up. "Listen," I said, "it was great to see you, Gabe, but Violet and I should probably go."

You nodded.

"I hope you find everything you're looking for."

"Thanks." Your voice cracked. "Me too."

"Say 'bye-bye,' Violet," I told my daughter.

"Bye-bye," she said, and reached out to you again.

You hugged her. You looked at me, clearly wanting to hug me too. But instead, you looked down and walked away.

I zipped us both into our coats and snapped Violet's hood. Even though the day was overcast, I fumbled in the diaper bag for my sunglasses. I didn't want anyone to see the tears in my eyes, just like you didn't want me to see the tears in yours.

lvi

THAT SUMMER, DARREN AND I GOT DRESSED UP FOR the first time in a long time and went to Gavin's wedding. We hadn't seen him much since Violet was born, and I barely knew his fiancée at all.

Darren wolf-whistled when I walked into the living room in a navy dress with a plunging neckline. "Hot mama," he said.

I smiled. "Let's go, handsome."

We had to get to the wedding early because Darren was a groomsman, and Gavin greeted us when we walked in. "I got my own paper doll now," he said, laughing.

I hadn't thought about that in years, how he'd called me Darren's paper doll the first time we'd met. "So what does that actually mean?" I asked.

"It's not important," Darren said. Then he turned to Gavin. "What do you need me to do, man?"

The guys walked off, and I headed toward the wives and girlfriends of the other groomsmen who were standing by a tray of champagne glasses. Very thoughtful. Very Gavin.

LATER, AT THE WEDDING, I found myself next to Gavin at the bar. We'd both had a lot to drink. Everyone at that wedding had.

"So really," I said. "What is a paper doll?"

He laughed. "Darren's going to kill me for telling you this, but he had a girlfriend checklist that summer. You ticked every box. Brunette. Ivy League educated. Brooklynite. Between five-two and five-five. Grew up on the East Coast. Good body. I don't remember the rest. But anyway, you worked on paper, so we called you—"

"The paper doll," I finished.

"Exactly!" Gavin said, clinking his Johnnie Walker against my vodka martini before he took a sip.

Making a list like that was such a Darren thing to do, and I shouldn't have been surprised. But it somehow made his love for me seem less real, more calculated. I didn't like how it made me feel, reduced to a series of attributes.

Darren walked over. "I heard I worked on paper," I said

to him. "Good thing I'm not an inch taller, or I would've been disqualified."

He laughed. "You'll never find what you want unless you know what you're looking for." The Jäger shots he and the other groomsmen had done had made him less measured than he usually was. Louder. "I was looking for you that summer."

"Or someone just like me," I answered. I was less measured than I usually was too.

"Stop it, I wanted *you*," he said, sliding an arm around my waist and pulling me close. "The checklist just helped me focus my attention on women who were worth it."

"Women who were worth it?" I echoed.

"Come on," he said, knocking back another shot Gavin had handed him. "Let's go dance."

I let him lead me to the dance floor, and once we started to Twist—which we were both terrible at—the two of us began laughing and thoughts of his girlfriend checklist vanished. But I've been thinking about that list a lot recently. If I'd made a list back then, I don't think either you or Darren would have ticked all the boxes. And if Darren made a list now, I don't think I'd still be his paper doll.

lvii

I ONCE READ THAT BIRTHDAYS ARE CELEBRATED MORE elaborately in New York City than they are anywhere else in the world. I have no data points, no study to cite, which is what I'd ask someone at work to provide if they made a statement like that, but from anecdotal evidence, I wouldn't dispute that claim.

For my thirtieth birthday, Darren treated me, Kate, and Julia to a spa day at Bliss, and booked the two of us a week-long trip to Australia.

"It's on your bucket list!" he said.

At least this time he asked first. Darren and I were doing pretty well on our bucket lists. He'd even gotten to ride a Segway at a bachelor party in Miami a few months earlier and crossed off number 1. "But what about Violet?" I asked. She was almost two and a half years old, and while we'd left her with my parents or Darren's parents for long weekends before, we'd never been away for longer than that, and had never been farther than California.

"I think Violet could probably use a vacation from us," he said.

Violet was on the floor next to Annie, with triangle-shaped safety crayons. She loved those things—could scribble for hours. I'm not exaggerating.

"Hey, Vi," he said.

"Hey, Daddy," she answered.

"I have exciting news. You're going to get to stay with Nana and Pop-Pop for a whole week while Mommy and I go on a trip!"

"Pop-Pop!" Violet's eyes opened wide. "Yes, please," she said, and went back to coloring.

"I think she'll be fine," Darren said.

And so we went. A plane from New York to San Francisco. Then San Francisco to Hawaii. Hawaii to Fiji. Fiji to Sydney. I don't love planes. Have we ever talked about that? The smallness of them, the recycled air, the inability to leave—it all rattles me if I think about it for too long. So Darren figured if we took a lot of shorter flights, there would be less time for me to panic while flying. I think it was a good idea, actually, because each time a flight started to feel too long, too constraining, we were just about to land. I've tried to employ that flying strategy ever since.

Though I did fly direct from New York to Tel Aviv. It was the fastest way to get here.

Anyway, we landed the day before my birthday, and a limo picked us up at the airport, taking us to the Four Seasons.

"I booked us a suite," Darren told me as we relaxed in the back of the car.

"You're ridiculous," I said.

He shrugged. "We haven't really traveled anywhere exciting since our honeymoon. And who knows when we'll have the chance to do it again."

When we got to the room, I hooked into the Wi-Fi and called my parents. "Violet's fine," my mom said. "Jason and Vanessa are here with the triplets. She's having a blast on your old swing set."

I wasn't sure if it would be better or worse if we talked on the phone, and since she was having fun, I figured I could call back later.

"You have to see this!" Darren was saying from the bedroom.

"I'll call again soon, Mom," I told her. "Give Violet an extra kiss from me."

"Of course," my mom said.

I walked into the bedroom, and on the dresser were chocolate-dipped strawberries and champagne. There was a box of a dozen long-stemmed roses on the bed.

"What did you tell them?" I asked Darren.

"That we were celebrating," he said. "And to send their best." Then he kissed me, and I relaxed into his arms. Being with him felt like kicking off a pair of heels after a long day at work. Natural, freeing, effortless.

"I love you," I told him, as he slid his hand under my shirt and unclasped my bra.

And those beautiful roses ended up scattered all over the floor.

I woke up in the middle of the night feeling panicked, like I'd forgotten something. I went through a list in my head. I'd packed my phone charger and the outlet adapters. I'd remembered bras and underwear and socks. Makeup. Deodorant. Sneakers. I'd called my mother, I'd spoken to Violet. Then I realized what it was. I poked Darren.

"I forgot my birth control pills," I whispered to him, when he was awake enough to hear me.

"That's good," he muttered. "It's a good time for a second baby."

Then he went back to sleep, but I didn't. I spent the night staring at the ceiling, wondering how upset Darren would be if I asked him to wear a condom.

The answer was: very.

Liam was conceived in Australia.

lviii

ONE OF THE THINGS I'VE FOUND THE MOST INTEREST-ing about being pregnant is that no one seems to experience it quite the same way. And symptoms can change from one day to the next. I'd always heard that the same woman could have different symptoms with different children, too, which seemed especially odd to me. Shouldn't a body react the same way each time? But it's true. Each of my pregnancies has been slightly different—though the exhaustion and the nausea have been there each time. But with Liam, even though I was exhausted, I was also an insomniac. That's how I ended up watching *The Daily Show* alone in the living room, while Darren was already getting ready for bed. That's how I ended up seeing you.

After the commercial break, Jon Stewart came on and said, "Welcome back. My guest tonight is a photographer with the Associated Press who has just come out with his first book, *Defiant*, a pictorial narrative of the Arab Spring. Gabriel Samson, everybody."

And there you were, in my living room, a year and a half after I'd left you in that Starbucks on Montague. As Jon Stewart displayed pages from your book, and you talked about your experiences, I couldn't help but feel a small sense of pride. The recognition you'd gotten for your work was huge—awards, it seemed, lots of them—and from the questions you were being asked, it appeared that the response to your book was magnificent, too. Apparently a *Times* review was due out the following weekend, and you had some offers from museums and galleries to stage an exhibit of your photographs.

"It looks like they want you everywhere from London to New York to Omaha, Nebraska," Jon Stewart said. "I'd suggest Omaha. Great steaks."

You laughed, and then you said, "As much as I like a good steak, the offers I'm considering the most are in New York. That city means a lot to me."

"New Yorkers get a bad rap," Jon said, picking up the banter. "But we're pretty great people. And I'd choose New York pizza over an Omaha steak any day, if you want to get down to it."

"Absolutely," you said. "New York women, too."

And then the segment was over, but I kept staring at the

screen. You looked great. You seemed happy. And I was glad for you. But I couldn't help wondering who you were talking about when you mentioned New York women. Was it me? Someone else? Or just a funny thing to say on TV? I tried to put it all out of my head. But that's hard to do when you're lying in bed, still staring at the ceiling at three a.m.

lix

As bad as the pregnancy insomnia was, the fact that by the time Liam was four months old, he had never in his life slept for more than four hours at a clip was even worse. I was a zombie. And the surest way to get him back to sleep was by nursing him. Which meant I had a lot more time to read the news on my phone than I used to.

At nine forty-five at night on May 2nd, while I was feeding Liam, an alert pinged that the president was going to address the nation that evening.

"What do you think that's about?" I asked Liam. His only answer was to continue sucking on my nipple.

By eleven, with Liam back in his crib, I was reading articles from tons of different news outlets. By eleven thirty-five, I was in the living room listening to President Obama say: *Good evening. Tonight, I can report to the American people and to the world that the United States has conducted an operation that killed Osama bin Laden, the leader of al-Qaeda, and a terrorist who's responsible for the murder of thousands of innocent men, women, and children.*

And then I was on Twitter and saw photos you were tweeting—retweets of your colleague's photos—of the jubilation at the gates of the White House. I didn't feel joy in bin Laden's death, but I felt relief. I felt whole, like his death completed a puzzle that had been left unfinished since 2001. I think you did too. The one tweet that was your own that night said: *The world is a better place today than it was yesterday. #OperationNeptuneSpear*

I watched your feed fill with more and more photos, links to articles, messages from politicians and journalists.

I opened up a direct-message box and sent you a note. *I can't believe it*, I wrote.

I know, you wrote back. *I feel like the world has shifted on its axis.*

I did too.

lx

TWO MONTHS AFTER THAT, I GOT A CALL FROM JULIA at work. Since she left television and went into book publishing, we saw each other less than we used to but tried to get together at least once every couple of months to catch up. And we still talked on the phone a lot. Her life was pretty different than mine, though, since she was still single, still going out on dates, still taking advantage of what New York City had to offer in a way I hadn't in years.

"Have you read *Time Out New York* today?" she asked.

"Oh, Jules," I said, "I can't remember the last time I even saw a *Time Out New York*."

I turned my chair sideways so I could look out the window of my office. I'd had a window office for almost a year now, and never tired of checking out the buildings across the way and the traffic below.

"You're going to want to get it today," she said. "There's an article on Gabe—your ex, Gabe. He has a photography show up at the Joseph Landis gallery in Chelsea. I haven't had a chance to read the review or the interview they did with him, but the headline and pull quote are great."

I watched a taxicab stop and pick up two passengers—an older couple with suitcases.

"Lucy?" Julia asked.

I was trying to figure out what I wanted to do.

"Do you want to go?" I finally said. "Today at lunch? Meet you there?"

"Just so happens my lunch plans canceled this morning," Julia said. "Twelve thirty?"

I looked at my calendar of meetings. "Can you make it one?" I asked.

"One it is."

We met at the gallery, and even though it was the middle of a weekday, we weren't the only ones there. Between how successful your book had been, and the review of the show in *Time Out New York*, you'd drawn a bit of a crowd. *Light*, it said, stenciled onto the wall, *A Photography Retrospective by Gabriel Samson*.

Julia and I shuffled from photograph to photograph with a group of ladies-who-lunch in front of us and a few NYU students behind us. It started with images of the Arab Spring, some of the same ones Jon Stewart showed, from the interior of your book. They were arresting, like all of your photography—the kind of images that draw a viewer in right away, like Steve McCurry, like you'd dreamed about.

"So hopeful," the ladies kept saying, at pretty much every shot. "Look at the hope in their eyes."

It got to the point where Julia mouthed their words along with them and rolled her eyes.

But as much as she was rolling her eyes, she was also saying, "These are spectacular." And they were, the way you captured emotion, the way you framed the people, the way everything seemed saturated with color and feeling and determination.

"I heard this guy's a real badass," one of the NYU kids said. "Like, he climbs on mountains of rubble and lies in puddles and shit to get these shots. I heard he once got beat up in Iraq because he took a picture of the wrong person's wife."

I realized, when I heard those words, that I had no idea why you'd gotten beat up in Iraq. Just that you had. Just that you'd called me afterward. Should I have asked more? Is that why you never called me from Arizona?

I noticed, as we were walking, that the photographs were in reverse chronological order. You could actually see the hope and determination increase—the earlier photos even more powerful than the later ones. Then the accompanying narration on the wall told us we were going further back in time, before the Arab Spring, before the photographs in your book, and we were looking at images from Afghanistan, from Pakistan, from Iraq. I hadn't read the review of the exhibit but had assumed it was all from *Defiant*. It was interesting to see the other countries in comparison. Then I took another step to the right and saw images I recognized from New York—the little girl behind the barred window was there, the one who inspired the dream episode of *It Takes a Galaxy*. And then I turned a corner and was confronted with a wall of myself.

"Whoa," Julia said, when she turned the corner a moment after I did.

There I was, at twenty-four, laughing, my head thrown back, a drink in my hand. There I was on the couch, smiling, my arms reaching for you. I was in the kitchen, looking delighted, holding a plate of waffles. Then I was twenty-three, slipping on a pair of high heels, my hair loose, swinging next to me. The final image in the show was one I'd never seen before: me, asleep on the couch, with one hand still on my laptop and the other clutching the pages of a script.

Stenciled on the wall it said: *A woman filled with light makes everything she touches brighter. Lucy, Luce, Luz, Light.*

When we got to the end of the exhibit, there was a pile

of books on the counter next to a little note that said: *Signed by the artist*. I stopped.

"Are you okay?" Julia asked. "I—"

"I don't know," I said. "I don't think so."

I couldn't even name the emotions I felt then. What were you thinking, putting up a wall of pictures of me without telling me about it?

"I'm going to buy a book," I said, pointing to the stack.

The woman who rang me up kept staring at me. Then she looked at the name on my credit card.

"You're her," she said. "Lucy."

I nodded. "I'm her."

She looked like she wanted to say something else, but instead she handed me a receipt to sign and slid a book across the counter.

When I handed her the receipt back she said, "He's very talented."

"I know," I said. "He always was."

My brain was still turning inside out by the time I got back to the office and slipped your book in my desk drawer. I couldn't concentrate on anything. So I opened up an e-mail and sent you a message:

Hi Gabe,

I saw your exhibit today at the Landis gallery. I don't know what to say. It's a lovely tribute, though

I wish you'd asked. Or at least told me. It was a bit
of a shock to turn the corner and see myself on the
wall.

-Lucy

Your response came instantaneously:

Lucy!
I know I should have asked. But I was afraid you'd
have said no. And the exhibit didn't feel complete
without you in it. I learned how to capture lightness
of spirit while photographing you. You were my
muse, my inspiration for all of those shots.

I'm glad you went to see the show.

-Gabe

I didn't write back after that. Being in touch with you
seemed too dangerous. And I still hadn't untangled the
knot of emotions, hadn't teased out how I truly felt about
seeing myself on that wall.

I READ THE INTERVIEW in *Time Out New York* on my way
home from work. The interviewer had asked you about me.
You didn't say much, but you called me your muse, your

light. In print. That was so brazen of you, Gabe. So . . . I don't know. Is *selfish* the right word? Did you think about how Darren would respond? What that would mean for me? Probably not. Almost definitely not. I know you wanted to be true to your art, to capture your world in the way that felt the most honest, maybe to send me a message, I don't know. But, God, you put me in an uncomfortable position. Because I knew I had to tell Darren about it before someone else did. And I knew he wasn't going to be happy.

I waited until after dinner. Until the kids were in bed. Until Annie was walked and fed.

"Want a drink?" I asked him.

"Drinking on a Wednesday," he said. "Look at you!"

I gave him a wan smile.

"That rough at the office?" he asked. "Sure, pour me in."

We'd discovered raki on our honeymoon and both loved it, so I poured us some, a subtle reminder of the fact that we were a couple, together, married. I thought he might need that.

"So, which show's giving you trouble?" he asked, when I handed him his glass and sat down on the couch.

He'd made peace with my work, finally started asking about it after I had Liam, when I made it clear that even with two kids, I wouldn't stay home. And once in a while, when we passed by a store that had a *Rocket Through Time* lunchbox in the window, or a bus stop with a *Sparkle On!*

poster—my girl-empowerment show, a nod to having a daughter—I could detect a note of pride in his smile that made me smile too.

Instead of answering him, though, I said, "I went to a photography exhibit with Julia today during lunch."

"Oh, yeah?" He turned to look at me, already, I'm sure, trying to figure out where I was going with this. "How is she?"

"Good," I said, carefully. "The show was Gabe's. My ex, Gabe's. She read about it in *Time Out New York* this morning, so we went."

Darren's body went still. "I see," he said.

I took the magazine from the coffee table and opened it, then handed it to him. "There were pictures of me in it, Darren. I swear I didn't know."

"This is for real," he said, quickly reading the words in front of him.

"It is," I said. "I was shocked. I . . ." I felt guilty, like I should apologize, like it was my fault, but it wasn't. It was *your* fault, Gabe.

Darren looked up from your interview, stricken. His face had gone pale. "Is this your way of telling me that you and he—"

"No!" I said. "No! There's nothing between us. I haven't seen him since that time Violet and I met up with him for coffee. Before I was even pregnant with Liam. And I

280

exchanged one Twitter message with him the night bin Laden was killed. That's it! Really. I swear."

The color was returning to Darren's face. "You really haven't seen him. He really didn't ask you."

"I swear on the lives of both of our children," I said.

Darren started getting angry then. He crumpled the magazine. "What a prick. What a self-important prick. Let's call the gallery. We can ask them to take it down."

"It's okay," I said. "We don't have to do that. We don't need to start anything." My emotions were unknotting, and as angry as I was with you, I didn't want the exhibit to come down. A part of me liked being up there. A part of me felt special. Chosen. Important.

He took a deep breath. "You're right. I wasn't thinking. We don't need to make this bigger than it is."

I took a sip of raki. Darren did too. Then he drained his glass. I followed suit, relieved that this wasn't worse. I don't know what I expected would happen, what I thought he would do, but this was okay. Darren and I were okay.

He rattled the ice in his glass. "Tomorrow night we're going out for dinner after work," he said. "I'll get us reservations somewhere fantastic. And then we're going to see the exhibit. If there are pictures of my wife in an art gallery, I want to see them."

I nodded. "Of course," I said. "Whatever you want."

THE NEXT MORNING I put on a tight black dress and heels to go to work. It was an outfit I knew Darren liked on me. One that had once made him whisper, after a couple of glasses of wine at a dinner party, "I have the hottest wife in this whole damn place."

After the promised fantastic dinner at Del Posto we took a cab straight to the gallery. When we walked in, I moved to the end of the line of people so we could go from country to country, following your journey of hope and light back in time. But Darren grabbed my hand and said, "Where are you?"

"At the end," I answered, indicating the corner at the other side of the gallery.

Darren pulled me through the crowd—and there really was a crowd that night, so many more people than when Julia and I were there—until we turned the corner. And then he stopped. His hand went slack and dropped mine. He stared. And stared. And didn't say a word.

I looked at myself on the wall. I tried to put myself in his shoes. I was someone he thought he knew better than anyone in the world, and he was seeing a different version of me. He was seeing Lucy-before-Darren, Lucy who loved someone else, Lucy who shared someone else's secrets and dreams. Who inspired them. I don't think I ever inspired Darren. And it couldn't have been easy for him, seeing me through your eyes. I took a step closer to him, but he didn't reach out to me.

When he finally looked over, I could see the anger simmering in his eyes. The jealousy. The hurt.

We fought about you for the first and only time that night. Darren wanted me to promise never to be in touch with you again, but despite understanding how he felt, I couldn't agree to it. Eventually my reasonable, chess-playing Darren returned and he took back his request. But it was the most insecure, the neediest I'd ever seen him.

"Do you love me?" he asked.

"I love you," I told him. "I do."

Then his voice cracked. "Do you love him?"

"No," I said. "Just you." And it was true then, or I thought it was. I promised him that I loved him more than I'd ever loved you, that there's no way you could compete, when he and I had a family together. By the end of the night, he and I were okay again. We had sex. We slept with our arms wrapped around each other.

I FORCIBLY PUT YOU out of my mind for a while after that. I focused on my anger at the position you put me in, my anger that you hadn't asked first. I was doing it for Darren, for Violet and Liam, for our family. But I couldn't stay angry with you. Because I really was flattered that you wanted me in your retrospective. Flattered that I meant so much to you, to your work. In that knot of emotions, a piece of me thrilled at being called your muse.

lxi

SOMETIMES LIFE SEEMS TO CHUG ALONG, MOVING FOR-
ward at a near-glacial pace day to day, until something happens that makes you stop and take notice and realize that a
ton of time has passed while you weren't looking. An anniversary, a birthday, a holiday. On September 11th, 2011,
Violet was almost four. Liam had just turned eight months
old. I was a producer on three different kids' shows and
developing pitches for two more. And Darren and I had
been married for almost five years. It was more than seven
years since you left New York. And a decade, exactly, since
the first time you and I met. A decade since the attacks that
set both of our adult lives in motion and caused our individ-
ual journeys to intertwine and separate.

At Violet's preschool, September 11th was Heroes Day.
There was a special gathering in Prospect Park where the
kids learned about firefighters and police officers and

EMTs. After that, whenever Violet saw a fire truck or a police car or an ambulance, she stopped and chanted, "Go, heroes, go! Go, heroes, go!" She still does. Liam, too. It always makes me smile.

Memorial events took place across the city. Services at St. Pat's and Trinity Church, and a photography exhibit at the Historical Society. There were two blue columns of light, beaming up from Ground Zero, shining even taller than the towers, visible for miles. And you called. I'd actually been contemplating calling you, even though I knew I shouldn't.

I'm sure you remember this.

You were in Kabul. "I've been thinking about you all day," you said, when I picked up the phone.

"Me too," I confessed, ducking into Violet's bedroom and shutting the door.

"I didn't know if you would pick up," you said.

I thought back to all of the times you'd reached out to me. "Have I ever not picked up?" I asked.

"Never," you said softly.

I sat down on Violet's bed and told you about Heroes Day, about what was happening in New York. You said you wished you were here.

"It feels like you should be," I said. "It feels like we should go to the roof of Wien and take stock of the city."

"I wish," you said.

Neither of us knew what to say after that, but neither of

us wanted to get off the phone. We sat there in silence, receivers pressed to our ears.

"Let's imagine we're there right now," I said.

"And there's no smoke, just a beautiful skyline," you said.

I closed my eyes. "And birds, and a blue, cloudless sky, and people walking up and down the streets," I added. "And you can hear children's laughter wafting up from a playground below. And no one's afraid that the next breath they take might be their last."

"What else?" you asked.

"The Empire State Building," I told you. "We can see that too."

"Standing strong and proud," you said.

"Yes, strong and proud." I opened my eyes.

"I like that," you said. "Thank you, Lucy."

"You're welcome," I answered, though I wasn't quite sure what you were thanking me for.

"I should go to bed now, it's late over here." You yawned through your words.

"Okay," I said. "Good night. Sleep well."

You yawned again. "I'm glad you answered," you said.

"I'm glad you called," I responded.

Then we hung up, and I realized how much it meant to talk to you that day. How I would have felt incomplete otherwise.

Did you feel the same way?

lxii

SOMETIMES IT SEEMS LIKE WORDS, PHRASES, OR people's names get stuck in my brain, and then I hear them everywhere. I don't know if they actually are everywhere, or if I'm just on high alert for them so I notice them more.

After you called, *Kabul* was one of those words. *Afghanistan* was another.

And three days later I heard those words on NPR. The U.S. embassy was bombed in Kabul. My thoughts went to you. I grabbed my phone before I could even think straight.

Are you okay? I texted.

I stared at the screen until I saw those three dots that meant you were writing.

I'm alive. I'm unharmed. I wasn't there. But my friends were, you wrote.

Then more dots.

I'm not okay.

I didn't know how to respond. So I didn't.

I'm sorry.

lxiii

I OFTEN THINK ABOUT HOW THROUGHOUT LIFE, WE acquire people. More like People, with a capital *P*. The ones we go to in an emergency—the ones we know we can count on. If we're lucky, our parents are our first People. Then our siblings. A childhood best friend. A spouse.

Maybe it was because you moved around so much, or maybe it was just because of who you were, but you didn't seem to collect People like the rest of us. You had your mom. I knew from the pictures on Facebook that you went to see her often. And I guess you had me. But otherwise, you had a web of acquaintances and friends, like your college roommates, whom you visited from time to time, but didn't seem to feel comfortable leaning on. At least, not while we were together, and I assume not afterward, because I was the one you called.

It was a Saturday afternoon, and your number popped onto my phone. I was pushing Violet on a swing in Coxsackie Park. That's not actually the name of the park, but it's what this woman Viviana started calling the park the summer before, when her son, Mateo, and four other kids came down with the Coxsackie virus after playing on the playground there. Word spread through the neighborhood parents like the virus spread through our kids, and no one went there for months. But common wisdom was that the virus must've died over the winter, and that day I wasn't the only parent at the swings.

Darren was with Liam at a father-child swim class.

I gave Violet a big push, and then hit the green accept button on my phone. All I could hear was you sobbing. I watched Violet flying back toward me and pushed her again.

"Gabe?" I said. "What's wrong? Are you hurt? Where are you?"

You took a deep breath. "JFK," you said. "My mom's gone, Lucy. She's gone."

And then I heard your ragged breaths and gulping sobs. My heart twinged, the same way it did when I heard Violet or Liam or Darren cry. When I heard Jason cry.

"What terminal are you at?" I asked. "How long are you there?"

"United," you said, when you were able to speak again. "I have a four-hour layover."

"I'm coming," I told you. "I'll be there in forty minutes."

I hung up my phone and stopped Violet's swing, functioning in the crisis-averting mode I used at work. Act now, plan on the fly, make things better. At least show up.

"No more swinging?" Violet asked, pumping her legs in an attempt to get the swing to move again.

"Vi," I said, "we have an important job to do: we have to go to the airport to see Mommy's friend. He's a little sad right now because his mom had to go away for a long time, so he might be crying. But we're going to try to make him feel better."

She raised her arms so I could take her out of the swing. "Sometimes I'm sad and I cry."

"Yeah," I told her, lifting her up. "Me too."

After Violet was settled into her stroller, I checked the time. Darren's swim class was over, but he usually hung out with the dads and babies at a coffee shop near the pool for a while afterward. I steeled myself and called him. This wasn't going to be easy.

"I have to take a trip to JFK," I told Darren, when he picked up. I could hear Liam babbling in the background.

"What?" Darren said, clearly distracted. "Why?"

We hadn't talked about you since the night of your exhibit. I knew he wasn't going to take this well. But I couldn't leave you, sobbing, alone at Terminal 7. It was those pomegranate seeds again. I was stuck, like Persephone.

"I just got a call from Gabe—Gabe Samson," I said. "His mother died and he's at JFK. He's falling apart."

Darren was silent on the other end. I heard Liam saying "bagel" over and over again in the background. "And you have to put him back together?" Darren asked. "No."

"He doesn't have anyone else," I said.

"He doesn't have you, either," Darren said to me. "I'll get you a bagel in one minute," he told Liam.

"Of course not," I answered. "You have me. Liam has me. Violet has me. But his mother died, and he called. He shouldn't be alone right now. You wouldn't want to be alone, if it were you."

"But I wouldn't call someone else's wife," Darren said; I could hear the tightness in his voice.

"To him I'm not someone else's wife, just an old friend, someone to call when he's hurting."

"He called you his fucking light," Darren said.

"And I call you my husband. It doesn't matter what he called me. Please, let's not do this on the phone. In front of your friends. In front of the kids."

I imagined his jaw clenching. His eyes closing and slowly opening again. "You're taking Violet?" he asked. "You know I don't trust him."

"I'm taking Violet," I said. Mostly because I didn't know

who I could drop her with last minute, and Darren was clear on the other side of Brooklyn.

"Fine," he said. "But I don't like it."

I knew I'd have to smooth this over later, I'd have to do a lot of smoothing, but in the meantime, I was going to the airport. I was going to see you.

AFTER A QUICK STOP to leave the stroller just inside our gate, the taxi dropped us off at Terminal 7 and we walked inside. You'd come out of the secure area, since we couldn't get in without a ticket, and you were waiting by the doors, slumped on a bench, broken. Your elbows were on your knees, and your chin was resting in your hands. The moment you saw me, you started to cry again. I ran toward you with Violet in my arms, and sat down, leaving her on my lap. I wonder now what was going through her head—and what was going through yours. In hindsight, I think that was a parenting fail on my end. There was no reason Violet should have had to process that, to see someone so distraught. If I were thinking more clearly, I would've called some of the moms who lived on our block, and I would've told Darren I wasn't bringing her with me, even if it made him madder. And that might have changed so much.

You reached over Violet's head to put your arms around

me. I hugged you back, and so did Violet, her little arms wrapping as far as they could around your rib cage.

"You're okay," Violet said to you. "There's no blood or anything."

AFTER YOU CALMED DOWN a bit, and after I found a pen and a pad of paper in my bag for Violet to play with on the floor, you told me about your mom's brain aneurysm. About how gutted you were that you hadn't been to Arizona to see her in almost a year. About how you felt unmoored, like no one was connecting you to the earth anymore, like you could float away and no one would notice.

"I'd notice," I told you.

While you were talking, Violet had wrapped her left arm around your calf, half hugging you while she colored.

"I think she'd notice, too," I said.

You smiled slightly, sadly.

We walked over to a food stand, and you got some water. I suggested a sandwich, or at least a banana, but you said you didn't think you could eat.

When Violet and I left, you seemed a little bit calmer than when we'd found you, but I kept thinking about what you said, about feeling unmoored. I was tied to so many people, I couldn't even imagine what that felt like. And I didn't think I'd want to.

lxiv

KIDS ARE AMAZING. REALLY, TRULY THEY ARE. THEY'RE open and caring and loving, four-and-a-half-year-olds especially.

Seeing you so distraught at the airport tugged at my heart. But it tugged at Violet's too, apparently, in an even more powerful way.

"Mommy's friend Gabe was crying," she told her dolls the next day. "He's really sad."

"Can I give Gabe this picture?" she asked me. "It's a heart and a sun and a lollipop. And smiley face stickers. Because they're happy."

"How about I take a photo of it, and we send that to his phone?" I asked her.

She nodded and solemnly held out her picture for photographing. "Don't forget to charge your phone so it'll work," she told me, which tells you a lot more about me than it does about her, I think. Or maybe a little bit about each of us.

I took the picture and e-mailed it to you with an explanation. Do you remember? Your response came back a few minutes later: *Tell Violet thank you.*

"Good," she said. "Tell him you're welcome."

Then at dinner Violet told the story to Darren. And to my surprise she added, "I need to cheer him up more. So I think he should come over for a play date. I'll show him how to make cookies."

We'd just started baking together, and Violet thought it was one of the most magical experiences in the world. She'd stare and stare through the oven window at the pan of batter until it bloomed into a cake, often narrating in real time.

Darren lifted his eyebrows at me.

"It's the first I'm hearing of this too," I said.

"He was so sad, Daddy," Violet told him. "He was a grown-up crying like a kid. And when people are crying we're supposed to cheer them up. That's what Miss Melissa says at school."

I bit my lip. I knew Darren's feelings, but I also knew that I was as worried about you as Violet was and wouldn't mind seeing you once more before you went back overseas.

"She's right. That *is* what Miss Melissa says . . ." I shrugged at Darren, kind of at a loss. I wasn't going to push it. I was going to let him decide. Because you did put another man's wife in your photography retrospective, Gabe. And even if you hadn't, I would've understood if he said no. Darren had every right not to want my ex-boyfriend at our home. To be honest *I* probably should've said no. I should have thought more about it, about what it would mean to have you there, but I didn't. My marriage felt strong enough that I didn't even wonder if letting you into my world would crack it, dent it, change the way I thought about Darren. But it did. I didn't realize it at the time, or even in the months afterward, but if I trace things back, I think this was one of those fork-in-the-road moments, a decision that pointed us down the path we ended up traveling.

Darren thought about it, his chess-playing crease appearing between his eyes. "Fine," he said, after a few moments of Violet looking at him with imploring eyes, of me looking down at my plate, cutting salmon into bite-sized pieces. "You're right, Vi. We should cheer people up when they're sad." I wondered then if he'd maybe stopped seeing you as a threat—because of something I'd said or Violet had said. Or if he thought that being in our apartment, with photographs of our family all around, would somehow make me less desirable to you. Or if he simply thought, like I did, that our marriage was solid enough that it wouldn't matter. I never asked him why he said okay.

I just accepted it. But I'm sure there was a reason. With Darren there's always a reason.

And that's how you ended up with an invitation to my apartment, to bake cookies with my daughter. I have to admit, I was surprised when you said yes.

WE CHOSE A DATE over e-mail—a day that was supposed to be a work-from-home Friday for me, though I ended up taking the day off. You were planning to be in New York for forty-eight hours, and were going to come straight from the airport. Violet insisted we decorate the apartment with balloons for you, and that we draw happy faces on each one. So we did, some with tongues, some without. Some had eyelashes. Others, eyebrows.

"Do you want one?" she asked Liam. He was almost eighteen months old, and Maria was going to take him to the Transit Museum—he loved running up and down the trains.

"Green," he said. She nodded and handed him a green balloon before he left with Maria.

I started the kids' laundry, and then Violet and I got out all the cookie-making ingredients. As we were taking out the mixing bowl, the buzzer rang, and my daughter went running. Annie followed her, barking.

"Hello?" I said through the intercom.

"It's me," you answered.

"It's him!" Violet said.

I buzzed you in and opened the door. A few minutes later, you arrived in my living room. The first thing I noticed was that you'd shaved your head. Violet noticed too.

"Where's . . . where's your hair?" she asked, her tiny brow furrowed. It was the one expression that made her look like Darren.

Your eyes went quickly to me and then back to her. "It's . . . in the laundry," you told her.

"The laundry?" she echoed.

You shrugged, your dimple making a brief appearance. "Don't you wash your hair when it gets dirty?"

Violet nodded. "But in the bath!"

You put the bags you were holding down onto the floor. "I thought the laundry would be easier."

Violet looked up at me. "Can I wash my hair in the laundry?" she asked.

"We'll talk about it later," I told her.

She took off into the kitchen, assuming you'd follow, reciting the cookie-baking plans. But you stopped next to me. I held out my arms, and you fell into them. I felt your tears on my neck. "Why'd you shave your head?" I asked, quietly.

You straightened up and rubbed a hand over your eyes.

"It's a mourning ritual," you said. "It felt right. Do I look that different?"

"Different, but still like you," I said. "Are you sure you're okay enough to make some cookies?"

"Of course," you said. "And thank you. For having such a sweet daughter. For indulging her desire to cheer up a sad old man. For being there for me. It may sound absurd, but part of how I made it through everything in Arizona was by looking forward to today."

After we mixed the dough and dropped it in different shapes on the cookie tray, after I slipped the tray into the oven, Violet got out a pasta pot.

"This is what we do so we don't burn ourselves," she told you. Then she turned on the oven light, put the pot in front of the oven door, and sat behind it. "We can't reach the door now," she said, and patted the spot next to her on the floor.

You sat there with her, the two of you watching the entire twelve minutes while the cookies baked, neither of you saying a word. I wondered what you were thinking. What she was thinking. But I didn't ask. I watched you both, hoping that this day would help you, that Violet's concern would mean something, that you would feel like you still had people who cared about you even though your mom was gone. I didn't want you to feel untethered.

When the timer rang, Violet brought me the oven mitt

that hung on the drawer next to the sink. "They're ready!" she said. "And we can play Hide and Go Seek Castle while they cool."

"Hide and Go Seek Castle?" you asked, standing up and taking the pasta pot with you.

Violet turned to you while I opened the oven door. "We dress up like people from a castle, and play hide-and-seek. You can be the king."

I almost dropped the cookie sheet when she said that. Darren was the only person she'd ever let be the king. When Jay came over she had him be the magician. And my father and Darren's father were always court jesters.

"Are you my queen?" you asked Violet, as she took your hand and brought you to her box of dress-up clothes.

"No!" she said, as if that were the most ludicrous idea anyone had ever come up with. "I'm the fairy! Mommy's the queen."

You looked over at me as I turned off the oven and walked toward you two.

After she'd put crowns on both of our heads, Violet slipped on her fairy wings and said. "Okay, king and queen, I'm hiding in your castle now! Count to twenty-three and then come find me!"

Twenty-three? you mouthed to me.

I shrugged. Violet ran off and we started counting.

"Louder!" she yelled from the hallway.

We'd gotten up to thirteen when I heard her say, "Hey! There's a moat in this castle!"

I stopped counting. "A pretend moat?" I called.

"A real one!" she called back. Then I heard the unmistakable sound of small feet jumping in a puddle.

I ran out of the living room to the hallway. "Where are you?" I asked.

"It's Hide and Go Seek Castle!" Violet said. "I can't tell!"

She'd left the door to the laundry room open, though, and the puddle was expanding into the hall. "Oh, God," I said, running toward the puddle.

You raced past me to Violet. "Found you!" you said to her. "I think this is the part where the king picks up the fairy and makes her fly!" You lifted Violet up and out of the puddle.

"Higher!" she shouted, laughing. "Fairies fly higher."

I stood in front of the laundry room, staring. *Shit*, I thought, *Shit, shit, shit*. The water was still coming from the back of the washing machine. I pulled my phone out of my pocket and dialed Darren.

"You okay?" he answered after the first ring.

"Me, yes," I said. "The laundry room, no. There's a huge puddle. I think the washing machine's broken. Who's our plumber?"

"Oh, hell," he said. "I'll e-mail you the number. Unless you want me to call?"

"No, no," I said. "I'll do it. Should I turn it off? Unplug it?"

"I have no idea," Darren said. "Ask the plumber. I just e-mailed you. Let me know how it goes."

I hung up and flicked to my e-mail. You came flying by with Violet. "Where's your fuse box?" you said. "You need to cut the electricity to the washing machine."

"Are you sure?" I asked, checking for Darren's e-mail. "I was going to ask the plumber."

"I'm sure," you said, flying Violet in a circle. "You need to turn off the washing machine to stop the water from running, and you don't want to deal with anything electric while standing in a puddle."

"Oh," I said. "That makes sense. It's in the kitchen."

You flew Violet into the kitchen, and then said, "Fairy coming in for a landing!" as you put her down on the countertop.

"More flying!" she said.

"The king needs to fix a few things," you told her. You still had your crown on your head, only now it was slightly crooked.

She and I both watched as you adjusted your crown and flipped the fuse that said *laundry room*.

"Should I call the plumber now?" I asked.

You were already taking off your socks and shoes. "Let me take a look," you said, rolling up your pant legs.

I picked Violet up off the counter and carried her to the laundry room, where we watched you pull the washing machine away from the wall and fix a loose connector in the hose. Since the water had stopped running, the puddle was already smaller, thanks to the drain in the middle of the laundry room floor.

"That should take care of it," you said. "You may still want to call a plumber to be sure, but you can also try running the washing machine again and see whether or not it leaks."

You stood up with that ridiculous crown still on your head. *This is what life would be like if things had gone another way*, I thought.

"You okay?" you asked, looking at me funny.

I smiled. "Thanks to you," I said. "You're more knight in shining armor than king, I think. Thanks for saving my laundry room."

You laughed. "I'd hate to trade in my crown, but I *have* always liked Lancelot." Did you want me to go there? To Lancelot and Guinevere? I have to assume you did.

I swallowed, wishing you couldn't read me as well as you could, then turned to Violet, who was still in my arms. "Well, my fairy princess, I think our cookies are probably cool enough to eat. Do you want one?"

She squirmed down to the floor and went running into the kitchen shouting, "Yes!"

"A cookie, my queen?" you said, straightening my crown.

I looked into your eyes and saw the sadness there, even though you were trying to camouflage it. In the chaos of the laundry room flood, I'd lost sight of why you'd come. "How are you doing?" I asked.

"Better," you said. "Thank you for today."

"I'm glad—and you're welcome." I wanted to reach out and hug you, like I had when you walked in, but I held myself back. Guinevere's married to Arthur, after all. Instead I said, "We should get to the kitchen before Violet tries climbing the cabinets."

And then we sat down with Violet and ate the cookies the three of us had baked together.

I NEVER TOLD DARREN that you and I stayed in e-mail touch for a while after that. And then you were traveling so much I could barely keep track: the Philippines, Russia, North Korea, South Africa. The time between our messages got longer and longer until I realized it'd been months since we last spoke. Violet seemed to forget about you, for the most part. But every once in a while she'd ask if she could put her hair in the laundry, and I'd pause for a moment to send up a wish to the universe, hoping that you were safe and happy.

lxv

THE FALL AFTER YOU FIXED MY WASHING MACHINE—
and you *had* fixed it, I told you that, right?—I got a call
from Kate that I found unsettling. Darren was watching
golf and the kids were playing in the living room. Annie
was nosing under the couch, probably on the hunt for the
Cheerios Liam seemed to drop everywhere. I was trying to
get through a backlog of *New Yorker* magazines and thinking that I should just cancel my subscription because seeing
the pile grow every week made me feel inadequate. And
reminded me how little time I actually had to myself, time
that wasn't consumed by work or family.

"What are your thoughts on crotchless panties?" Kate
asked when I picked up.

"Um," I said, making sure that Liam and Violet were still

building a tall tower before I walked into the kitchen. "I've never really thought much about them, but I guess they seem a little useless to me? Like lensless glasses or cupless bras."

"Are those a thing?" Kate asked. "Cupless bras?"

"I have no idea," I said. "I was just making a point. Why are you asking about crotchless panties?"

Kate sighed on the other end of the phone. "Do you ever feel like . . . I don't know. Do you ever want to spice things up?"

"You mean sex?" I asked. This was so unlike Kate. Until this point I'd never in my life heard her utter the words *crotchless panties* or talk about spicing things up. Her bachelorette party was at a spa. No penis straws allowed.

"I told Liz things with Tom just felt so . . . stale. She told me to get crotchless panties."

This was starting to make a little more sense. Liz probably wears crotchless panties on the regular. And cupless bras, if that really is a thing. "Is it sex that's stale?" I asked again.

Kate sighed. "It's everything," she said. "I take the same train into the city every morning, and the same one home each night. Tom asks me the same question every day when he gets home, two trains after me. I always wash my face while he brushes his teeth, and then while I brush my teeth, he pees. Every night. The other day I brushed my teeth

308

before I washed my face, and it was like he didn't know what to do. Is this forever?"

I hadn't really thought about things feeling stale, but if I was honest with myself, sometimes they did feel a bit . . . rote, routine.

"I know what you mean," I said. "Darren calls me every day at five oh two to ask me what time I think I'll be home. My assistant jokes about it. We've been buying the same brand of toilet paper—Charmin Ultra Strong—for as long as we've been together. Last month I wondered what would happen if I bought Charmin Ultra Soft. But I didn't do it."

"You should," Kate said.

"You should take a different train," I told her. "Get a haircut. Or maybe take a trip, alone with Tom. You can leave the girls with us for a weekend."

"Would you really watch them for the weekend?" she asked.

"Of course," I said. "Do it. Book a trip."

"What about you?" she asked.

"I'll buy some new toilet paper," I said.

We both laughed. Tom and Kate did leave their girls with us and go away for a weekend. And I did buy Charmin Ultra Soft. But there's so much to do every day, so many things that have to get taken care of, that it's easier when there's a routine, when you don't have to think. Even using that smidgen of extra brainpower to choose a toilet paper brand can turn things from "manageable" to "overwhelming."

But Kate got me thinking: Sometimes my life with Darren did feel stale. And stale can lead to something worse if it goes unchecked.

lxvi

THAT WINTER, A FEW MONTHS AFTER LIAM TURNED
two, our whole family got sick. It was the kind of horrible
cold that had Violet out of kindergarten for a week. She was
listless and clingy and my heart just about broke every time
that she coughed, a deep rattle in her tiny chest. Your heart
would've broken, too, Gabe. She was so sad and pathetic.
Annie wouldn't leave her side. Darren wasn't feeling well
either, and on top of that a deal he was handling at work
wasn't going as smoothly as he'd expected, so he was
short-tempered—with the kids and with me.

After four days of that, Violet and I were curled up
together on the couch with Annie watching *Sparkle On!* and
Liam was on the floor with his favorite wooden trains.
Darren was pacing the apartment holding some company's
financial report in his hands, reading while he walked.

During his third or fourth circle into the living room he said to me, "Liam's nose is running."

"There are Boogie Wipes on the kitchen table," I told him.

He stopped walking and looked at me. "I'm working," he said. "You're their mom."

"Excuse me?" I said, as Violet rubbed her own drippy nose against my sweater.

"I'm working," he said again.

I stared at him. Sometimes he came out with these things that made me think: *Is this really the person I married?* Not often, but it happened. It was usually about childcare, about my role in the family as a wife and a mother.

Without another word, I got up off the couch, lifting Violet with me, got the Boogie Wipes from the kitchen, and wiped Liam's nose.

Later that night, I woke up to the sound of Liam crying. We'd just switched him from a crib to a bed, but he still hadn't figured out that he could get out of it by himself in the middle of the night. I looked over at Darren. He was half awake too.

"Liam's crying," he said, his eyes barely open.

"I hear him." My head felt like it was filled with cotton.

"You're going?"

It wasn't really a question. "Mm-hm," I said, getting out of bed.

When I got to Liam's room, Violet was standing in the door frame. "He woke me up, Mommy," she said, following me inside.

"Me too," I told her, as I lifted him out of his bed. "Why don't you go back to sleep?"

"Can I stay?" she asked.

I was too tired to argue. "Okay," I said, then turned to Liam. "What's wrong, baby?"

Upright, in my arms, Liam's cries turned to a whimper. I wiped his face, which was covered in snot. "Too hot," he said, his breath still shuddering.

I put my lips against his forehead, the way I had with Darren so many Christmases ago. But I was sick too, and my lips weren't reliable. I took his temperature. 101.4. I sighed.

"Okay, buddy," I said. "You don't like this part, but it'll make you feel better."

While Violet watched, I syringed Tylenol into the back of Liam's mouth and then stuck his sippy cup between his lips. He was too sick or too tired to put up much of a fight. He swallowed, then coughed. "I know, baby," I said. "Being sick is no fun."

"Sick is no fun," he echoed, his lower lip trembling a little.

Violet coughed, covering her mouth with her elbow, like she'd learned at kindergarten.

They looked as miserable as I felt. "How about we all sleep together tonight?"

She nodded and climbed into Liam's bed. I slid in next to Violet and propped Liam's head on my shoulder, hoping the elevation would help him breathe.

"Love you, Mommy," he said, as his eyes closed.

"I love you too," Violet said, as she snuggled against my other side.

"I love you both," I told them, "to the stars and back."

And I thought about you, then, Gabe. I hadn't in a while, but lying there I remembered the day, not quite a year before, that we baked cookies and you fixed my washing machine. I remembered the feeling of what could have been. And I wondered how you would have reacted to two sick kids. Would you have gotten out of bed and told me to sleep while you comforted a crying child? Would you have wanted them in bed with both of us, a family of runny noses and fevers? You wouldn't have expected that it would all fall on me, that I'd be the one wiping faces and syringing Tylenol. I know that for sure.

That night, with my babies in my arms, I dreamed about you in Darren's place. We were making waffles for Violet and Liam. You were wearing that ridiculous crown. We were all in matching Christmas pajamas.

When I woke, I chalked it up to a fever dream. But, really, it was much more than that.

lxvii

THAT YEAR, 2013, SOMETIMES FELT LIKE A YEAR OF disillusionment. I seemed to disappoint Darren constantly with my choices. And he disappointed me with his reactions. And his expectations. It was small things—Violet started first grade at a new school and he thought I should go in to work later so I could walk her there in the mornings instead of Maria. I got invited to speak at a conference in Los Angeles, and he wanted me to turn it down because it meant I'd be gone for six days, which he thought was too long for the kids to be without their mom. He was still trying to turn me into the woman he'd imagined when he made that inane checklist. But he was not my Pygmalion. I was not his Galatea.

I'm being unfair, though. We had fun times too. We spent two weeks at a beautiful house in East Hampton in August and invited Vanessa and Jay and the triplets to join us for a week. The kids had a great time swimming and building sand castles and digging holes deep enough to stand in, and Darren and I were better together out there, without work getting in the way. We took Violet and Liam to their first Yankees game in September and had seats right behind home plate. Austin Romine signed a ball for each of the kids, and they talked about it for weeks afterward. We hosted our first Thanksgiving and invited Darren's whole family and mine, and everyone got along wonderfully. On the balance, we were fine, but we weren't great.

Which is probably why when I saw a woman's name— Linda—appear on Darren's phone the week we were both off from work between Christmas and New Year's Day, my mind immediately went to an affair. The way people interpret a situation often says more about them than it does about the situation. Like how during our five-year reunion, when I saw that woman with her hand on your arm, I assumed she was your girlfriend, or at least someone you were interested in taking home that night. We see everything through the filter of our own desires and regrets, hopes and fears.

When I saw *Linda* with no last name, my body flushed hot and cold all at once. I'd never imagined Darren would cheat on me. He seemed too stable, too solid, too loyal. So I set out to prove to myself it wasn't true. I scanned through my mental Rolodex for Lindas—someone from his office, from college, from the gym—but came up blank. Then I went onto his Facebook page to look for Lindas. The only two I could find were a cousin who lived in New Mexico and a college acquaintance's wife who lived in Philly. I took a deep breath and decided it could be either one of them. I should give him the benefit of the doubt, even though leaving off a last name in a contact entry felt like a deliberate choice, like there was something to hide.

"Have you spoken to your cousins recently?" I asked over a dinner of macaroni and cheese and chicken cubes we were eating with our kids. For some reason, Liam preferred to eat meat in cubes, so that became our default shape. Personality-wise, he reminds me a lot of my brother.

Darren shook his head. "I should call them, though, and wish them a happy new year."

"Yeah," I said. "I should do that too."

So it wasn't Cousin Linda.

"What would you think about going out to Philly for a day with the kids this week?" I asked. "Have you been in touch with any of your college guys there? We haven't seen them in a while."

Darren shrugged. "It's a long trip, and really I haven't spoken to any of them since Josh got married last spring. Are we getting to that point where we're trading in our old friends for newer models?"

I took a sip of the Merlot I'd poured us both, even though

it didn't really go with the mac and cheese and chicken. I never like white wine in the winter. "What do you mean?"

Liam was building his chicken into a tower. Violet was eating her mac and cheese one noodle at a time.

"Just that we've been spending most of our time with people in our neighborhood who have kids our kids' ages. I can't even remember the last time we saw Kate and Tom and their girls, and they're only an hour away in Westchester. Maybe we should make plans with them this week."

"Good idea," I said. "I'll give her a call."

"Auntie Kate?" Violet asked. "Do you think she'll have new dress-up clothes I can wear with Samantha and Victoria?"

Samantha was a year and a half younger than Violet, and Victoria was six months older, but the age differences didn't seem to matter as much now as they had when the girls were smaller. "I think that's quite possible," I told her.

She nodded and went back to her noodles.

I'd struck out with the Lindas.

Two weeks later, though, Darren left his phone at home when he went to the gym. After staring at it for fifteen minutes, I picked it up and decided to find out, once and for all, who Linda was. I typed in his unlock code—our anniversary—and his iPhone buzzed and shook its dots at me. The hot-and-cold feeling that had flooded my body when I first saw Linda's name returned. I tried Violet's birthday and then Liam's. Then Darren's. Then mine. Nothing worked, and I knew that if I put in a sixth wrong code, the phone would be disabled. But truly, I didn't have a sixth guess anyway. Linda's birthday? I put the phone down on the coffee table, where I'd found it.

I thought about telling Kate my suspicion but felt like too much of an idiot. There was no real proof. Besides, she and Tom were working through their own issues. The last thing she needed was to be dealing with mine, too. But even though I didn't feel like I had enough evidence to warrant a phone call to Kate, I was still afraid to ask Darren why he'd changed his phone code. Who Linda was. Why she didn't have a last name. Because once I knew he was cheating for real, there was no going back—the hurt, the betrayal, the arguments, the tears. I shuddered at the thought of living through that, of what it would do to the kids, to me, to all of our lives. It was easier to pretend things were fine.

I kept my ears open for the next few months, and noticed three or four times that he'd be talking on the phone in the hallway as he came home from work, but would say goodbye before he entered the apartment. Could that have been Linda?

He worked a couple of Saturdays in March. Linda?

He went on a golf weekend with some friends from the office. Or did he?

I barely slept those six months. I would lie next to him,

wondering how he could sleep so soundly while he was keeping such a horrible secret, while he was betraying me like that. I couldn't get the images out of my head, him in some other woman's arms. Sometimes I'd imagine her as a blonde, sometimes a redhead, sometimes a younger version of me. No matter how I pictured it, it was terrible. I ate less. I drank more. I wondered why he'd given up on us. What made him do it.

Sometimes I wanted to hurt him as badly as he hurt me—physically, emotionally, anything to show him what he was doing to someone he'd promised to love until the day he died. Sometimes I just wanted him to tell me that he was sorry, that he'd leave her, that he loved me still and would love me forever; sometimes I thought that was all it would take for me to forgive him everything. My heart felt like a yo-yo, or maybe like a ping-pong ball, bouncing from one side of the table to the other. Through all of it, though, was this overwhelming feeling that I'd failed somehow. I hadn't been sweet enough or smart enough or a good enough wife. That it was my fault he was doing this. I was paralyzed by the idea of that failure.

I think that's why I didn't tell anyone, really. Once I said it out loud, it became real. Our marriage had failed. We had failed. I had failed.

Darren and I weren't having sex as often as we used to—maybe once or twice a month—which had become the norm after Liam was born. I didn't even bother with birth control. Once I saw Linda's name on his phone, though, there was this paradox of being so upset with Darren that I didn't want to touch him at all, but at the same time, I didn't want to give him a reason to fall into someone else's arms. A few months into my spiral of suspicion, when I was staring wide-eyed at the ceiling, torturing myself with mental images of Darren zipping up some other woman's dress, fixing her collar, sliding on her shoes, I reached my hand over to his side of the bed and slid it under the band of his boxer briefs. He was already falling asleep.

"Not right now," he muttered, as he rolled farther away from me.

I felt like I'd been kicked in the chest. The rejection hurt, physically. How could he want some stranger, but not me?

I questioned everything he did or said in my head, my hurt and mistrust growing, but didn't bring anything up out loud. The only good thing about believing Darren was cheating was that when I fell into a fretful sleep and dreamed about you, I didn't feel guilty anymore.

I started reading your Facebook page more that spring. I liked more of your photos. Even commented on an article you posted. Did you notice? Did you wonder why?

lxviii

TIMING IS EVERYTHING. THAT'S SOMETHING I'VE learned. With work, with friends, with romantic relationships—with us in particular.

You were in New York for a long weekend in mid-June. The AP was sending you to Jerusalem after three Israeli teenagers were kidnapped by Hamas. You'd told them you wanted a breath of America before you dove into a new country and a new conflict, and they said okay. You were a pretty well-known photojournalist by then, so I guess the Associated Press gave you what you wanted. You'd been in Ukraine and then Moscow. I don't know how you did it—a new country every few months, sometimes every few weeks. Or did moving around like that help? Make you think about your mom less, what you didn't have less?

When you e-mailed me that you were landing on the

thirteenth and asked if I would be able to get together, I wrote back *yes*, without even clearing it with Darren. I decided he didn't deserve to be consulted. He was keeping secrets from me, so I could keep secrets from him.

Darren had been talking about bringing the kids to see his parents out in Jersey, and I suggested he do it that Saturday without me—that I could use a day to relax, get my nails done, have lunch with some friends, and his mom could help him with the kids.

"Sounds good," he said. "And maybe next Sunday I can go play golf?"

"Deal," I told him, wondering if *golf* meant *Linda*. I'd initially felt guilty that I'd lied to him, or at least omitted my plans with you from my explanation of the day, but when he said *golf*, I shrugged off my guilt. My omission felt justified.

I texted you that morning: *How about we meet in Manhattan? Darren has the kids for the day in New Jersey.* Manhattan was our borough, after all.

Great, you texted back. *How about Faces & Names? Is that still around? I'm Googling.*

I laughed while I waited for your follow-up text.

It is. See you there for lunch? Noon?

Sounds good to me, I wrote. Then I went and got a manicure and pedicure so my lie to Darren would be partially true. I'd never lied to him before—not like that. And I didn't like doing it. But making part of it true helped.

It took me half an hour to figure out what to wear to see you. It was sunny and in the seventies—ideal weather—so I could go in any direction I wanted: dress, skirt, pants, capris. I settled on something simple. Jeans, black T-shirt, ballet flats, some jewelry. I did my makeup the way I used to when we were together, with a black line at the base of my top lashes. Did you notice?

I walked into Faces & Names, and you were already there, sitting on a couch next to the fireplace.

"They won't turn it on for us," you said. "They said no fires in June."

I sat down next to you. "They do have a point."

I took you in. Your hair had grown back, your dimple was there, but your eyes looked weary, tired, like they'd seen too much.

"Are you okay?" I asked.

"I might be getting too old for this," you answered. "I was just thinking about that. I'm not looking forward to this assignment, and that's the first time that's happened." Then you looked at me closely. "Are *you* okay?" you asked.

I hadn't said a word to anyone for months, but with you I felt safe. Besides, you weren't in my regular life; there wasn't anyone you'd tell. Darren and I wouldn't become gossip at preschool drop-off.

"I think Darren's cheating on me," I whispered. I tried to stop the tears, but I couldn't. You held me to your chest.

You didn't say anything, you just held me. And then you kissed my forehead.

"If he is, he's an idiot," you said. "And he doesn't deserve you. You're smart and sexy and the most amazing woman I know."

You kept your arm around me as I ordered an apple martini and you ordered a whiskey—for old times' sake. I leaned against you as we drank them. And ordered a second round. Your body felt so good next to mine. I remembered that fever dream I had, where we made waffles in our Christmas pajamas, and I wondered what it would be like to come home to you every day, your compassion, your strength, your understanding.

My brain started clouding.

"I need food," I told you. "I'm not used to drinking this much, this quickly."

We ordered fried mozzarella bites and a plate of mini Cuban sandwiches. Things I hadn't eaten in years, but devoured, trying to soak up the alcohol. Even so, when I stood up to go to the restroom, I had to use the top of your head for balance.

"Are you okay?" you asked me for the second time that afternoon, placing a steadying hand on my back.

"Better than I've been in months," I answered.

In the restroom, I kept thinking about how it felt when you held me, how distant I was from Darren, and how much hurt I'd kept bottled up these past months. I craved the kind of closeness I felt in your embrace. I closed my eyes and thought about your lips against mine. The warmth and pressure of them, the taste. I imagined giving myself over to you, completely, the way I used to, abandoning all control, letting you be in charge. I wanted that. I needed that. I'd been trying so hard to hold everything together, to hold myself together, and I was done. I needed someone else to take over. I needed *you* to take over.

When I got back to our couch, you'd already paid the bill.

"Want to go for a walk in the park?" you asked. "We can get some water from the bodega out there."

"Sounds good," I said, putting my hand out. You grabbed it and stood. That moment of skin-to-skin contact felt charged. You looked at me, and our eyes locked. My breathing slowed, unconsciously mirroring yours. You took a step closer to me.

"Gabe—" I started.

You let go of my hand. "I'm sorry," you said, looking down. "I forgot myself."

"Gabe," I said again, trying to put a whole sentence's worth of meaning in that one word.

You looked back at me, and this time neither one of us could break the connection. I reached out and touched your lips with my fingertips.

"We shouldn't," you said, holding my hand in both of yours.

And then I don't know who leaned in first, if it was you or me or maybe we moved at the exact same time, but my mouth was against yours, and all of a sudden everything wrong in the world felt right.

You pulled me closer so our bodies were pressed together, thigh to thigh, stomach to stomach, chest to chest.

"Where's your hotel?" I whispered.

"I'm staying at the Warwick on Sixth Avenue. But . . . Luce."

"It's okay," I said. I've never wanted anything as much as I wanted you in that moment.

I kissed you again and you moaned, slipping your hand into the back pocket of my jeans, just like you used to.

WHEN WE GOT to your hotel room, I think you asked me four times if I was sure this is what I wanted to do. I said yes every time. I was drunk, but I wasn't incapacitated. I knew what I wanted. What I needed.

"Do *you* want to do this?" I finally asked.

"Of course!" you said. "But I don't want you to regret it."

I kissed you harder and concentrated on the taste of you. Gabe plus whiskey was a flavor I knew well.

"Lucy, Lucy, Lucy," you whispered, like you couldn't

believe you were getting the chance to say my name again.

You grabbed for the hem of my T-shirt. I put my hand on yours, self-conscious all of a sudden.

"My body doesn't look the same," I whispered.

You pulled the T-shirt up and over my head.

"Your body is gorgeous," you whispered back.

We wrestled each other out of our clothes and you lifted me up and tossed me onto the bed. A move you'd used on me eleven years before. I reached up and pulled you down with me, running my hands along the muscles of your back, feeling them contract under my fingers. The line from that E. E. Cummings poem kept running through my head. *i like my body when it is with your body.* I do, Gabe. I like my body better when I'm with you, I like myself better.

"There is no one like you," you whispered as you slid into me. "There is nothing like this."

I answered with an arch of my back and a moan. "No one," I breathed. "Nothing."

Afterward, we lay naked on top of the blanket, your body curled around mine the way it used to. Your hand was on my stomach. I thought about the first time we went to Faces & Names, the trip to your apartment afterward, your confessions in the dark.

"What if you came with me," you said, "to Jerusalem."

"What if we traveled down a rainbow highway and danced on the moon," I answered.

"I'm serious," you said, kissing my neck.

"This feels like déjà vu," I answered. "Though now I could probably figure something out with my job. Working remotely. A satellite office. They wouldn't want to lose me."

Your teeth tugged my earlobe. "Brilliant beauty," you said.

I flipped over to face you. "I can't," I told you. "You know I can't. My kids are here, I can't leave them, and there's no way Darren would let me take them to Israel. Especially if it meant I'd be taking them to you." I twined my hand with yours. "But if it were just me, I'd be there in a heartbeat."

I still can't believe I said that. That I was truly considering your offer after one afternoon in bed with you. Though it wasn't one afternoon, was it? It was one afternoon thirteen years in the making. And I'd thought Darren was done with me, that he'd found somebody who ticked all the boxes in whatever new checklist he'd made.

You didn't say anything more, then, just bent your head down and ran your tongue in a circle around my nipple. I felt you, hard, against my leg.

"Again?" I asked.

You took your mouth off my breast. "You make me feel like I'm twenty-three."

"So again," I said.

You kissed your way down my stomach in response.

IT WAS LIKE we were that binary star again, orbiting around each other, no planets or asteroids for light-years. I should've been thinking about my children or my husband, but I was thinking only about you and how you made me feel. How, with all the years between us, our connection felt deeper than it did when we were twenty-four. We'd both changed, but in ways that made us more compatible instead of less so. We talked about us, about staying in touch, about whether I'd be able to visit you in Jerusalem. You typed your new address into my phone.

"I want to see you again, like this," you said, running your hand down my naked body.

My skin goose-bumped, from my shoulders down to my ankles. My nipples stiffened. I rolled over and wrapped my arm around your chest. "Me too," I said. "But I can't figure out how we can make that work."

"If he's cheating on you, you should leave him," you said, your chin resting on the top of my head. "You should be with me."

I kissed your neck and sighed. Lying next to you was intoxicating—I felt the euphoria of that Gabe high; the addiction was back. I'd have to go back to day one, kick the habit all over again. Except I didn't want to. "It's not that easy," I said. "But I'll see if I can figure out a reason to travel to Jerusalem for work . . . Maybe London? That's more plausible. Could you meet me there?"

"Lucy," you said, your arm tightening around my back, "I'll meet you anywhere. I never thought I'd have a second chance with you; I'm not going to screw it up. You're my light. You always have been."

"I know," I said quietly, absorbing your words. "But I'm responsible for other people now. That's partly why I haven't said anything to Darren about this other woman. What would it do to Violet and Liam if I left their dad? You and your mom were so hurt when your dad left."

You were quiet for a while, and then you said, "But what will it do to you if you stay with him?"

I pulled myself closer to you. "They're more important than I am," I said. "But maybe Darren will make the first move. Let's see what the universe has in store."

"Take the current when it serves?" you said.

I smiled at the reference. "It always comes back to Shakespeare with us, doesn't it?"

"'When to the sessions of sweet silent thought, / I summon up remembrance of things past,'" you said. "I have a book of his sonnets that fits in my backpack. I've read Shakespeare in every hellhole this world has to offer, and that's my favorite line. It always makes me think of you, no matter where I am."

I was in your thrall again, Gabe, because even though so much of you had changed, so much of you hadn't. And that part of you—the part that quoted Shakespeare at the drop of a hat—made me feel young and hopeful and infinite. I thought for a moment about asking you to stay. I wondered if your answer would be different than it was ten years before. But I was afraid that it wouldn't be. And that my question would ruin the beauty of our afternoon.

"I'll let you figure things out," you said. "I'll give you some space."

"That's probably best," I said, wishing it weren't.

You grabbed my hand. "But know I'll be thinking about you," you said.

"Me too," I whispered.

We shared one final kiss, and I took the subway home, still orbiting around you in my mind.

lxix

THERE ARE SO MANY KINDS OF SECRETS. THE SWEET ones you want to savor like candy, the grenades that have the potential to destroy your world, and the exciting ones that are more fun the more you share them. Even though our secret was a grenade, it still felt sweet to me. I went home and took a shower, thinking about your touch, your words, your body against mine. I put on an old Columbia sweatshirt that I'd worn when we lived together and a pair of leggings. Instead of turning to my computer to answer e-mail, I pulled out a worn copy of *Lady Chatterley's Lover*. I hadn't read it since college. I'm not even sure how it escaped getting sold back to the Strand for so many years, but I was glad it had. I skipped right to chapter fifteen—John Thomas and Lady Jane. Do you remember that chapter? It's the one where Lady Chatterley and Mellors escape together into the garden shed and weave flowers into each other's pubic hair. I found the scene so sexy in college. I still do.

For the next hour I read about Connie and Mellors and Hilda and Venice. I thought about how our afternoon together was like the night Connie and Mellors spent together before she traveled to Italy.

Then I heard Darren's key in the lock.

"Mommy!" Violet came racing into the apartment.

"Mommy, Mommy!" Liam came racing after her.

They both jumped onto the couch with me and I kissed their hair.

"Daddy told a secret," Liam informed me.

"Shh," Violet said. "A secret means we can't *tell*, Liam. Remember? It's been a secret for a long time and we're not even supposed to know."

The name Linda flashed into my mind again. He couldn't have told them anything about her, could he?

Darren dropped the kids' bag of stuff in the entrance to the living room. "Well, they kept that quiet for all of thirty seconds."

"We didn't tell, Daddy," Violet said. "Pinky promise, right Liam?"

Liam held out his little pinky.

Darren groaned. Then he disappeared up the stairs.

"Hey, wait!" I called after him. "Do I get to know this secret or not?"

"You do!" he said. "I'm just getting something to show you."

"How was your day?" I forced myself to ask the kids.

"Grandma and Grandpa took us to their park," Violet said. "You remember it, right? It's smaller than our park, but has a maze with really tall walls."

"I do," I told her. "And it has seesaws."

She nodded.

"We did seesaws," Liam said.

"But he's littler, so Daddy needed to help so I wasn't stuck on the bottom." Violet jumped off the couch. "I'm going to check on my dolls."

"Checking on my Legos," Liam said, jumping after her.

I followed them up the stairs to find Darren. He was in the study, the room that he always reminded me would become a bedroom for a third kid if we had one, and had booted up his laptop.

"Those little stinkers," he said, as he clicked open a few windows. "I hadn't been planning to tell you until I'd had all the work done, but they heard me talking to my dad about it. I was trying to time it with our anniversary. Can you believe it's almost ten years?"

"Eight," I answered. "We'll be married eight years in November."

Darren smiled. "Ten since the first time we met."

Then he turned the computer so the screen faced me. "I bought the house."

My brain was having trouble processing what he was saying. "You what?"

"That's the secret!" he said. "I've been stalking this house since the summer after Violet was born. I wanted to buy the place where we met. And I finally convinced them to sell in January."

I was still struggling to unravel what was going on. Darren stood up and took my hand.

"I know things haven't been the best this past year or so," he said, "but we were so happy last summer out in East Hampton, and I thought with this house . . ."

Tears pooled in my eyes. "Oh, Darren," I said, squeezing his hand. He really did still love me, he did still want us to work. I hadn't been sure until that moment. But it made his affair even more confusing. Why would he be doing that while he was planning this?

He squeezed my hand back. "I've been secretly communicating with the Realtor, a really lovely older woman named Linda, since the fall. The weekend I said I was golfing with my friends in March, I actually went out there and closed on the house."

The Realtor? I felt sick.

For all those months I let myself believe he was cheating on me. I created a new image of who Darren was, what he wanted, how he'd betrayed me; I thought I'd understood what was happening. I'd thought I understood him in a way he'd never understood me. But I didn't. Not at all.

"And it's being renovated as we speak," he said. "The place was pretty trashed when I saw it. So did I surprise you? Did you suspect anything?"

I thought about the Darren I first fell in love with—the one who'd made me laugh so hard my cheeks hurt, the one who'd turned storm clouds into sunshine. Even though I couldn't remember the last time we'd laughed until there were tears in our eyes, that Darren was still there, and I'd ignored him. I'd chosen to focus on what was wrong instead of what was right. And all the while he was trying to buy the house where we first met. He was trying to fix things. But he was doing it in the exact way I'd asked him not to, over and over. He'd cut me out of a big decision again.

It was all too overwhelming. I started to cry.

"You like it?" he asked. "Are those happy tears?"

"It's beautiful," I answered, wiping my eyes. The guilt threatened to swallow me whole. The shame.

Darren wrapped his arms around me. "Only the best for you," he whispered into my hair. Then he kicked the door shut and kissed me with a passion I hadn't felt from him in a long time.

I kissed him back, and for the second time in five hours, a man was taking off my shirt. For the second time, a man had his mouth on my breast. For the second time, I felt a man hard against my leg. But this time, even though my body responded, I felt numb.

"I HATED KEEPING SECRETS from you," Darren said after, as he put my sweatshirt back on me. "But your reaction was totally worth it. Maybe next weekend we could head out there and get reacquainted with the house."

"Great idea," I said, making sure that my eyes were dry, that there was a smile on my face. "I love it."

He kissed me again, and then opened the door, yelling for the kids. "Mommy knows about our new secret house! Who wants pizza for dinner to celebrate?"

I didn't think I'd be able to eat a bite.

lxx

On Monday morning, at work, I tried to put everything out of my mind—you, that hotel room, Darren, the beach house—and concentrate on the new show I was developing. It didn't have a name yet, but the idea was to invite famous musicians to write songs introducing kids to different aspects of government. The pilot was going to be about monarchies, and we were in talks with Elton John to compose the songs for that episode. The concept had actually come out of something Violet had said to me last Election Day—she wanted to know who I was going to vote for to be princess.

But I couldn't focus on the call I needed to make to Elton John's manager or the notes I was typing up on the proposed script. I needed to talk to someone about what had happened—with you and me, with Darren and me—but I felt so ashamed. I knew my brother would still love me, that Kate would still be my best friend, but I didn't want them to change their opinion of me, even a little, when I showed them what I was capable of. And I thought they might. If I were in their position, my opinion would probably change.

Julia might understand, though. Ever since she and I went to your gallery show together, she asked about you. And since she wasn't married, maybe she wouldn't be as disturbed by all of it as I imagined Kate or Jason would be. I called her at her office.

"Hey!" she said when she picked up. "I was going to call you today. I have news."

I stretched my phone cord and looked out the window. "Good news?"

"Great news," she said. "I gave my notice this morning."

"You got a new job?" I asked. Julia had been looking for the last few months, but art director positions were few and far between, especially because she didn't want to leave children's books.

"I did." I could hear her smiling over the phone. "You're talking to the newest art director of Little Golden Books at Random House. I start in three weeks!"

"Congratulations!" I said. "That's fantastic. Violet loves those Little Golden Books. We have like twenty of them."

"Well, let me know if there are any other titles she wants. I can pull some extra copies from the book room once I start." Julia lavishes gifts on my kids whenever she sees them. She's probably gotten both of them half the books on their shelves.

"Thanks," I said. "I'm sure Violet will love that."

"But you called to tell me something," Julia said, "and I hijacked the whole conversation."

"You didn't hijack anything," I said. "I was just calling to say hi."

I couldn't do it. Even with Julia, I couldn't confess to what I'd done, what I'd let myself believe, what I said to you, how wrong I was. And I certainly couldn't confess that deep inside, in spite of everything, I still wanted to leave Darren and be with you.

You just—you made me feel so alive, Gabe. I don't even know if I can put it into words. The world seemed bigger when you were around, filled with possibility. I seemed smarter, sexier, more beautiful. You saw me in a way that no one else did. You understood who I was at my core, and you didn't want to change me. You wanted me *because of.* Darren wanted me *in spite of.* I think that's the best way to describe it. And it took every ounce of self-control I had not to give in to my desire to call you, to be with you. But I would never forgive myself if I hurt my kids. Even if it meant surrendering that feeling forever.

lxxi

IN THE WEEK AFTER WE SAW EACH OTHER, I KEPT TRY-
ing to push you out of my mind, but news of what was happening between Israel and Gaza filled newspapers and
Internet feeds. *He's there!* the universe kept saying. *Think
about him!* I scoured every photo for its credit, looking for
your name. I found it on a particularly arresting image. Five
women, all in headscarves, all wailing. One was reaching
out in front of her, as if to stop whatever was going on outside the frame. It was a funeral, I read, for a Palestinian boy
who was killed. So I knew—you'd left Jerusalem and were
in Gaza City.

A few weeks later, the news media started calling the
conflict an actual war. I was glued to the television, horri-
fied as battles erupted while I watched. There were so many
children there; some looked like they could have been in

first grade like Violet, or in Liam's preschool class. I watched a journalist interview a woman who explained that she didn't let any of her three children sleep in the same room at night, so that if a bomb hit one part of her house, it wouldn't kill all her children at once. Then I saw the families who didn't have houses left at all.

"Want to watch *CSI*?" Darren asked, dropping next to me on the couch, while I had the news on.

"Sure," I said, changing the channel. But I couldn't follow the storyline. My mind—and my heart—were still in Gaza City.

lxxii

I WAS AT WORK WHEN YOU CALLED.

"Gabe," I said.

"I can't do this anymore," you answered. "I'm coming home."

My heart sped up in my chest. "What's going on?" I asked.

"I've never seen anything like this before," you told me. "The women, the children." Your voice broke on the word. "I just keep thinking about you. About the Warwick. I was wrong when I asked you to come to Jerusalem. I should have offered to stay in New York. Is Darren still with that Linda? Have you talked to him about it?"

My breath caught. That was what I'd wanted—that was the offer I'd hoped for. But it didn't matter now. I stalled.

"Gabe, you're doing good work there. I saw your photograph on the front page of the *New York Times*. You're showing the world what's happening. You're living your dream."

I heard you take a ragged breath. "I thought I'd be able to make a real difference, but . . . they're just pictures, Luce. They haven't changed a thing. The world is still shit. And now . . . it feels like too much of a sacrifice. I miss you. I think about you all the time."

"I miss you too," I said. "But, Gabe, if you come back . . . I can't promise . . . don't come for me, Gabe. Don't make me choose. Darren wasn't cheating. He . . . he bought me a house. The house where we met. Linda was the real estate agent." It broke my heart to say it, but I knew it was the right thing to do—for my kids, for my life. I needed to be responsible, to focus on my marriage, to keep my family together.

I listened to you inhale, exhale, inhale, waiting for your response.

"Is that what you want, Lucy?" you said softly. "Will that fix everything?"

I closed my eyes. "No," I said. "It's not. It won't. But it's a start. I told you I won't leave my kids. I won't break up my family."

I imagined the pain I knew would be visible on your face. I tried to harden my heart to it.

"I think I need to come back anyway," you said, your

voice filled with emotion. "I think I have to come for *me*. I'm going to give my notice. Hopefully I'll be home by the end of the summer. And . . . I won't expect anything from you. But life is so short, Lucy. I want you to be happy. I want us both to be happy."

I didn't know how to respond because I wanted us both to be happy too. I just didn't see a way to make it happen. "Okay," I said. "Stay safe until then. We'll . . . talk when you're back home."

"I love you, Lucy," you said.

I couldn't leave your words hanging there, not when I felt the same way.

"Me too," I whispered, tears filling my eyes. "I love you, too, Gabe." I did, I do, I always have. I realized that then. I love Darren, too, but what you and I have is different. If I'd never met you, maybe Darren would be enough. But I've taken a bite of the forbidden fruit. I've eaten from the tree of knowledge. I've seen how much more there is.

I knew I'd have to forget that, ignore what could be. Because *I like Gabe better* didn't seem like an acceptable reason to destroy my marriage with a good, generous man. It didn't seem like an acceptable reason to do that to my kids.

I took the rest of the day off from work. I went home and fell asleep on the couch holding on to *Lady Chatterley's Lover*.

lxxiii

THERE ARE SOME THINGS WE KNOW WITHOUT KNOW-
ing them.

I should have realized it when I fell asleep in Liam's bed
at eight thirty, in the middle of reading him *If You Give a
Mouse a Cookie*.

I should have realized it when my period was five days
late, and then ten.

But I didn't realize it until I woke up knowing I was
going to vomit before I made it to the bathroom. I reached
for the garbage pail next to my nightstand.

"Oh, God," Darren said, jolting up in bed. "Are you
sick?"

I wiped my mouth with my hand as my brain quickly put
the pieces together. "I'm going to go with pregnant," I told

him, groaning. "Do we have any pregnancy tests in the cabinet?"

I tied the plastic bag that was in the trash can in an airtight knot, as the rest of the information filtered through my brain. I was counting weeks. I'd been so sure I wasn't ovulating when you and I were together, when Darren and I were together later that day. But I must've been wrong. My whole body flashed hot as one thought engulfed my consciousness: *Whose baby was it?*

"Wait, are you serious?" Darren asked.

"As serious as the Defenestration of Prague," I told him, trying to keep the shock from registering on my face. The horror.

Darren jumped out of bed and enveloped me in a hug. "This is fantastic!" he said. "We're filling up this whole apartment with tiny humans! You know I always wanted more. Our new house must be a good-luck charm."

"It must," I said, thinking the exact opposite, my mind spinning.

Do I tell him? Don't I tell him? If I told him, would he leave? Kick me out? Would that be it, our family up in flames? I couldn't tell him. But what if it *was* yours? How could I let him raise your son?

"I'm going to puke again," I said to Darren, running into the bathroom.

I couldn't believe that this was my life. It was like a soap opera.

I knew you'd planned to be back in New York again soon. I decided I should wait. I didn't need to tell you. At least not over the phone. At least not yet.

I wish I'd made a different choice. If I'd known our time was limited, if I'd known we'd end up here, like this, I would have reached out that day. I wish I could rewind time and make that call. Maybe you would've come home. Maybe this wouldn't have happened to you at all.

lxxiv

THERE ARE SO MANY MOMENTS THAT CHANGE A PER-
son's world. Some are because of a decision that's made.
Others, I think, might be because of the universe, fate,
God, a higher power, whatever you want to call it. I don't
know. I've been wrestling with this question for thirteen
years now.

That Tuesday I was on my way to work in a taxicab.
Maybe it was the uncertainty or the guilt or the fact that I
hadn't spoken to you about it yet, but the nausea those few
weeks after I realized I was pregnant was so awful that I
didn't want to risk riding the subway and vomiting on the
stranger next to me. So I was taking cabs. Darren offered to
get a driver to take me to and from work, but that felt exces-
sive. Instead, I hailed a cab each morning. And sometimes
on the way home too. Whoever named it "morning sick-

ness" was an optimist. I carried at least two plastic bags in my purse at all times, but so far I hadn't actually thrown up in a cab. My office was another story. I think I might have scared my poor assistant into celibacy.

I was breathing slowly, in through my nose, out through my mouth, trying to calm my body down. And then my cell phone rang. It was a number I didn't know, but I picked up, in case it was something having to do with Violet or Liam. Becoming a mother changed my call-screening habits. The last thing I ever wanted to do was not pick up when one of my kids needed me.

"Hello?" I said.

"Is this Lucy Carter Maxwell?"

"Yes," I answered, though there wasn't anywhere other than Facebook that I was listed that way.

"This is Eric Weiss," the person said. "I'm an executive editor at the Associated Press. I work with Gabriel Samson."

"Yes?"

"I'm calling to let you know that Gabe has been hurt."

He stopped talking. I stopped breathing.

"Hurt, but he's okay?"

"He's in a hospital in Jerusalem."

Then my brain started catching up with my heart.

"Wait," I said, "why are you calling me about this?"

I heard Eric take a deep breath on the other end of the

phone. "I'm looking at Gabe's personnel file, and you're listed as his emergency contact and his medical proxy. It says you're a good friend of his? We're going to need you to make some decisions."

"Decisions?" I repeated. "About what? What happened?"

"I'm sorry," Eric said, "let me start over."

Then he told me the story. You were in Gaza City. There was fighting in Shuja'iyya. There was an explosion, and you were too close. It happened too quickly for you to run. An Israeli medic took care of you in the field and the AP got you to a hospital in Jerusalem, but you hadn't been responding to any stimuli and you couldn't breathe on your own. He told me he didn't think you'd recover. You had signed a DNR, but no one knew until you were already hooked up to machines, and now they needed my permission to take you off them.

"No," I kept saying into the phone. "No, no, no, no, no."

"Ma'am?" the cabdriver asked me. "Is everything all right?"

"Please turn around," I whispered to him. "I need to go home."

I went back to the apartment, climbed back into bed, and cried. For hours. Then I called Kate, giving her the broad strokes of what had happened to you.

"I think I have to go to Jerusalem," I told her. "I can't tell them to take Gabe off those machines before I see him

352

again. I can't let him die with no one there but strangers—or wake up, confused and hurting, all alone."

"There's a war there," Kate said, as if the thoughts were unspooling in her mind as she was verbalizing them. "But I work with a corporation that's headquartered in Tel Aviv, and they seem to be business as usual. So I don't think it's as dangerous as it sounds. At least not on the Israeli side."

"And I'm pregnant," I said, talking over her.

"You're pregnant?" She sounded disconcerted, jumping from one train of conversation to the next. "When did . . . I didn't think you wanted any more children. Hold on. Let me just—"

I heard the door to her office shut.

"Okay, so what's going on?"

"It might be Gabe's baby," I said, quietly. "I don't know." I still hadn't told her anything about us or about what had happened at the Warwick, which was why I hadn't told her I was pregnant either. I was too ashamed, too worried about what she would think of me. But I'd reached a point where I didn't care. I needed her. I needed someone to lean on.

"Oh, Lucy," she said. "Lucy." She paused for a moment. Then she said, "Why didn't you tell me? Never mind, we can talk more later. For now: do you want me to come to Jerusalem with you?"

I made a sound that married a sob with a sigh of relief.

"I love you," I told her. "I'm sorry I didn't . . . You're the best best friend in the world."

"Don't you forget it," she said.

"But even though I'm pregnant, even though there's a war, I think I need to go to Jerusalem by myself."

I KNEW EXPLAINING the situation to Darren—especially without explaining what had happened at the Warwick—wasn't going to be easy. And probably I shouldn't have tried. If I'd been serious about focusing on my marriage, I would've signed what I needed to sign from New York and told Eric Weiss that the doctors should do whatever they felt was best. But even though I knew that was what I *should* do, I couldn't. Especially not if the baby I was carrying was ours. How could I explain to that child that I'd abandoned its father when he needed me most?

"Are you kidding?" Darren asked, his face incredulous, when I pulled him into our bedroom right after he got home from work. "You want me to let my pregnant wife fly into a war zone so she can sit at her ex-lover's bedside?"

The way he said it made me more resolute. "It's not as dangerous as it sounds," I said. "And, Darren, I'm not asking you to *let* me do anything."

"So you're telling me you're going? I have no say?" He was pacing in front of our bed. "Why the fuck did that asshole make you his medical proxy?"

I felt my eyes widen in shock. Darren almost never swore, and his voice was laced with such vitriol.

"I'm telling you I want to do this," I said. "I'm telling you I need to do this, or I'll regret it forever." My voice choked up, and as I was saying those words, I was wondering: Would I break up my marriage over this? I'd asked you not to come back to New York for me, not to make me choose, but when it came down to it, I wondered if I'd choose you.

"Do you understand there's a war there? Are planes even flying?"

I'd checked before he came home. "El Al is," I said, stopping the trembling in my voice. "And they have the Iron Dome. It's not like I'm going to Gaza. I'll be safe."

"What if something goes wrong with the baby?"

"Their emergency medicine is even better than ours," I said. "I read about it online." It was not the time to tell him that the baby might be yours. I wondered if it would ever be the time to tell him.

I could see Darren was calming down. I could see he was playing out the scenarios in his head and realizing this was an argument he wasn't easily going to win.

"Please trust me," I said. "This is something I need to do."

He massaged his forehead for a moment.

"So help me God, Lucy," he said finally. "I don't know what it is about you and that man, how he keeps pulling you back into his orbit. He left you ten years ago. I'd think you wouldn't forget something like that. If you have to go, go. But I want you back as soon as possible. By Sunday at the latest. It's not safe there."

"Fine," I said. If I left tomorrow, that would give me three days in Jerusalem. I'd have liked more time, but if I wanted to come back to a marriage that wasn't going to disintegrate upon reentry, I knew I had to compromise. And Darren really is a good man—even as upset as he was, he still agreed. That's why all of this is so hard. It would be easier if he were a jerk.

So I booked my flight, and a return trip for Sunday morning. I packed my bag. I called Kate and told her my plan.

After everything that had happened between you and me, I couldn't believe that this was where life had led us.

lxxv

I BOARDED WITH THE REST OF THE FIRST-CLASS CABIN and found myself seated next to an older Orthodox woman. Her head was covered with a patterned silk kerchief, tied behind her neck. She smiled at me when I sat down.

I smiled back but was already concentrating on breathing slowly, trying to will away the nausea, trying to ignore the briny taste in the back of my throat. It didn't matter, though. While the rest of the plane was boarding, I knelt down in the airplane bathroom and vomited. "Please don't let this happen the entire flight," I said out loud as I flushed and wiped my mouth.

"Okay?" the woman asked me in heavily accented English, when I sat down again. My face must've been pale.

"Pregnant," I told her, placing my hand low on my stomach. Then added, "A baby." I wasn't sure how much English she knew.

She nodded and rummaged around in her purse. Then she handed me a bag of candy with Hebrew writing on it. "This helps," she said. "I eat it on the airplane."

I held one up to my nose and sniffed it. "It's ginger?" I asked.

She shrugged. She hadn't understood the word. "It helps."

I figured I didn't have much to lose, so I unwrapped the candy and popped it into my mouth. I sucked on it and actually did start to feel a bit better. "Thank you," I told her.

"I have five," she said, pointing to my stomach. "I was sick always."

"This is my third," I told her.

"You are Jewish?" she asked, I guess trying to figure out why I was pregnant and on my way to Israel in the middle of a war.

"No," I said.

"Your . . ."—she searched for a word and then settled on one—"man is in *Yisroel*?"

I embraced her use of the word *man* instead of *husband*.

"He is," I said. "He's a journalist. And he's in the hospital. He was hurt badly in Gaza."

As I said it, I felt tears welling up in my eyes. Other than Kate and Darren, I hadn't talked about you, about what happened to you, with anyone.

The next thing I knew, the woman had her arms around

me and was murmuring words in Hebrew or Yiddish—a language I didn't understand but found comforting just the same. It's embarrassing to admit, but I cried on her shoulder, let her stroke my hair. When I finally pulled myself together, she held my hand. And then after our food came, she kept patting my arm, as if to say without words, *It's going to be okay.*

When I woke up, having fallen asleep for a few hours, I found myself covered with an airline blanket.

"Thank you," I said to her.

"God has a plan," she said. "And a child is always a blessing."

I'm not sure if I believe her about either of those things. I don't like the idea that God had this plan for you. And I can think of instances where having a child may not be a blessing. But her belief and her quiet strength, they helped. There is an element of peace in believing that we're only players on a stage, acting out stories directed by someone else.

Is this God's plan, Gabe? Is there even a God?

lxxvi

We landed in Tel Aviv just on time. I let Darren know I was safe and then took a taxi straight to the hospital. It felt strange not texting you to say I'd arrived. Or calling to ask what room you were in, how I'd find you. But there was no one to call. No one to talk to. It was just me—and the baby.

"I'm glad you're with me," I muttered to my stomach. It seemed less lonely, somehow, to know there was another living being there, experiencing this alongside me.

At the hospital there were two security guards checking everyone's bags. "I need to find a patient's room," I told them frantically as I handed mine over, before I could even wonder if they spoke English.

"Information is over there. She can help you," one of the guards said, after I went through the metal detector and got my bags back. He was pointing to a desk behind him.

I ran to the information desk as quickly as I could, rolling my suitcase behind me.

"Please," I said when I got there. "I need to find a patient's room. Gabriel Samson." The woman behind the desk must've noticed how distraught I looked. The ten-and-a-half-hour flight and time change didn't help. I'm sure my eyes were bloodshot and my hair and clothes rumpled. She found your name on a computer in no time.

"Floor eight," she said. "Intensive care. Room 802." Then she pointed me toward the elevator.

I hit 8 and tried to remember what floor your hotel room was on in the Warwick. Closing my eyes, I imagined your finger pressing the button. It was 6. Or was it 5? A tear rolled down my cheek. If you died, I realized just then, it would mean that I'd be the keeper of our memories. I'd be the only one on Earth who had experienced them. I have to do better. I can't forget the details.

The elevator pinged and the doors opened. I went to the woman behind the desk and told her I was there to see you. She nodded and then said I could take a seat. That the doctors would be there shortly. Then she picked up the phone and started speaking quickly in Hebrew.

"Wait," I said. "But I want to see Gabe. Can I see him now?"

She covered the mouthpiece of the phone with her hand. "Soon," she told me. "But the doctors want to speak first."

I had my suitcase and my oversized handbag from the plane. I carried them to a gray institutional-looking chair and sat. I closed my eyes and tried to remember the first time I saw you. Were you wearing a white T-shirt, or was it gray? Was there a pocket? An emblem on the left side? It had a slight V-neck, I remembered that part.

I opened my eyes when someone cleared his throat in front of me. "Mrs. Maxwell?" the man asked. He was wearing a lab coat. It reminded me of Jason's.

I nodded and stood. "I'm Lucy Maxwell," I said, holding out my hand.

The man shook it. "I'm Yoav Shamir," he said. "Mr. Samson's neurologist." His English sounded nearly perfect, except for the way he swallowed the letter *r*.

"Thank you for caring for him," I said.

Two women standing a bit behind Dr. Shamir stepped forward.

"I'm Dafna Mizrahi," the taller one said, her accent more pronounced. "I'm the intensive-care doctor."

I shook her hand too. "Nice to meet you," I said inanely.

Then the third woman introduced herself. She wasn't wearing a lab coat. Instead she had on a bright summer dress.

There was a scarf draped across her shoulders. "I'm Shoshana. Shoshana Ben-Ami," she said. "I'm a social worker here. I've reserved a room for the four of us—shall we head over?" She sounded British. I wondered if she'd been raised there and moved to Israel recently, or perhaps one of her parents had and she'd grown up speaking both languages.

"Okay," I said, following all three of them. Between the flight and the time difference and the surreality of the situation, I felt like I was floating, like this whole thing was happening in a dream world, where sound was traveling through cotton wool to make its way to me.

"Do you know what happened?" Dr. Mizrahi asked me, as we all sat down in a small, quiet room. There was a table, a few chairs, a telephone.

"Some," I answered, putting my handbag at my feet.

"Do you want to know more?" she asked. "I have the medic's notes."

Usually, I want to know everything. Usually the more information I have, the more I feel in control. But this time I said no. "I just want to see him," I said.

She nodded. "You will, very soon, but we want to give you some information first."

Dr. Shamir had sat down across from me. "As you know," he said, "your friend had a very significant, traumatic injury to his brain. Would you like me to go through the test results?"

I took a deep breath. "Just tell me this," I said, "what are the chances that he'll recover? How long will it take?"

A look passed between the two doctors. "The lower portion of his brain was affected," Dr. Shamir said. "That's the part that performs essential life functions."

"Swallowing, breathing," Dr. Mizrahi clarified.

"But could he gain those back?" I asked. Hope, it had perched in my soul. It was singing a tune without words. Did you take that class at Columbia? The one on Dickinson? I can't remember. I wish I could remember.

They looked at each other again. Dr. Mizrahi started this time. "Dr. Shamir and I both performed the test for brain death," she said. "And your friend's brain . . . it doesn't function."

"But will it again?" I asked. "Like a broken leg, or a sore throat. Can he get better?" As I rode in the cab from Tel Aviv, I'd imagined you hearing my voice and waking up. I'd imagined you whole and happy in my arms.

Dr. Shamir looked straight at me. His brown eyes were magnified through his glasses. "Mr. Samson is brain-dead," he said. "That means he will never breathe again on his own, he'll never swallow, he'll never speak, he'll never walk. I'm so sorry."

Mr. Samson is brain-dead. A powerful wave of nausea swept through me. I looked frantically around the room for a garbage pail and lunged toward the one in the corner, just

364

as I started to dry heave. *Brain-dead. Brain is dead. Dead.* You were gone. Forever. My body was rejecting that, rejecting everything.

My stomach muscles contracted in waves, trying to rid my body of anything it could.

Dr. Mizrahi came over and knelt beside me. "Take a deep breath," she said. "Through your nose."

I tried and stopped gagging.

"Now another." She helped me off my knees and back into my chair. I wasn't crying. I was numb. I felt like my consciousness had split in two. The part that felt things had detached itself from the rest of me. It was on the ceiling, watching the meeting.

Shoshana left the room and came back with a cup of water. "Do you need some time?" she asked.

I shook my head. I felt like a robot. Like my body and mouth were moving mechanically. "I'm sorry," I said to all of them.

"No need to apologize," Shoshana told me, patting my hand with hers.

"I'm pregnant," I said, trying to explain. "I've been feeling sick anyway. I think—"

"How far along?" Dr. Mizrahi asked.

"Just over eight weeks," I said.

She nodded and sat in the empty seat right next to me.

"You can keep him on life support," Dr. Mizrahi told me.

"We can talk about the length of time and what risks there are. But I always tell the families and friends to consider what their loved one would want. How would he want to live the rest of his life?" She reached across the table for a file, then shuffled through it for a piece of paper. "This is a copy of the DNR that the Associated Press sent to us."

I took the paper and looked at your signature, so familiar—all angles where one expected curves. It was dated October 3rd, 2004. I began to read the form, but stopped. I knew what it meant. I still felt numb, robotic, like I wasn't all there. I wasn't sure what to say next. I wished I weren't so alone. I wished you were there with me.

"When can I see him?" I asked.

"Dr. Mizrahi can take us now," Shoshana said. "Or you and I can stay, and we can talk. About anything you'd like." She handed me a plastic bag. "I have Mr. Samson's camera for you—and his cell phone and wallet. His house keys as well. And a hotel key. That's what he had on him." I looked inside the bag. Your phone was shattered. Your camera looked surprisingly intact, but I could see splatters of mud—or was it blood—dried onto the lens.

I took a shaky breath. This was all too much. My fogged-up mind jumped to all the things you left behind. Would I have to deal with them too? For a moment I wished Darren were there with me; he'd know what to do. Or Kate.

I decided I'd call Kate. But first I needed to see you. That was why I'd come. That was why I'd traveled so far.

"Thank you," I said to the social worker. "But I just want to see him. Can I see him now?"

"Of course," she said, standing and picking up my suitcase.

"We've got to be strong," I muttered to the baby. Or maybe to myself. I followed Shoshana and Dr. Mizrahi out the door. Dr. Shamir turned in the other direction, saying he was available if I wanted to talk further.

I nodded and he left.

Then I stopped walking. "There is one thing," I said, in the hallway.

Shoshana paused and looked at me. "Yes?"

I took another deep breath. I couldn't believe I was asking this. "How far along does a pregnancy have to be before you can do a paternity test?"

Dr. Mizrahi had stopped too. Her gaze dropped briefly to my stomach before it returned to my face. "There's a blood test that can be performed as early as eight weeks," she said. "It can also tell the baby's sex."

I clutched the plastic bag tighter. The things you'd left behind. "Thank you," I said.

And then Dr. Mizrahi led us in to see you.

lxxvii

I WALKED INTO YOUR ROOM AND HAD TO STEADY MY-self against the door frame. The nausea returned and I battled it back.

There was a breathing tube jammed down your throat. Your lips were dry and cracked around it. Your head was bandaged, and the soft area below your closed eyes was bruised purple. Someone had wrapped your left arm in a splint, from elbow to wrist. There were tubes and machines beeping everywhere. But it was you. You were there. Your chest was rising and falling. You were alive. I knew what the doctors had just said, but I ignored it.

"Gabe," I breathed. The room smelled metallic and medicinal, like antiseptic mixed with sweat and blood. I knelt next to your bed and took your hand. Your fingers felt reassuringly warm. I held them to my face, wishing you would trace my lips with your thumb, wishing I could hear your voice.

I thought about the last conversation we had. The one where we said we loved each other. The one where I told you to stay in Jerusalem, not to make me choose. "I take it back," I said to you. "I didn't mean it. Just come back. Come back, Gabe. Please. Don't leave me."

Nothing happened. You didn't move. Not a twitch, not a blink.

A sob escaped my chest and then I couldn't stop them from coming. My throat constricted. My ribs ached. My body shook. I collapsed onto the floor.

I don't know when she'd entered the room, but Shoshana was at my side, her hand on my shoulder. "Mrs. Maxwell," she said. "Lucy."

I looked at her instead of at you. I tried to stop the body-racking sobs. She lifted me up off the floor.

"Let's take a walk," she said. "Is there anyone who can be here with you?"

I shook my head. "No one," I choked out. I thought about Kate, about asking her if she could get on a plane that night. She would come if I asked. I took a quivering breath.

"It's going to be okay," Shoshana said, as she steered me out of your room and back down the hall. "Visiting hours are almost over. Why don't you try to get some rest? You don't have to make any decisions today."

"Okay," I said, my voice as shaky as I felt.

"Do you need a car to take you to a hotel? Or to Mr. Samson's apartment?" Shoshana asked.

I'd booked a hotel, but I thought about the keys to your apartment in the plastic bag. I had your address in my contacts, where you typed it while we were in bed together. I felt like I had to go there. "A car," I said. "That would be great."

Shoshana nodded and came back a few minutes later with my suitcase. "Let me take you outside to meet the driver." She handed me a card. "I don't usually do this, but here's my private line. If you need anything, please call. I've added my mobile number on the back."

"Thank you," I said, slipping the card into my handbag.

She picked my suitcase back up and I followed her through a revolving gate to the parking lot. A thought flashed through my mind quickly, gone as fast as it entered: If this was fate's way of granting my wish, making me not have to choose between you and Darren, then I didn't want to live in this world either.

What do you think, Gabe? Was it your choice to report from Gaza? To take those pictures when you did, where you did, how you did? Did your choices lead you here? Or was this preordained? Your fated end? Our fated end? I have my own thoughts about this, but I wish I could hear yours.

lxxviii

THE TAXI DRIVER TOOK ME DOWN SOME WINDING streets, trying to give me a bit of a tour as we went. It was the first time I'd ever been to Israel, and I knew I should have been paying more attention, appreciating the significance of where I was, but I was still in a fog. Images of you in that hospital bed flared in my brain. Dr. Shamir saying the words "Mr. Samson is brain-dead." *Don't think about it*, I told myself. *Focus on what you're doing now. Stay strong. Think about his apartment.* Would it seem familiar? Would it feel like home? Would I find something out about you that I didn't know before—and wouldn't want to know now? For a moment, I wondered if I should go to the hotel after all, but we were already on the way. And to be honest, I wanted to see where you'd lived. I wanted to surround myself with you.

"Ah, Rehavia," the taxi driver had said, when I gave him your address. "Very nice."

He was right. Your neighborhood was lovely—inviting and calm. I concentrated on the buildings we passed instead of what I'd just seen and heard at the hospital. I imagined what it would have been like if I'd said, *Yes, I'll come to Jerusalem with you.* Would I have shopped at that market? Had coffee at that little store? Would we have enjoyed being together, or would everything have been tainted? Through the fog and numbness, I felt a pang for Violet and Liam. I'd been gone for less than a day, and I missed them already. I wished I could hold them, feel their little bodies warm against mine, their arms wrapped around my neck. I never would have been able to leave them.

When we stopped in front of your building, I took my bags and stood at the entrance. There was a wooden door behind a metal gate, both set into a beautiful stone archway. I would've chosen a building like this too. It looked solid, comforting, like it had protected families, kept them safe, for centuries. I fumbled in the plastic bag for your keys, and then tried a few before I found the one that opened the gate and then the door. I took the stairs to the third floor, and then struggled again to find the right key.

Inside, by myself, all of a sudden I felt like an intruder. I'd forgotten that you'd only been in Jerusalem briefly before you were in Gaza. And that even when you were here, you were working like crazy. Your apartment hadn't really been set up yet. There were boxes of books opened but not unpacked. A few photographs framed and leaning against walls, but not hung. There were rugs patterned in bold colors, like I'd seen at the bazaars in Turkey. A brown couch. A wooden desk piled with electronics and wires. A chair. I imagined you working in that chair, at your computer, cropping, adjusting color saturation, increasing contrast, the way you did when we lived together. I did my best to think of you here, and not in the hospital. You were alive, you were doing what you loved, you were smiling. In my mind at least.

I pushed open the door to your bedroom and saw, folded on the foot of your bed, the same blanket I threw at you the night you told me you were leaving. I picked it up and touched it to my cheek. It still smelled faintly of you. There was a nightstand with a copy of *All the Light We Cannot See*. I sat down on your bed, noticing a piece of paper that marked your place. Page 254. That's the farthest you'll ever read in that book. You'll never finish it. Your life was interrupted, cut short. A film that snapped on its reel and wouldn't get to its natural end. There is so much you left undone. So much you'll never complete, never see, never know.

"I'll finish the book," I said out loud. "I'll read it for you, Gabe."

Then I looked at your bookmark. It was the receipt from our afternoon at Faces & Names. I traced the date with my fingertips. Even if I'd known that was the last time I'd ever see you, I don't think there's anything I would have done differently. I still would've pressed my body against yours in the bar. I still would've made love to you over and over in your hotel room. And I still would've told you I couldn't come with you to Jerusalem.

Still, I can't help but wonder if this would have happened if I'd said yes. Would you have been more careful, if I was home, waiting for you? Would you have been more careful if you'd known there was a baby that might be ours?

I touched my stomach. Did we conceive a child that afternoon?

Numbly, I wandered back into your living room and then into the kitchen. The refrigerator was almost empty—mustard, a few bottles of beer. There was a bag of coffee beans and a half-empty box of chai in the cabinet, along with two bags of pretzels, one unopened, the other closed with a binder clip. I didn't know you liked pretzels that much. Why didn't I know that about you?

Back in the living room I found an iPhone cord on your desk and plugged in my phone to charge. There were two cameras there and an iPad. I assumed your laptop was wherever you'd been staying in Gaza. I wondered if I'd have to figure out how to get that back. *Maybe the AP could help*, I thought. *I should call them. I should call Kate. I should really call Darren.*

As soon as my phone had enough power to turn back on, it started dinging with text messages and voice mails. My mom, my brother, Kate, Darren, Julia, the office. I opened your desk drawer to look for paper and a pen to make a list, and instead found an envelope, the only thing in the drawer, that said *Last Will and Testament of Gabriel Samson*.

I bit my lip and opened it. Your pointy handwriting filled the entire page. I have the letter here with me now.

I, Gabriel Vincent Samson, being of sound mind and body, declare this to be my last will and testament, and revoke all former wills I have written.

I appoint Adam Greenberg as the executor of my will. If he is unable or unwilling, I appoint Justin Kim.

Do they know what happened? Did your boss call them too? I should call them. I should call Adam.

I direct my executor to pay, out of my accounts, any taxes or fees associated with my death and burial, and any outstanding bills or debts I owe.

I bequeath to Lucy Carter Maxwell the rights to all my creative work—any photographs I have taken, along with my book Defiant, *and the new book I've been working on, which is saved on my laptop in a folder called "New Beginnings." I grant her complete control over and ownership of my copyright.*

I was surprised when I read that part, Gabe. I wondered if it was an apology of sorts for putting those pictures of me in your gallery show in New York without asking. I realized, too, that it would tie me to you for the rest of my life. I'll die before your copyright expires. Were you thinking about that when you wrote your will? Did you want to hold us together for as long as you could?

The remainder of my monetary estate, after all taxes, fees, and bills are paid, should be divided equally between two charities: the National September 11 Memorial & Museum and Tuesday's Children.

If Lucy Carter Maxwell would like any of the physical items I own, I grant them to her. Otherwise, I would like my executor to find an appropriate place to donate those.

I attest to all of this on the 8th of July, 2014.

Was that the day you left for Gaza? Did you write a new will each time you left for a new conflict zone? Or was it different this time?

There are so many conversations I want to have with you, so many questions I want to ask, I wish I had asked. And so much I wish I'd told you. I decided then, after I finished reading your will for the first time, that there was one thing I needed to tell you before you died, even if you couldn't respond, even if I wasn't sure you'd be able to hear me say it.

I pulled out the card Shoshana Ben-Ami had given me, and I dialed her number.

"How quickly," I asked, "can the hospital run a paternity test?"

lxxix

I met Shoshana at the hospital the next morning. She had made me an appointment with an OB in the hospital who'd examined me and then agreed to order the test. And Dr. Mizrahi was able to order that your blood be drawn too.

Shoshana hadn't known how long the test results would take when we'd spoken on the phone. "I can find out for you," she'd said. "But my best guess is that it might take a few days. The Sabbath starts tomorrow night."

I'd forgotten about the Sabbath. But I'd figured as long as I had the results by Sunday morning, that was good enough. The machines could breathe for you until then. I could stay with you until then.

But the universe had other plans. Dr. Mizrahi met us at the phlebotomy lab.

"He's all right now, but Mr. Samson had a bit of a rough night," she said soon after she said hello.

"Please call him Gabriel," I told her and Shoshana. They knew our secrets. It felt strange for them to refer to you so formally. "What happened?"

"He spiked a bit of a fever," she said, as I followed her inside. "The resident in charge thought he might have been developing sepsis, but they increased his antibiotics and gave him acetaminophen. The fever came down. He's stable now."

"Sepsis?" I asked; hardly anything after that word had registered.

"Unfortunately, it happens sometimes with patients on life support. It's a serious infection. But Gabriel seems to have avoided it, at least for now." Dr. Mizrahi had stopped walking once we entered the lab. I'd stopped next to her.

"He could die at any time?" I asked. "From sepsis?"

"There are many risks to being on life support," she answered.

I thought about asking her to lay them out for me, but instead I said, "Is there a way to get these test results today? Or tomorrow? I don't want him to die without knowing." I felt my throat constrict and wondered, for a moment, if that would actually be easier, to let you die of another cause instead of making the decision myself. But the idea of your body becoming septic, poisoning you from the inside out, made me shudder. I couldn't let that happen. I couldn't let anything like that happen.

"I'll see what we can do," Dr. Mizrahi said.

Then a man with kind eyes and a long, curly ponytail took my blood and promised to send the results as soon as they were in. And then we came here, to you.

SO HERE WE ARE, GABE. I did better when I walked into your room this morning. I didn't fall apart. I'm steeling myself. I'm being strong. For you. For the baby. I'm pretending this is a job I'm responsible for that has to get done. I'm doing the best I can.

The nurse who was in here when I arrived said that you could hear me. I know what Dr. Shamir said about your brain, but the nurse said to talk to you anyway, and so I did. I am.

I've told you our story. I've asked you questions you'll never be able to answer. I let you know about the baby. The baby that might be ours. Or might not.

I don't know what would be worse—if it is, or if it isn't.

I'm holding your hand now. Can you feel my fingers on yours?

The hospital never should have put you on these machines, but no one knew, and now you're here and they can't take you off them unless I say it's okay. I'm trying so hard not to be angry at you for that. But really, Gabe, how could you have put me in this position? How could you ask me to kill you? Did you think at all about what making that choice would do to me? I'm going to have to live with this the rest of my life, Gabe. I know, already, I'll experience this in my dreams, over and over. I'll feel the starched sheets, I'll hear your steady mechanical breaths.

Do you think it's okay if I climb in there with you? I'll be careful. I won't touch any of your tubes. I won't hurt your broken arm. I just . . . I want to hold you again. My head feels so good on your chest. So right. It always has.

You've shaped me. Did you know that? You; September 11th. The person I am, the choices I've made. They're because of you. Because of that day.

Is it all right if I kiss your cheek? I just want to feel you against my lips once more.

Nothing I do will bring you back, will it?

I have to accept that.

lxxx

My son,

I don't know when I'll give you this letter, if I do at all—when you turn eighteen? When you graduate from college? Will I wait and leave it to you in a safe-deposit box to open after I die? Or maybe you'll grow up knowing all of this. Maybe the secret will be too much to keep.

I need to tell someone what happened these past two days—they've been the hardest days of my life so far—and I've been so grateful that you've been here with me, a part of me. I read an article once, when I was pregnant with your sister, about prenatal consciousness. It's possible that somewhere deep inside your mind, you have your own record of this, your own memories. But in case you don't, I'm sharing mine. Because these last days should be memorialized.

Yesterday I found out who your father was. And this morning I killed him. I was sitting with him when it happened. His head was resting on my shoulder. My lips were pressed into his hair.

His doctor, Dr. Mizrahi, walked in and asked me if I was ready.

I tried to say the words. I couldn't. I just nodded.

"You're doing the right thing," she told me.

Your father was brain-dead. He'd been in an explosion in Gaza. He would never recover. I'd talked about that with her, over and over. He had no chance of getting better.

I nodded again. Even though I knew I was doing the right thing, it was so hard. So hard it was nearly impossible.

She watched me for a moment; I could see the well of sympathy in her eyes. I was glad it was her doing this and not someone else—she's been so kind to me, and to your dad. "You can hold him," she said.

That's when I pulled him closer to me, when I wrapped my arms around him and rested my own head on his. "Is this okay?" I asked her.

She nodded.

I closed my eyes and pressed my lips to his hair. I couldn't bring myself to watch as she detached the breathing tube. The machine next to me beeped its panic and my heart felt the same way, alarm bells going off in one long wail. I opened my eyes and watched Dr. Mizrahi silence the machine as its screen flatlined. There was one long, rattling breath, and then nothing.

Complete silence.

Your father was gone.

Tears blurred my vision. I apologized to him. Over and over. I hated what I had to do. "I'm sorry," I whispered. "I'm sorry. I'm sorry. I'm sorry."

For years your father and I talked about fate or free will, destiny or decision. I think I have an answer now. It was my choice. It's been my choice all along. And his. We chose each other.

Right now, you and I are in your father's apartment. We're surrounded by him, even though he's gone. We can see him everywhere, in the golden light that comes in through the bedroom windows at sunrise, in the crimsons and midnight blues of the Persian rug on the floor, in the fragrant coffee beans stockpiled in his kitchen—coffee he'll never get to drink. But we'll drink it for him, you and I.

If I'm gone when you're reading this, look up your father's name: Gabriel Samson. Look up his art. Look up the exhibit he showed at the Joseph Landis gallery in Chelsea in 2011. I hope you can see, from his photographs, how deeply he felt for the world—and how deeply he and I felt for each other. He was an artist, your father, a brilliant, sensitive, beautiful artist who tried to make the world better with every photograph he took. He wanted to share stories across borders, across boundaries, across races and religions. And he did. But he gave his life for it.

He wasn't perfect. You should know that. Neither am I. He was selfish sometimes, self-centered, self-important. He thought sacrifice was noble.

He never knew you were coming. I should have told him. Maybe it would've changed things. I can only imagine that if he knew about you, his mind-set would have been different, he'd be less willing to jump into the fray, throw himself into the battle. I can't imagine he would've been willing to sacrifice his time with you. Or maybe it wouldn't have made a difference. Maybe it wouldn't have changed a thing.

You were conceived in love—I want you to know that. Whatever comes next, whatever happens after I write this letter, whatever our lives look like when you read this, whoever you grew up calling "Dad"—I need you to know how much I loved your father. It was a passion that transcended time, space, and all logic. I hope that you find a love like that—one that is all-consuming and powerful, that makes you feel like you're going slightly mad. And if you do find that love, embrace it. Hold on to it. When you give yourself over to love like that, your heart will get bruised. It will get battered. But you will also feel invincible and infinite.

Now that he's gone, I don't know if I'll ever feel that way again. If anyone else will make me feel as special or as chosen or as desired as he did. As seen. But I count myself lucky to have experienced those feelings at all. I count myself lucky to have met him. And to have you.

You haven't entered the world yet, but already I love you, my son. And I know that wherever he is, your father does too.

acknowledgments

I wrote the first vignette that later became *The Light We Lost* in 2012, after a relationship ended that I'd thought would last forever. For the next four years, I worked on this novel during the extra bits of time I had between other book deadlines. And those four years turned out to be some of the most tumultuous years of my life. During that time, I thought a lot about love, loss, destiny, decision, ambition, and regret—and I was thankful, many times, to have had Lucy's world to create when my own world began to feel overwhelming.

I am so grateful for the friends and family who supported me in those four years, during both the celebrations and the sorrows. But while I send thank-yous to each and every wonderful person in my life, I want to call out specifically the ones who helped turn the vignettes I was writing into a novel. So: Thank you to Amy Ewing, who read the first twenty-eight pages and told me to keep going; to Marianna Baer, Anne Heltzel, Marie Rutkoski, and Eliot Schrefer, the best writing group on the planet, who read more than one iteration of this story and—as they always do—encouraged and criticized in just the right way; to Talia Benamy and Liza Kaplan Montanino, whose feedback—and multiple follow-up conversations—was invaluable; and to Sarah Fogelman and Kimberly Grant Grieco, my focus group of two, whose insightful thoughts about Lucy as a mother and a wife informed the final drafts of this book.

Thank you to my sisters, Alison May and Suzie Santopolo, who offered their expertise on hospital and medical matters; to my aunt, Ellen Franklin Silver, who helped with TV producer information; to Atia and Conor Powell, who answered questions about reporting from Gaza; and to Bari Lurie Westerberg, who told me a story about Jeff's hair being in the laundry and then agreed to let me borrow a version of it for this book. And thank you a million times to Nick Schifrin, who finalized the plot with me on a cocktail napkin, who made sure Gabe's career in journalism rang true, who fixed my Jerusalem facts, who explored Rehavia with me, and who read and talked through almost every scene in this book with me at least three times—pushing me to go deeper and suggesting lines himself when I wasn't sure what should come next. Nick, a ticket to Hamilton doesn't even begin to express how grateful I am for your help.

This book would still be a manuscript on my computer, though, without two incredible women: my agent, Miriam Altshuler, and my editor, Tara Singh Carlson. Miriam, I'm so appreciative of all you do for me and for my work, and am so thankful that my path in life led me to you. And Tara, your insight and vision changed Lucy, Gabe, Darren, and their story for the better. Thank you for championing my manuscript, thank you for asking the perfect editorial questions, and thank you, Ivan Held, Sally Kim, Helen Richard, Amy Schneider, Andrea Peabbles, Kylie Byrd, Claire Sullivan, and the entire team at Putnam and Penguin—especially Leigh Butler, Tom Dussel, and Hal Fessenden—for giving me the opportunity to share *The Light We Lost* with the world. Thank you, also, to Charlotte Mursell, Lucy Richardson, Lisa Milton and the rest of the team at HQ for so passionately bringing *The Light We Lost* across the pond.

But I never would have thought I could write a book in the first place if it weren't for two other people. The final thank-yous go to my mom, Beth Santopolo, and—even though he won't ever see this—my dad, John Santopolo, for never once acting like my dreams were disposable and for always encouraging me to go for it, whatever "it" happened to be. I will never take that for granted.

lucy and gabe's reading list

Books, plays, and poems have been important to me for as long as I can remember, and in this novel, they're important to Lucy and Gabe and to their relationship. Some of the book references are rather clear, and others are less so. Below is a list—in order of appearance—of all of the pieces of literature Lucy and Gabe reference throughout *The Light We Lost*.

Julius Caesar by William Shakespeare
Titus Andronicus by William Shakespeare
The Iliad by Homer
"The Road Not Taken" by Robert Frost
Mythology: Timeless Tales of Gods and Heroes by Edith
    Hamilton (the Persephone myth)
Romeo and Juliet by William Shakespeare
The Giver by Lois Lowry

Le Morte d'Arthur by Sir Thomas Malory

Metamorphoses by Ovid (the story of Pygmalion and Galatea)

"i like my body when it is with your body" by E. E. Cummings

"Sonnet 30" by William Shakespeare

Lady Chatterley's Lover by D. H. Lawrence

If You Give a Mouse a Cookie by Laura Numeroff, illustrated by Felicia Bond

"'Hope' is the thing with feathers" by Emily Dickinson

All the Light We Cannot See by Anthony Doerr

HQ
One Place. Many Stories

The home of bold, innovative
and empowering publishing.

Follow us online

 @HQStories

 @HQStories

 HQStories

 HQ Stories

 HQMusic2016